Morning Light could feel the anger simmering inside him.

His eyes, which had been glazed, suddenly focused on her. "Who are you?"

"I am Morning Light. Sister to the Comanche chief, Two Moons."

Dan smiled. "Then I know I must be dreaming. Where the hell am I?"

She moistened her dry lips and whispered, "You are in the camp of the Comanche. My brother asked me to see to your needs."

"Comanche camp." A sound issued from deep within his chest, and she thought it might be laughter. "So that's what they call heaven."

She did not understand.

"And you're the angel assigned to me?"

She tried again. "I am Morning Light, sister—"

Her words were abruptly cut off as his fingertip began to trace the outline of her lips. "God in heaven," he muttered thickly. "If I'd known angels were like you, I'd have let them kill me long ago...."

Dear Reader,

This July, Harlequin Historicals brings you four titles that you won't want to miss.

Texas Healer from Ruth Langan is the long-awaited sequel to *Texas Heart.* After years of study in the East, Dr. Dan Conway finally returns home to Texas...as a wanted man.

With *Temptation's Price,* contemporary author Dallas Schulze has turned her talented pen to writing a historical. Matt Prescott married young Liberty Ballard for the sole reason of preserving her good name, and promptly left town. But five years of haunted dreams have got Matt wondering whether life without Liberty is really worth living.

In Deborah Simmons's *Fortune Hunter,* set against the backdrop of Regency London, a viscount looking for a rich woman and an heiress looking for a title discover that they've both been had.

Dangerous Charade by Madeline Harper is the story of a prince who is unaware of his royal heritage and the headstrong woman who convinces him to rescue his birthright.

We hope you enjoy this month's selection.

Sincerely,

Tracy Farrell
Senior Editor

Harlequin Historicals first edition July 1992

ISBN 0-373-28731-3

TEXAS HEALER

Texas Healer
Ruth Langan

Harlequin Books

TORONTO • NEW YORK • LONDON
AMSTERDAM • PARIS • SYDNEY • HAMBURG
STOCKHOLM • ATHENS • TOKYO • MILAN
MADRID • WARSAW • BUDAPEST • AUCKLAND

RUTH LANGAN

traces her ancestry to Scotland and Ireland. It is no surprise, then, that she feels a kinship with the characters in her historical novels.

Married to her childhood sweetheart, she has raised five children and lives in Michigan, the state where she was born and raised.

To the Ryans and Langans,
pioneers, dreamers, healers, adventurers.
And to Tom,
who joined me on the greatest adventure of all.

Prologue

Texas, 1872

"This is a day like no other." Two Moons, the great chief of the Comanche, caught his wife's hand and, in a rare display of affection, brought it to his lips. "This day I will have my firstborn."

"And your sister, Morning Light, will become a bride." His wife, Shining Star, who lay upon the buffalo robe, gave him a weak smile before another pain caused her to gasp. "Leave me now," she whispered. "For my time is here."

He strode from the tepee while the old women took up their positions on either side of his wife. Under a cloudless Texas sky, a breeze ruffled the tall prairie grass, adding to the festive air in the Comanche camp.

Morning Light, sister to the great chief, Two Moons, had been led to the stream where the women had helped her bathe and perfume her hair. Now, dressed in her finest buckskin gown, her hair entwined with wildflowers and pretty beads, she stood in the doorway of her brother's tepee for the last time.

From this moment her home would be with One Who Will Lead, a great warrior among her people.

All of her earthly goods had been bundled and set outside her brother's tepee. On this day she would become an honored wife, with a tepee of her own. Soon, she hoped, she would be like Shining Star, giving her husband a child of their love.

In a formal ceremony, the chief accepted the string of ponies from the sun-bronzed brave. With the bride-price paid, One Who Will Lead strode forward with an air of confidence to claim his woman. He led the horse upon which she would ride away with him.

To Morning Light he looked like a young god as he strode confidently toward her. Stretching out her hand to him, she smiled shyly, then glanced up at the sudden sound that broke the stillness. The smile froze on her lips. Seeing the look of sudden horror on her face, he turned, then placed himself in front of her for protection.

Nearly two dozen soldiers astride horses crested the hill and raced through the camp, their guns blazing.

The first bullet hit One Who Will Lead directly in the chest. He collapsed against Morning Light. With a cry of pain and outrage, she fell to the ground and cradled the handsome brave in her arms. His blood stained the front of her gown and flowed in ever-widening circles, until the grass beneath them ran red with his blood.

The air was filled with the screams of the women and children, and the thunder of hoofbeats as the armed men raced through the camp, destroying all in their path.

Morning Light had no idea how long she lay in the grass, holding the lifeless body in her arms. When at last she was lifted in her brother's powerful arms and carried to the edge of the stream, she looked around as though in a daze.

Black, acrid smoke drifted from the burned tepees. Bodies of men, women and children littered the ground.

"Shining Star?" she whispered.

He shook his head, and she saw the tear that squeezed from his eye before he turned away. He was, after all, proud chief of the Comanche. There must be no show of weakness before his people.

"She is dead?"

"The bullet found her before the child could be delivered."

With a cry of alarm she caught his arm. "And the baby?"

"A son." The words were wrenched from the chief's constricted throat.

"He—lives?"

He nodded. "For now. He seems very weak, but alive. The old women brought him forth with great difficulty. But one of the white soldier's horses trampled them and crushed his foot. Because of this I have named him Runs With The Wind. This will give him strength against his weakness." The chief's voice shook. "The journey before him will sorely test his strength."

He stood and offered his hand. "Come. We will mourn our dead. And then we must leave this place before the soldiers return with more men and more guns. We will make our way to the high country."

His voice roughened. "Because of this treachery, I turn my back on the white chief's treaty. I will raise my son in the ways of my father."

Morning Light's eyes narrowed in fury. "I give you my word, my brother. I pledge my life that no soldier's hand will be lifted against your son, unless it first strikes me down."

She stared at the blood that stained her hands and arms, the front of her dress. This was to have been her wedding day, the happiest day of her life. Instead it was a day of pain and horror.

Kneeling at the banks of the river, she was suddenly overcome with grief. She could not wash away the blood of One Who Will Lead. It was all she had left of the handsome brave who had pledged his heart. Instead she smeared the blood on her face, where it mingled with her tears.

As was their custom, they buried their dead in caves and crevices, facing the rising sun. When the last body had been laid to rest, Morning Light and Two Moons stood with the others who had survived this massacre and grieved without mentioning the names of the dead, for that would be disrespectful.

As she made her way from the burial site, Morning Light vowed she would never forget. Nor would she forgive those who had done this thing. She would carry this anger against all whites in her heart. And nurture it until she had extracted vengeance.

Chapter One

Texas, 1876

"Oooeee! Jessie. Cole."

At the commotion outside, Jessie and Cole Matthews looked up from the breakfast table and hurried to the front door, followed by a towheaded boy of six and a dark-haired girl of three. In Jessie's arms was an infant whose chubby fingers tugged on a lock of her hair.

Jessie's brother, Thad, didn't even wait until his horse had come to a halt before sliding from the saddle and racing toward them. Dust swirled around him in a cloud as his boots pounded the dirt. He held aloft a crumpled envelope.

"A wrangler who's a friend of mine in Fort Mason spotted Dan."

Jessie's eyes went wide with surprise and pleasure. "He's in Texas? Where is he now? When is he coming home?"

"Not so fast. He didn't say much." Thad thrust the letter into his sister's hand and reached down to easily swing his niece and nephew up into his arms. "Just says he knows of a doctor who wandered into the town and stayed long enough to see to a lot of people's needs. Then, just when he'd earned the town's respect, there was some kind of trouble, and the doctor left just as silently as he'd arrived. But I know it was Dan. Read it.''

Jessie scanned the words written in an almost illegible scrawl, then handed it to her husband without a word.

Cole read the letter. Seeing the way Jessie's eyes filled, he tousled her hair in a gesture of tenderness. ''Dr. Dan Conway.''

She sniffed back the tears that had surprised her. ''It sounds like Dan, doesn't it?''

Cole nodded. Glancing toward Thad, he muttered, ''We'd better send one of the hands to Fort Mason to find out all he can.''

''I've been thinking the same thing.'' Thad nodded toward the bunkhouse. ''I'll get my stuff together now.''

''What do you mean?'' Cole's brows knitted into a frown.

''He's my brother, Cole. I need to find him.'' His voice lowered. ''I don't mean to leave you without a wrangler. Jeremy Storm said he'd take over my chores until I get back.''

''To hell with the ranch chores.'' Cole gave a quick glance at his wife, knowing how she felt about swearing in front of the children. ''Look, Thad, I'm worried about Dan, too. But if you're going to run off every time some cowboy reports a doctor who looks like your brother, you could spend the rest of your life crisscrossing the trails of Texas and never find him.''

"I'm going," Thad said, turning toward the bunkhouse.

As he strode away, Jessie placed her hand on her husband's arm. "Let him go, Cole. Thad needs to do this. He spent all his growing-up years missing Dan. Now that he's a man, he has the right to try to find him."

Cole took the infant from his wife's arms so that she could read the letter again. He saw the way her hands shook.

"I know that something terrible happened to Dan," she murmured, carefully folding the paper. "Something that's keeping him from returning home like he planned."

"People change, Jess," Cole whispered.

She shook her head, then draped her arms around her husband and baby, and nestled her head on his shoulder. "If Dan has changed, something has happened to change him. All I know is, I won't rest until I find out what it was."

The horseman topped a rise and stared at the land spread out below him. The baked earth shimmered beneath a blazing sun. Towering buttes dotted the landscape, along with rock-strewn cliffs and dry, barren soil.

He lifted his hat and wiped his brow, then pulled the hat low on his head to shade his eyes.

He had never forgotten how relentless the sun could be in Texas. Nor how desolate the land. Despite the flow of people into strings of tiny towns scattered across the plains, Texas was still an uncharted wilderness. For that, he should be grateful. What he didn't need was civilization. Or recognition. He wanted to get swallowed up in this vast land and be left alone.

Alone. It struck him that that single word best described his whole life. Growing up in Texas had isolated him and his family from the rest of the world. His dream of being a doctor had isolated him, as well. Even his own father hadn't really understood his need to heal the wounded.

Big Jack Conway had wanted his son to be a rancher. And when Dan Conway had finally gone East to study, he'd found himself in a world into which he never quite belonged. Harvard Medical School in Boston was not just separated by thousands of miles from Texas. It was a separate culture, as well. But through dogged determination he had made a place for himself. Whether he walked amid the squalor of the docks or the glittering life of the scholarly and successful, he had been accepted as a man who charted his own course.

His musings were interrupted by the sight of a wagon hurtling along on the flat stretch of land below him. At first he thought it might be hauled by a runaway team. But as he watched he saw the driver crack his whip, urging the team even faster.

Damn fool, Dan thought. He'd probably wind up along the trail with a broken neck.

Minutes later a dozen or more horsemen raced past, following the trail of the wagon. From his position Dan could see that all the men carried long-range rifles. Buffalo hunters, he realized. They were overrunning this part of Texas. Probably on the trail of a herd. A big one, from the number of men he counted.

He veered off the path and followed a dry gully until he came to a small creek. Though it was little more than a mud hole, he stripped off his clothes and sought relief from the heat. A short time later he staked out his horse near the water's edge and took shelter beneath an outcrop of rock. He would sleep until the heat of the day was past. Then he would resume his journey.

It wasn't any sound that alerted Dan to danger. In fact, it was the absence of sound. No birds shrieked overhead. No insects buzzed. One moment his horse had been contentedly drinking from the creek. The next moment the sound ceased. As if, Dan thought, his eyes quickly opening, someone had muzzled the animal.

As he started to rise, he heard the sound of a pistol being cocked. The cold steel of a gun was pressed to his temple.

"I wouldn't move," said a raspy voice, "unless you like dyin'."

Dan froze.

"I'll take the gun," said the voice as Dan's pistol was yanked from his grasp.

Dan turned toward a man in dirty buckskins whose face bore a jagged scar from his temple to his jaw. Stringy copper hair fell to his shoulders beneath a black, sweat-stained hat. Two men stood behind the stranger. Both carried rifles aimed at Dan's head.

"What do you want?"

"You're on our land," the man said. "We thought we'd see if you were carrying anything of value."

"Your land? I thought this land belonged to the Comanche."

"Not anymore. Haven't you heard? The Indians have been sent packing to the reservation." The man gave a sly laugh. "We got friends in high places who let us use the land. And we don't like anybody trespassing on our property."

"Well, look here."

At the shout, Dan turned toward the creek and watched as a scrawny boy of about fifteen rifled through his bedroll and saddlebags. Spying the black bag, he untied it and lifted it in the air.

"Bring it here," called the scarred man.

The boy ran up the hill and said with a grin, "Looks like one of them doctoring bags, Cal."

The man studied the contents for a moment then asked, "You a doctor?"

Dan nodded.

The man gave a slow smile, revealing tobacco-stained teeth. "We just keep getting luckier all the time. Billy, fetch his horse."

The boy went running down the hill and returned leading Dan's horse.

"Come on," Cal cried, giving Dan a shove. "We got someone who needs you real bad."

The men pulled themselves into the saddle and gathered around Dan, to make certain he couldn't escape. Cal took up the reins to Dan's horse and led him. Some distance away, in a secluded campsite surrounded by evergreens, stood the wagon Dan had seen earlier in the day. The group of men clustered around a camp fire looked up as they approached.

When they came to a halt, Dan was hauled from the saddle and led toward the wagon. Lying on the ground beneath it was a man wrapped in several layers of blankets. Despite the heat of the fire, his teeth chattered uncontrollably.

"We found you a doctor," Cal said, staring down at the man.

The man's eyes opened and he struggled to focus on the figure looming over him. His eyes slowly closed.

"Fix him up, Doc," Cal said, tossing the black bag at Dan.

"What happened to him?" Dan asked.

"Damned if I know. He just keeled over when he was riding today. Said he couldn't go another mile. We thought we could get him to a town in the wagon, but we had to stop when he got half-crazy with the pain."

"He wasn't shot?" Dan was already kneeling beside the man. As he unwrapped the blankets, heat poured from the man's body in waves.

"Hell, no. Who'd shoot old Quent? He's the meanest, toughest trail boss in Texas. His hide is too tough for bullets."

The men all laughed at Cal's words.

Dan's fingers moved slowly over the man as he carefully probed. As he touched Quent's lower side he heard his sudden intake of breath. The man's face became contorted with pain.

Dan glanced up. "It's his appendix."

"Fix it," Cal said.

"It isn't that simple," Dan explained patiently. "It may have ruptured."

"And if it has—whatever you called it?"

"Ruptured."

"Yeah. Then what?"

"His body will be already filled with poisons. I won't be able to save him."

"And if it hasn't—whatever you said?"

"If it hasn't ruptured, I could try to remove it. But under these conditions..."

"Then quit talking about it and do it," Cal said. "But remember this, Doc. If Quent doesn't live, you won't either."

"I didn't cause his trouble," Dan said evenly.

"Didn't say you did. But you'll die all the same." Cal gave an evil laugh. "Life just isn't fair, is it, Doc?"

The others joined in the laughter.

Dan searched through the meager supplies in his bag. Until he replenished the medicines in a town, there was almost nothing left that he could use. He bit down on his frustration. It wouldn't be the first time he'd been forced to work under such primitive conditions.

"I'll need some whiskey," he said. "And a kettle of boiling water."

One of the men took a healthy swallow from a bottle of cheap whiskey, then handed it to Dan. The driver of the wagon wrapped a dirty rag around his hand and removed a blackened kettle from the fire. He dropped it beside the sleeping man. Dan plunged his instruments into the boiling water, then, with the aid of a stick, plucked out a knife.

"Give him a stiff shot of whiskey," Dan said. "And then hold him still."

Cal nodded and did as he'd been told. For a moment the men stared transfixed as Dan bent to his patient. But as he began to make an incision, the men beat a hasty retreat. As the blade of the knife bit into his flesh, Quent let out a scream of terror that filled the air. Then he fell deathly silent.

"There's no need to hold him now," Dan said softly. "He's beyond pain."

Cal remained, kneeling beside his friend. He seemed unmoved by the sight of the blood that spilled from Quent's body.

Dan studied the diseased organ and realized that the deadly poisons had already begun to spread through the man's system. Discounting the notion that his efforts would probably be in vain, he worked feverishly to do all that he could to save him. Moving quickly, he removed the appendix and closed the man's wounds. Any minute now Quent would come to and begin to thrash around. If that happened, he would surely bleed to death. Of course, that might be preferable to the slow, painful death that often resulted from a ruptured appendix.

Dan had no idea how long he worked over Quent. It could have been hours or mere minutes. But the sky had become streaked with thin red ribbons, signaling a brilliant sunset. At last Dan sat back on his heels and surveyed his patient. When he lifted a hand to his forehead, he was surprised to see that the hand was smeared with blood.

He plunged his hands into the bucket of water that had been used to sponge the patient. It now held dirty instruments. Instantly the water was stained the color of rust. Dan wiped his hands on his pants as he stood.

"I've done all I can," he said as Cal continued to kneel beside the still figure of his friend. "Now all we can do is wait."

"You'd better hope you did enough, Doc." Cal stood and waved his pistol toward the camp fire. "Make yourself real comfortable. You're not going anywhere unless Quent opens his eyes and tells us he's ready to ride."

Dan walked to the fire and filled a battered tin cup with strong black coffee. Then he sat with his back against a rock and stretched out his legs. The hot coffee seemed to sharpen his senses.

Out of the corner of his eye, he watched as Billy carefully went through the rest of his saddlebags, examining his meager supplies. Several times he saw the boy glance around before stuffing things into his pockets. When he was satisfied that Dan had nothing more of value, Billy led Dan's horse to where the others were tied. Dan noted that all the horses were tethered to a single rope. He stored the knowledge away for future use.

Draining the cup, he leaned his head back and pretended to sleep.

There was a chorus of sound in the camp. Men's voices, raised in anger, low with laughter. Someone swore, loudly, viciously. A horse nickered. Another whinnied in reply. The driver of the wagon, who was also the cook, banged blackened pots against each other as he cleaned them in the stream. On the far side of the camp fire, several men were engaged in a hand of poker. A wail of protest issued as the last card was dealt. Someone hooted as he stuffed a handful of money into his pockets.

At first Dan took little notice of another sound. High-pitched, like the bleat of a lamb, it seemed to come from inside the wagon. He heard it again. Higher now, almost a wail. A night bird perhaps? He strained to sort it out from all the other sounds. At last he heard it again. It was definitely coming from the wagon. It sounded like crying. A child perhaps. The hair on the back of his neck rose. A female child.

Dan sat very still, his mind whirling. His every move would be watched. He glanced around the camp. Young Billy was occupied with the horses. That was obviously his job with this crew. Besides the boy, Dan counted ten men. But the number of horses told him that at least two men were unaccounted for. That would mean that at least two men were in the wagon. Two men and a girl child. He felt the bile rise to his throat. His hands clenched into fists at his sides.

Twelve men. Twelve guns. And he was unarmed. Not the best odds he'd ever faced. But somehow, he would have to find out if what he suspected was true. And if it was, he thought, death would be too good for these animals.

Dan watched as two men climbed from the back of the wagon and sauntered toward the creek. Tossing aside the tin cup, he stood.

"Where're you going?" Cal asked, reaching a hand to the gun at his waist.

"Thought I'd check my patient."

With lazy, unhurried movements Dan made his way toward the man who lay as still as death beneath the wagon. He knelt, pretending to examine the man. As he did, he heard the unmistakable sound of muted weeping from inside the wagon.

"How is he?" Cal asked, coming up behind Dan.

"Still out." Dan touched a hand to his patient's brow and was alarmed by the fever that raged. Quent was fading quickly. The poisons had already begun to drain him.

Reaching into his bag, he removed a small amount of his precious laudanum. It was necessary to keep this man as quiet as possible. Then he poured a generous amount of whiskey on a piece of flannel and placed it over the wound to act as a poultice.

"Is he going to make it?"

Showing no emotion, Dan nodded his head. "So far everything seems fine." He made a great show of taking the man's hand and feeling for a pulse.

A fight erupted between two of the cardplayers, and Cal swung away, determined to end it before it grew into a full-blown gunfight. Seizing the moment, Dan made his way to the back of the wagon and peered inside. At first he thought there was nothing but a pile of rags in the far corner. But as his eyes adjusted to the dim light, he made out a small, crumpled figure half-hidden by a tattered blanket.

As he crawled toward her, he saw her cringe until her back was pressed against the rough wood of the wagon. He was dismayed to discover that she was, as he had feared, a child, no more than perhaps ten or twelve years. Her hair was dirty and matted and fell over her face in wild tangles. Her buckskin dress was torn and bloody. She held the gaping bodice together with a small fist. Her eyes were glazed with pain. But, he noted with relief, she was still prepared to fight him.

He struggled to recall the simple Chinook jargon he had learned as a boy. That was a common language used to communicate with the various Indian tribes that had often crossed their rangeland.

In halting words he whispered, "I am friend. When I leave here, you leave with me."

Her eyes widened at his words.

He touched a finger to his lips. "Watch," he said tersely. "And listen. When the time comes, we move with all speed."

He saw her lips move. But no words came out. Instead, tears filled her eyes. Without another word he slipped from the wagon and returned to the man who lay unconscious.

He knelt beside the still figure and watched as Cal stepped between the two angry poker players. Despite Cal's daunting presence, one of the men threw a punch and the other followed suit. Soon it had erupted into an all-out brawl, with the other cardplayers joining in, and several of the other men leaping in to put a stop to it.

Dan glanced around. Only Billy stood between him and the horses, and the boy was busy watching the fight. This might prove to be the best chance.

He got to his feet. At the back of the wagon he said simply, "Now." Then he forced himself to walk slowly toward the line of horses.

Billy glanced at him as he approached. Dan forced himself to appear unhurried.

"Where you going, Doc?"

"I need something from my saddlebag," he said. "For Quent."

Billy glanced at the prone figure, then back at Dan. "I don't know. I'd better wait till Cal gives me the word."

Dan shrugged. "Suit yourself, boy. But don't blame me if something goes wrong with your trail boss. I'll just tell him you didn't think it was very important."

Billy was torn between a desire to witness a good fight, and to follow Cal's orders. With a shrug he said, "All right. Get what you need. But don't try anything or I'll blow you to bits." The pistol he waved seemed too big for his bony hands.

Dan strolled past him and paused beside his horse. Billy stood beside him as he rummaged through his saddlebags. When one of the poker players knocked another to the ground, Billy turned to watch. That was all the time Dan needed to deliver a blow to the boy's jaw that sent him crumpling to the ground. Kneeling over him, Dan quickly removed his belongings from the boy's pockets.

The girl, who had been watching, bounded from the back of the wagon and raced toward Dan. Dan pulled himself into the saddle, then lifted his knife and cut the rope that held the string of horses. Reaching down, he caught the girl and hauled her up in front of him.

"It's the doc," someone shouted.

"Stop him," Cal screamed.

A shot rang out as Dan wheeled his mount and dug in his heels. He felt his body jerk slightly, and he struggled to hold on to the string of horses. If he were to drop it now, the men would be on their trail before they could reach safety.

A second shot rang out and Dan jerked again before bending low over the girl, determined to keep her safe. His left hand tightened around the rope, and the horses streamed along behind him, their hooves thundering.

He heard voices shouting and swearing. But as his horse continued its pace, the voices grew dim.

His arm circled the girl and he leaned heavily on her. He felt her shift as she turned and took the rope from his hands. The sound of the horses behind him grew faint, and he wondered idly if she had turned them loose. But still he could hear them, as if from a great distance, keeping pace.

The wind whistled past their heads as their mounts continued speeding across the hard-packed earth. Dan wondered why the nighttime had come so early. It was dark. So dark he could no longer see.

He was now hunched far over the girl. And he had grown very warm. The heat seemed to radiate from his back and shoulders, and trickle along his spine in warm, sticky rivers.

He slumped over the girl and wrapped the reins around his wrist because he could no longer feel his fingers. And though he felt weary beyond belief, he knew he could not stop.

He knew that he was losing consciousness. He shook his head to clear his mind, but the movement only made him feel more light-headed.

At least the girl was safe.

He had forgotten where he was headed. Or why. His mind refused to function. But he sensed that in this direction was safety.

The pain came over him in great waves.

With an iron will he urged his horse on.

Chapter Two

"I am Comanche," came the young girl's voice. "Do you understand?"

Nodding his head seemed too great an effort for Dan. He squeezed her hand and allowed his head to bob against her shoulder.

"I am Little Bear. And you are the pale wolf I saw in my dream. I knew you would come, just as the dream promised."

Her words made no sense to him. He gave no response.

Their mount stumbled then righted itself. Dan gritted his teeth against the pain.

"I will take you to my people."

He wanted to resist. He needed a doctor, and they could be found only in a town of some size. But he couldn't find his voice. All his energy went into staying alive. She would have to decide for him.

The girl urged the horse into a hard, jarring run. When Dan's hands on her waist went slack, she gripped them firmly, knowing that he was once again unconscious.

* * *

Dan struggled to focus on the view spread out before him. The Comanche had chosen their campsite with careful attention. The animal hides of their tepees blended into the wooded setting. The rock wall behind them and the river in front made their camp accessible from only two sides. Beside the banks of a swollen river, women spread out their wash on low-hanging bushes while the children played nearby.

As the dusty horse and its riders made their way through the camp, a sudden hush seemed to fall over the inhabitants. The women and children watched somberly from a distance. The braves formed a wall that gradually closed in until the horse came to a halt.

There was a great cry as the girl's parents, recognizing their long-absent daughter, raced to her side.

The girl spoke softly, and many hands reached up to lift the man from the horse. The girl slid from the saddle and fell into her parents' arms. After a jubilant reunion, the sea of silent observers parted, as the man was half dragged, half carried toward a tepee in the middle of the camp.

Before they could reach their destination, a young brave barred their way, glowering at the girl.

"Why have you brought this white man to our camp?" the brave asked.

"He saved me from the buffalo hunters who stole me."

Dan heard snatches of the conversation and struggled to make sense of the words. Words he had heard in his childhood, he realized. Comanche. If he could only rouse himself, he would make himself understood. But the pain came in great black waves, searing his mind and body. He clenched his teeth and fought to hold on.

Maybe this angry brave would kill him, he thought. But he experienced no fear. At least then the pain would end. Maybe death would be a welcome relief.

As his eyes closed he heard a new voice. One filled with quiet authority.

"Little Bear said you make good medicine."

Dan's eyes flicked open. It was plain that the blurred figure standing before him was the chief. It was evident in his stance, in the way the others stood back a respectful distance. Dan's eyes closed. With a grunt of pain he croaked, "Hell, I can't even heal myself." He was unaware that the words were no more than guttural sounds.

"Take him to my tepee," the chief said.

Dan tried to walk, but his legs refused to obey. He felt himself falling, before strong hands caught and lifted him. The pain was so intense, he swore loudly, viciously. Then a soft black cloud enveloped him. He slipped beyond the pain.

Morning Light, sister of the great chief, Two Moons, stood in the shallows with the other women and watched from a distance. Several of the mothers caught up their infants and hurried to their tepees, convinced that an army would soon converge on their camp. Others wore worried frowns as they saw their husbands circle the horse and riders.

Hearing the cries from Little Bear's family, Morning Light scooped up the little boy who clung to her skirt and began to run toward them. Then, as she realized they were cries of joy, she paused and watched as the girl was embraced by her father and mother.

She let go of a long, slow hiss of breath and began walking slowly toward the crowd. There seemed to be no danger here, only rejoicing.

As the stranger was hauled from the saddle, she caught a glimpse of his blood-soaked shirt. For a moment she swayed, seeing in her mind another, whose bloodstained body writhed in her arms until he had given up his life. She felt the unexpected ache around her heart before she shook off her feelings and forced herself to continue walking.

As she approached, the chief said, "Morning Light, you will see to the stranger. You must use your healing powers on his wounds."

She nodded and followed the braves to her brother's tepee, all the while clinging to the child in her arms. She had been taught the power of healing by their old medicine man. But it had never occurred to her that she might one day use it to heal the wounds of a hated white man.

It was Dan's worst nightmare. It had dawned on him in one of his rare lucid moments. He had been shot in the back. Twice. Someone had to get the bullets out, or he would bleed to death.

Two braves stripped his clothes from him and held him down while a ghostly maiden, her face painted eerie white, advanced on him with a knife. She spoke to the braves in Comanche, unaware that Dan understood her words.

"I do this only because my brother has commanded it. As for me, I would rather plunge my knife into his heart. Then there would be one less white man to bring harm to our people."

The braves rolled Dan over and placed a strip of rawhide between his teeth before they held him down.

He heard the hiss of the fire and knew that the medicine woman had plunged her knife into the flame. At least, he thought with bitter irony, the blade that killed him would be clean.

As the blade sliced through his flesh, he felt white-hot pain exploding through him. A flash of sunlight seared his brain until he thought he would go mad from the blinding light. He bit down hard until he tasted his own blood. And then, just when he thought he could bear it no longer, he felt himself catch fire and begin to melt. His bones became liquid. His flesh burned away. He floated on blood-red waves. Angel hands cradled him against a soft breast. A heavenly voice crooned to him in words that were unintelligible. Dying was easier than he had expected.

Morning Light knelt beside the man and sponged his fevered flesh. In the tepee, all was silent. But the sounds of laughter and jubilant singing drifted on the air. Everyone in the camp was celebrating the miraculous return of the young maiden, Little Bear. She had been given up for dead. And now she had been returned to them. Little Bear told and retold the story of this white man's heroic rescue. Though the presence of the white man caused much fear and speculation, he had earned the gratitude of Little Bear's family. And though this white man was unknown to them, his story had already become legend. This man, whom her people called Pale Wolf, had become larger than life.

The man moaned and Morning Light murmured softly as she drew the buffalo robe around him. Beneath his dark, bristly beard, his face showed the ravages of pain. He looked as fierce and frightening as the cunning animal for whom he had been named. Tentatively she touched a hand to his forehead. Fever raged through him. He sighed and she abruptly withdrew her hand.

Morning Light did not know this stranger whose presence caused a prickly feeling along her spine. And yet she had the distinct impression that she had seen him before. Yet how could that have been possible? Surely she would remember a man such as this, who would stand taller even than her brother, the chief.

Wringing out the cloth, she placed it on his fevered forehead. Suddenly his eyes opened and his hand clamped over hers, pinning her when she tried to pull away.

Where had such incredible strength come from? She struggled, but he only held her more firmly.

"I have to go." His voice was little more than a whisper.

"You must not," she said, struggling against the hand that held her in a painful grasp.

"You keep saying that." His voice lowered. "What would you have me do? Stay here and grow sleek and rich like the others? You knew why I came here. You knew from the beginning that I would take what I learned back to the people who need me."

His words made no sense. But they did not disturb Morning Light as much as the anger she could feel simmering inside him.

"You are weary," she said softly. "You must rest."

His eyes, which had been glazed, suddenly focused on her. "You aren't Sarah. Who are you?"

"I am Morning Light. Sister to the Comanche chief, Two Moons."

He smiled, and she was amazed at the transformation in him. "Then I know I must be dreaming. Where the hell am I?"

She moistened her dry lips and whispered, "You are in the camp of the Comanche. My brother asked me to see to your needs."

"Comanche camp." A sound issued from deep within his chest, and she thought it might be laughter. "So that's what they call heaven."

She did not understand.

"And you're the angel they assigned to me?"

She tried again. "I am Morning Light, sister—"

Her words were abruptly cut off as his fingertip began to trace the outline of her lips. "God in heaven," he muttered thickly. "If I'd known angels were like you, I'd have let them kill me long ago."

The effort he made to speak had been too great a task. A dry cough caused him to wince in pain. "Water..."

She reached for the buffalo paunch filled with cool water from the stream, and poured some into a buffalo horn, while he continued holding her by the wrist.

She tipped the horn to his lips and watched as he drank his fill. But as she attempted to set it down, he suddenly pulled her into his arms until she was flattened against his chest. The water seeped into the earth beside them.

"Thank you, angel." His hand cupped the back of her head, drawing her close until his lips brushed hers.

Morning Light was too stunned to pull away. Wave after wave of feeling washed over her as his lips moved over hers. Icy needles raced along her spine. Her heartbeat accelerated until she could barely breathe.

She was aware of so many things about this man. The hair that darkened his chest was soft against her palms. The breath that fanned her cheek was warm. Her heart thudded in her breast as she forced herself to meet his gaze.

Her mouth opened in surprise. His hands, which had held her in a painful grip, were now slack. His eyes were closed; his breathing slow and steady. He had drifted once more into sleep.

She would have to be more careful of this stranger. Pushing herself away, she paused a moment to study him. Even in repose, he seemed dangerous.

A rawhide strip around his neck caught her eye. Attached to the rawhide was an amulet. She lifted it and by the light of the fire studied the intricate markings.

She gasped and dropped it against his chest. What games were the spirits playing with her? This amulet had belonged to her mother, many years ago. She had worn it until her death, when it became Morning Light's. It had remained around her neck until the day she had given it away, to a white youth who had saved her life.

From some corner of her mind she produced the name she had thought long forgotten. Dan Conway. Da-Nee. She studied the face beneath the heavy beard. There was no trace of the boy she had once known. Her eyes narrowed. This stranger had probably killed Da-Nee and stolen his amulet. That was why he had fallen into disfavor with the spirits. She lifted the amulet once more and closed her hand around the copper disk. Someday soon, she would reclaim her mother's amulet for herself.

His eyes opened, pinning her. For a moment she feared that he could read her thoughts. Then she scolded herself for such foolishness. His eyes were merely glazed with pain. Almost at once they blinked shut.

Picking up the empty buffalo paunch, she made her way from the tepee and hurried to the stream to fetch more cool water. The impression of the stranger's lips was still warm upon hers. Her legs were still unsteady. Her breathing was still ragged.

Dan knew that this was only a dream. He knew it because the beautiful face swimming in and out of his vision kept reminding him of someone from his past.

"You must drink this," she said as she lifted his head to her lap and held a buffalo horn to his lips.

The liquid tasted foul as he swallowed it and he decided he didn't like this dream. He struggled to wake up, but the dream wouldn't let him go.

"One more taste," she said in that lyrical voice that soothed.

He winced as the vile liquid trickled down his throat.

The vision disappeared. In her place was the white-faced devil, with hard, clever hands. But her face was no longer streaked with eerie white paint. Her face was unsmiling. Her voice was low with anger.

"My dreams are troubled. I should have disobeyed you, my brother, and killed this Texan while I had the chance."

The chief's voice was low, reasonable. "He brought Little Bear back safely to us. Is his life not worth as much as the one he saved?"

"I tell you, he will bring death and destruction upon our people. Ishatai is concerned that..."

"We will speak no more of this, Morning Light," said the calm voice of the chief. "He must rest if he is to return from the spirit land." Two Moons, chief of the Comanche, turned and left.

Dutifully she placed Dan's head upon a soft animal hide. She wrapped his chilled body in a buffalo robe. She took his hand between both of hers and began chanting. The words were strange to Dan, and at first he resisted. But gradually he stopped fighting. The effect of the chant was soothing. In his mind he traveled back to his childhood. He was standing beside his sister, who was facing a stern Comanche chief. He couldn't hear the words they spoke, but he could hear the strange chanting in the camp in the distance. He was drawn to the Comanche village, but each time he got close, the people moved away and their chanting grew faint.

Though he resisted, more liquid was forced between his lips. He slipped into blessed unconsciousness.

The three figures darted between the tepees like shadows, then dropped to their knees in the dry grass.

"Have you persuaded your chief to join us?"

"Two Moons has decreed that the Comanche stand alone."

"Even the great chief, Two Moons, is helpless against such armies. We must band together if we are to turn back those who cover our land like locusts."

"What would you have me do? I have already spoken at our council. My voice is but one among many."

"There are other ways to persuade him."

The whispered voice was tinged with sudden suspicion. "What do you mean?"

"If someone close to him should be killed by white soldiers, he will be forced to seek vengeance."

"No." The protest was fierce. "The woman will be mine one day. And the boy is too precious to her. You must find another way to reach the heart of Two Moons."

The voice was low, commanding. "Return to your buffalo robe. Your sleep will be undisturbed."

One figure slunk away. The other two waited, before weaving their silent way between the tepees until they came to the one in the center of camp.

Dan was fighting the nightmare again. He felt the sweat break out on his forehead as the eerie figure moved toward him. The figure held a knife aloft, and he knew that he would have to endure once again the agony of having the bullets dug out of his back.

He blinked his eyes, expecting to see the white-painted face that he had seen so many times in his dreams. But this time it was not the maiden. It was a man in the uniform of a soldier, creeping silently between the figures wrapped in buffalo robes that ringed the fire.

God in heaven. The woman and child. A soldier was intent upon killing one of them.

For a moment Dan's body refused to obey the commands of his mind. Though he struggled to sit up, his body protested.

He saw the glint of the knife as it poised above the sleeping figure. Calling on every ounce of willpower at his command, Dan came to his knees and caught the man's wrist in an iron grasp.

The sounds of their struggle woke the others. Morning Light let out a cry, then instinctively reached for Runs With The Wind and pushed the boy behind her. The chief, seeing the intruder, rolled to his feet brandishing a knife. They watched helplessly as Dan and the intruder engaged in a life-and-death struggle.

Dan knew he could not hold on. Already his strength was ebbing. He felt the blade of the knife slice through his shoulder until it found muscle and bone.

The pain was too much. He had no strength left with which to fight this attacker. But when the man raised the knife again, Dan knew he had to protect the ones who had saved him. With a grunt of pain he threw himself onto the man, pressing him to the ground. He waited, expecting to the feel the knife buried in his chest. Instead, he felt nothing. The figure beneath him gave a final shudder, then went limp. The intruder's knife had found the wrong heart. Dan rolled to one side, enfolded in mists of pain.

The Comanche clustered around the bloody body dressed in the garb of a soldier.

"This man is not what he appears to be," Two Moons said solemnly. "He is a Kiowa Apache. If it were not for the bravery of the man who lies in my tepee, those of us who were sleeping would have joined the spirit world."

"Why would the Apache try to pass this off as a deed of the white soldier?" one of the braves asked.

"I have no answer." Through narrowed eyes Two Moons allowed his gaze to sweep the company of men who faced him. "But this much I know. We must leave this place. If this man did not act alone, others will follow."

"What of the white man who sleeps in your te-pee?" Ishatai asked.

"He has proved himself friend to the Comanche. Two times now he has saved one of the People. He goes with us."

"That is a mistake," Ishatai cried. "This one is only dressed like a white devil. But the one in your tepee is a white devil. He can bring only harm to the People."

"I have spoken," the chief said in a tone that left no room for further questions.

"When will we leave?" an old man asked.

"At first light."

In the chief's tepee, Dan was aware of none of this. He lay in numbing pain, enduring the ministrations of a grateful Comanche maiden.

Chapter Three

The Comanche broke camp and moved out in an orderly fashion. The very young were carried on the backs of their mothers. The old rode on horses behind the younger braves. The women and children laughed and chatted as they followed along behind the packhorses laden with the household goods.

"You will see to Pale Wolf?" the chief asked his sister.

She nodded as four strong braves struggled to lift Dan to the travois that had been tied behind his horse. He moaned but did not waken as they secured him between layers of animal hides.

Little Bear, who had visited the chief's tepee daily to chart the progress of her hero, caught up the reins of his horse and began to lead him on a slow, easy pace. Behind walked Morning Light, who kept her gaze on the man who had been given over to her care.

The two young women, who had been merely friends before, had now become inseparable. Little Bear had confided in the chief's sister about her ordeal at the hands of the white hunters. And Morning Light, who had endured such a captivity in her own youth, when she had been nearly the same age as Little Bear, understood the girl's need to unburden her heart.

Morning Light studied the man who had risked his life for the safety of Little Bear. Not many men would have survived such wounds. Already many of their people had decided that Pale Wolf was more than a mere man. They spoke of him as though he were possessed of great spirits.

Seeing the beads of moisture on his forehead, she dipped a cloth in water and pressed it to his fevered brow. His big hand closed over hers, startling her. For a moment she went very still, feeling a strange curling sensation deep inside. It was the same each time he touched her. Scolding herself for such distractions, she pulled her hand away and continued to walk beside the travois. But her gaze kept straying to the man who lay as still as death.

All day they walked. And when evening shadowed the land, they slept in the shelter of a towering butte. But in the morning, at a single word from their chief, they once again began to move. It was not until the evening of the second day that they came to a place of water and trees and game. There they pitched their tepees and set up camp.

Dan opened his eyes. They felt gritty, as if sand had been rubbed into them.

He studied his surroundings. There was nothing familiar. No bed or dresser. Not even a saddle beneath his head. Just the dim light of a fire nearby, casting shadows on the inner hide of the tepee. He struggled to put together the bits and pieces of memory. But it was all so vague.

"You have come back to us."

Dan turned toward the woman, who spoke to him in English. For a brief moment he felt as if all the air had been knocked from his lungs.

"Am I still dreaming?" Dan studied her bowed head and saw the light in her eyes as she glanced up at him.

"You have suffered many dreams since you came to us."

He lay a moment, enjoying the sound of her voice. He had heard it often, soothing him when the pain was severe; scolding him when he refused the vile-tasting liquids she had forced down his throat.

He studied the beautiful, graceful woman, whose coal-black hair streamed down the back of her fawn-colored dress in a cascade of silk.

Throwing off the buffalo robe, he struggled to sit up. As he did, pain washed over him, surprising him with its intensity.

The woman rushed to his side and helped him back down until he lay helplessly against the blankets. She could see the effort it cost him.

"You must lie still. You were gravely wounded."

She heard his sudden intake of breath as she drew a robe over him. His face was slick with sheen. He closed his eyes and she placed a damp cloth on his forehead.

He had never known such weakness.

He reached a hand to his back and probed the dressings. The wound beneath was raw and tender, but the area around it was not swollen. No infection. He felt a wave of relief. And then he felt a second dressing at his shoulder. He didn't understand. Had he been shot a second time? As he struggled to remember, the memory came back to him in half-remembered pieces.

"There was a struggle," he muttered.

"With a Kiowa Apache dressed as a soldier."

He lay still, digesting this. He remembered the struggle, the knife. The pain. But nothing else.

"Did he get away?"

"He is dead."

"So, Pale Wolf."

At a voice from the entrance of the tepee, Dan turned and studied the man who entered. He arched a brow at the strange name he'd been given.

"You have come back from the spirit world."

The chief was tall, with buckskins covering the lower half of his body. His chest and shoulders rippled with muscles honed through years of battle. His hair was tinged with gray. And though he had aged considerably in the years since Dan had seen him, he still carried himself with the same pride and arrogance that Dan could remember from his youth.

"Two Moons."

The chief's eyes narrowed. "How is it that you know me?"

"We met many years ago. My name is Dan Conway. My father, Big Jack Conway, owned a ranch near your hunting grounds."

Two Moons had a sudden flash of remembrance. Of a white woman who had long haunted his dreams. And of a boy who had the gift of healing.

"Woman With Hair Like The Sun," Two Moons breathed. "She is well?"

Dan chuckled at the name Two Moons had given his sister many years ago. "She lives on a big spread with her husband and three children."

"And you, Pale Wolf, still have the gift of healing?"

Dan's smile faded. "I do my best."

The chief took the measure of the man who was finally awake. He remembered the rancher who had always dealt fairly with the Comanche. Despite the serious injuries that had weakened him, it was obvious that this man was indeed Big Jack Conway's son. He had the same intense look in his eyes. Eyes as green as the prairie grass that grew lush and tall in summer. Like his father before him, he was tall, with arms heavily corded with muscles. He did not look like a man of medicine. Or of peace. The name the Comanche had given this man suited him.

Two Moons turned to his sister, who had been listening in silence. "This white man once saved your life," he said. "When he was but a youth and you were still a child."

She lifted her head to study the man more closely. She remembered those green eyes. She remembered also a painful, festering wound, and the gentle, healing touch of a boy almost grown to manhood. He was not a stranger. He was the one to whom she had given her most prized possession, her mother's amulet. With a flush she lowered her head and studied the toe of her moccasin.

"We are grateful for the return of Little Bear. She will long remember your kindness," the chief said.

"Little Bear." Dan thought of the bravery of the girl he had discovered in the back of the buffalo hunters' wagon. And then he thought of the brutality she must have suffered at their hands. "How is she?"

"You will soon see for yourself. She has visited you daily to see how you are recovering from your wounds." Two Moons smiled. "As soon as you are able to receive visitors, the family of Little Bear wishes to offer their thanks for the return of their daughter.'' He saw the fatigue etched on Dan's face. ''But for now, I will leave you to rest.''

When they were alone in the tepee, Dan turned to Morning Light. ''Why am I called Pale Wolf?''

She felt suddenly shy and awkward in his presence. Though he had surely forgotten pressing his mouth to hers, for he had still been in the spirit world, she would never be able to forget.

''A pale wolf appeared to Little Bear in a dream, and rescued her. That is why she never lost heart. And when you appeared at the wagon, she knew that you were the wolf of her dreams.''

He shook his head and the merest hint of a smile touched his lips. ''The wolf of her dreams.'' His eyes closed.

Morning Light knelt and drew the robe over him. She was surprised to note that her hand trembled slightly. It had been easy to care for him when he was in that otherworld, fighting the evil spirits. Especially when he had been nothing more than a stranger. But now, he was much more than a wound to dress and a body to heal. He was Dan Conway, who had once healed her. And touched her heart.

''Little Bear and her family can wait no longer to express their gratitude.'' Morning Light struggled to help Dan to a sitting position.

''I don't want their gratitude.''

He was grumpy. She smiled. That was a good sign that he was mending.

''It is expected. You must permit it. They wait now outside the tepee.'' As she brought her arms around his shoulders, she felt the jolt. It happened whenever they touched. And though she struggled to feel nothing, she was helpless to put a stop to this strange reaction.

Did he feel it, as well? She glanced toward him and saw the frown etched between his brows.

"How long have I been here?"

Their faces were very close. She could feel his breath warm against her cheek as she replied, "Five days and nights you have raged against the wounds. First there were the buffalo hunters' bullets. Then there was the knife of the Kiowa Apache."

"Five days?" Dan frowned. "I'm afraid I don't remember much."

"It will return to you. Come," she said, eager to put some distance between them. "You must welcome your visitors."

"Then bring me my clothes," he said.

"You are not strong enough...."

"Bring them."

Yes. Grumpy. He must be mending. With a shrug of resignation Morning Light brought him his clothes, then busied herself on the far side of the tepee.

As Dan struggled into his pants, he noted idly that they had been washed clean of the blood that had earlier soaked them. The same was true of his shirt. Clenching his teeth against the pain, he pulled on his boots, then retrieved his pistol. After checking to see that it was loaded, he strapped on his gun belt.

"Help me to stand." His tone softened. "Please."

She hurried to his side and was dismayed at the gun at his hip. It made him look even more dangerous.

Leaning heavily on Morning Light's shoulder, Dan got slowly to his feet. Taking a deep breath, he planted his feet and waved her away.

At her signal the chief entered the tepee, followed by a little boy of three or four. The boy had a slow, limping gait. As soon as he spotted Dan, he hid behind Morning Light's skirts.

Dan watched with a frown. Was the boy Morning Light's son? Of course. A beautiful maiden like Morning Light would have been a prize for any brave. The sister of a great chief would have had many suitors through the years. The thought deepened the frown that furrowed his brow. He experienced an unexpected feeling of jealousy, which he instantly denied.

He forced himself to turn to the others who entered the tepee. Little Bear preceded them, her face wreathed in smiles.

"I learned your language from the missionaries," she said boldly.

"You speak it very well. And for that, I'm grateful," Dan said with a laugh. "My command of the Comanche tongue is not as good as your command of the white man's tongue."

"I have visited you each day, though you never knew me. Morning Light said you were in the land of the spirits."

"Thank you for your visits," Dan said. "Even though I don't remember, I appreciate your concern."

Behind her were her father, Crooked Tree, a tall, handsome brave, and her mother, shy, plump Winter Bird.

"We bring greetings, Pale Wolf," her father said solemnly. "And we thank you for giving us back our daughter, who was lost to us."

Little Bear's eyes danced as she murmured, "I have told the others that I knew you were from the spirit world when I saw you open the white man's body and remove his heart."

Dan shook his head. "It wasn't his heart, Little Bear. I removed..." He paused. How could he explain an appendix? "I removed a part of his body that was very sick."

"I watched from a crack in the wagon," the young girl said. "Though you may deny it, I saw you pluck out the evil man's heart."

Dan held his silence. There was no point in arguing. The girl's mind was made up.

When he didn't speak, she blurted, "How can you deny that the spirits protect you? Even the white man's bullets could not kill you. All of our people talk about the pale wolf who will not die."

Little Bear's father stepped forward. Placing his hand on his daughter's shoulder, he said to Dan, "You gave our daughter back to us. In return, we give her to you. Though she is very young, she will grow to please you."

Standing off to one side, Morning Light's hand tightened on the shoulder of the little boy who stood beside her. She was surprised by the sudden shaft of pain around her heart. Though she had known that Little Bear would be given to her rescuer, she had not expected these strange feelings.

Because he understood the Comanche customs, Dan had anticipated this offer. And dreaded it.

"I cannot accept your kind offer of your daughter," Dan said. Out of the corner of his eye he saw the frown on the chief's face and knew that he was taking a chance on incurring the wrath of all the Comanche.

"I know that it is the custom to own the one whose life you save." He saw Morning Light stiffen and forced himself to continue smoothly, "But in this case, Little Bear also saved my life. If she had not brought me here, I would have died."

"You cannot die, Pale Wolf. You are of the spirit world," the girl protested.

Dan touched a hand to the girl's cheek, then firmly turned her into her parents' arms. "I am a man, not a spirit," he said softly. "There is no more debt between us."

The girl's mother, who had been prepared to lose her daughter a second time, gathered her close and fought back tears of relief.

Her father, too, seemed relieved. He had been prepared to follow their custom, even though it meant giving his beloved child to this white stranger.

Crooked Tree offered his hand to Dan. "I would be proud to stand beside you, Pale Wolf, if ever you need a friend."

"I ask no more than that," Dan murmured, accepting his hand.

With wide smiles the happy family left the tepee. Dan then turned to face the chief, who was still frowning.

"You should have accepted their offer of their daughter," Two Moons said sternly. "Little Bear has a good heart. She would have been much comfort to you."

"She's a child," Dan said abruptly. "She isn't ready to be with a man."

"You are not just any man, Pale Wolf. To the family of Little Bear, you are of the spirit world. It would be an honor to boast that their daughter was your woman.''

Dan turned away, to signal that the conversation was ended. He glanced at the woman who had so tenderly cared for him. Then his gaze slid to the little boy who still hid behind Morning Light's skirts. From time to time the boy stole a furtive glance at the man who was taller even than the chief.

"Is he yours?" Dan asked Morning Light.

The young woman remained silent while Two Moons said, "The boy is my son."

Dan experienced a wave of relief and had no idea why. He told himself that it didn't matter whether or not Morning Light had a husband and child.

But a nagging little voice deep inside reminded him that it did.

The chief dropped a protective hand on the boy's shoulder and added, "This is Runs With The Wind. His mother died during his birth."

When the boy glanced shyly up at Dan, the chief added, "A spirit has stolen his voice. He does not speak."

Dan was unaware that his look softened as he acknowledged the boy. But it was not lost on Two Moons. Or on his sister.

"Have you a woman and children, Pale Wolf?" the chief asked.

Beside him, his sister went very still.

Dan shook his head, unaware that his gaze strayed to Morning Light. The chief watched her reaction carefully, then turned to Dan. "Life is difficult without someone to share it."

Dan shrugged, then glanced at him. "How long ago did you lose your wife?"

"Four summers have gone now since Runs With The Wind was born. But the loss of his mother pains me still."

Dan decided to turn the tables. "There are many beautiful young maidens who would be proud to be wife to the chief."

Two Moons smiled. "Has my sister been filling your mind with her words?"

When Dan glanced at Morning Light, the chief explained, "She thinks another wife would soften my anger."

"And still your sharp tongue," Morning Light added.

Two Moons threw back his head and laughed. "You see why my sister still lives in the tepee of the chief? No other man would permit such bold words to be spoken in his presence."

He lifted his son, to the delight of the little boy. "Come, Pale Wolf. We will take nourishment. For your spirit has fought many battles since you came to us."

As they strode from the tepee, Dan remarked, "None of this looks familiar. Is my mind playing tricks on me, or is this a different camp from the one I rode into five days ago with Little Bear?"

Two Moons smiled. "I see your mind was not as wounded as your body. This is indeed a new camp. We left after the attack by the Kiowa Apache."

Dan shook his head. "So many things seem like only half-remembered dreams."

"In time it will all come back to you."

The chief led Dan toward a grassy knoll. As they sat, a young brave walked up to Dan. The look on his face was one of controlled anger.

He spoke to Two Moons, who explained, "This is Ishatai. The Coyote. I welcome his counsel. He has proved his bravery in battle."

Dan nodded at the young man, who gave him an arrogant glance before turning back to the chief.

"It is not right that this white man is permitted to stay in the lodge of the chief," Ishatai said in Comanche, unaware that Dan understood.

"You would send him away before his wounds are healed enough to sit a horse?" Two Moons seemed surprised at Ishatai's outburst.

"What if this stranger should rise up in the night and strike? The People would be left without a chief." The brave glowered at Dan. "Now that he is strong enough to move around, he is a danger to Two Moons and his family."

"The decision is mine," the chief said softly. "And I have decided to trust this man."

"Trust. Since when do the Comanche trust the white man?"

Two Moons held up a hand. "I have spoken."

Ishatai stalked away.

"It looks like I've stirred up a lot of fear among your people," Dan said softly. He understood their need to move their camp.

"We fear what we do not know." Two Moons cradled his son in his arms. "It will take time for them to know you, Pale Wolf."

Dan smelled the long-forgotten aroma of deer roasting over a fire. And he remembered the stale biscuits he had eaten—could it be five days ago? No wonder he suffered such weakness.

The chief studied the fatigue etched on Dan's face. "First you will eat, then you will rest once more. In resting, a brave gathers his strength for the next battle."

As Morning Light moved around the fire, Dan's gaze followed her. He was unaware that the chief watched him carefully.

"It was Morning Light who removed the buffalo hunters' bullets from your flesh," Two Moons said with a trace of pride. "And she who called upon the healing spirits."

"Then I am forever in your debt," Dan said as Morning Light knelt to place several dishes in front of them.

"I tended to your wounds because my brother commanded it, and he is a great chief. But I feared that you would bring others like yourself to our camp."

"My father was friend to the Comanche. I'd like to be your friend, as well."

"Will our 'friend' bring the white soldiers, now that he knows of our camp?"

Two Moons shot her a dark look and she clamped her mouth shut on any further outburst.

"Our guest," he emphasized the word, "Pale Wolf, will eat so that he can regain his strength."

Morning Light set out deer meat and wild plums, hot, steaming Indian potatoes mixed with wild onion, and hot, roasted acorns. Then she obediently took a seat beside her brother.

"...and you studied at the white man's university to be a healer?"

At the chief's question, Dan nodded and finished his meal, then leaned back, replete.

There was much, the chief deduced, that this man had left unsaid. It was there in his troubled eyes, his careful speech. But Two Moons had learned long ago that every man's heart harbored secrets. Secrets he carefully shielded from others.

"You have been gone a long time. The land has changed. The people have changed." Two Moons signaled his sister to remove the food. As Morning Light moved among them, Dan's gaze followed her.

"I guess we've all changed," he said tiredly.

Two Moons glanced at Dan, whose eyes were glazed with the pain he tried to hide.

"Come," he said as he stood and made his way to the tepee.

Dan struggled to his feet and followed.

"You must rest now. It is in sleep that your body will heal."

Dan nodded, too weary to argue. "I'm grateful for your hospitality." Bending, he entered the tepee and began to wrap himself in the buffalo robe.

"Sleep well, Pale Wolf. In the morning you will feel much stronger than you do tonight."

"He stays again in your tepee?" Ishatai had returned and was quick to voice his displeasure.

"He risked his life to return Little Bear to her family," Two Moons replied. He saw the brave's mouth open to issue another protest and cut him off sharply with a note of finality, "We will speak no more of it tonight. Now we will sleep."

Dan was grateful for the silence that followed the chief's command. With his eyes closed, he listened to the sounds of the others moving around the tepee. He heard Ishatai speaking in low, angry tones to the chief, before his voice receded. There were whispered com-

forts to the little boy, Runs With The Wind, in a quiet
voice that rippled over his senses.

He rolled to his side and closed his eyes. He was
weary. Bone weary.

Lulled by the hiss and snap of the fire, his breathing became slow and even. But despite his weariness,
his sleep was restless.

Chapter Four

Pain jolted Dan awake. For long minutes he lay in the darkness, listening to the sounds of slow, even breathing. His body was bathed in sweat. He felt as if he were suffocating. He needed to stand beneath an open sky and breathe cool fresh air.

Folding the buffalo robe over his arm, he slipped from the tepee and made his way to the banks of the river. He draped the robe over the low-hanging branch of a gnarled old tree. Rolling a cigarette, he held a match to the tip and drew smoke into his lungs. He lifted his head and watched as the smoke dissipated into the night air.

Texas. It had taken him ten years and thousands of miles. But he had made it home.

Strange, he thought as a frown etched itself between his brows. He had long dreamed of returning home. And he had pictured himself setting up a little practice in the town near his sister's big ranch.

He sighed and thought about the strange circumstances that had forever changed his life. Nothing, it seemed, would ever be as he'd planned it. Instead of a quiet little town, he was surrounded by Comanche, many of whom made no secret of the fact that they considered him an intruder.

Maybe he was, he thought suddenly. Maybe he would always be an intruder wherever he roamed. Maybe there was no place he could ever truly belong.

Morning Light lay wrapped in her buffalo robe, listening to the sounds of slow, steady breathing coming from those around her. Something had awakened her. And now that her sleep was disturbed, she knew that sleep would elude her for the rest of the night. Her heartbeat was too unsteady. Her mind was too troubled. And all because of the stranger in their midst.

She must not allow herself to think about Pale Wolf. Though he had once, in his youth, been kind to her and nursed her through a grave wound, he was a man now. A white man. An enemy to the Comanche.

She closed her eyes and thought about the way he had healed her when she had been little more than a child. His touch had been surprisingly gentle. His manner had been unexpectedly shy. Through the long months and years that followed she had relived the incident in her mind until it had become magnified. She had replayed over and over the touch of his hand, the gentleness of his words, until he had become larger than life. What a foolish child she had been. Like Little Bear, she had convinced herself that the man who saved her was possessed of spirits. To the white youth, however, it was probably no more than a passing event that had been quickly forgotten.

She stared at the glowing embers of the fire and shifted in annoyance. How was it that this man, this stranger, should disturb her so? She had finally, after years of struggle, managed to push his image to some distant corner of her mind. And now he was here, stirring up unsettling feelings, stealing even her much deserved rest.

Tossing aside the robe, she made her way from the tepee of her brother and stalked to the river. While the others slept she would enjoy an unhurried bath.

Clouds scudded across a full moon, casting the land in darkness. Dan heard the snap of a twig and was instantly alert. His fingers tightened on the trigger of his pistol. As the shadow drew near, he coiled, ready to pounce. He waited, gauging the distance, then sprang. His arm tightened around the throat of the figure in his grasp.

"Don't move a muscle," he breathed.

He pressed his gun to flesh, then muttered a low savage oath when he realized his mistake. His captive was small and slight and smelled faintly of wildflowers and evergreen.

As quickly as he had ensnared her, he released her. Dropping his arms to his sides, he watched as she whirled to face him.

"I..." She swallowed and tried again. Her breath was coming in short gasps, and she blamed it on fear. It was surely not the nearness of this man that caused such breathlessness. "I did not know you had come down to the river. I thought you were still asleep in the tepee of my brother."

"I wanted to be alone." His voice was low with repressed anger. Damn her. He'd nearly broken her pretty neck. And all because he was jumpy. The pain had caused him to become careless.

She watched as he jammed his pistol into the holster he wore low on his hips. Then her gaze moved to his eyes, dark, hooded in the moonlight. She felt a shiver course along her spine at the intensity of his look.

"It's dangerous to walk out here alone." Dan's voice was angrier than he intended. "Don't you care that what happened to Little Bear could happen to you?"

"I do not need you to remind me of the dangers lurking in the darkness." Her voice was low with resentment. "I have lived with danger from the moment of my birth."

In the silence that followed, she saw him wince as he took a step back.

"Your wounds still pain you?"

"Some. But it's tolerable." He glanced at her. "I never properly thanked you for taking care of me. From what I recall, I must have been a handful."

She almost smiled, then caught herself. "You were—burdened in your mind."

His head came up. "What did I say?"

She shrugged. "It made no sense to me." Morning Light knew that it would be impolite to repeat the secrets he had revealed while the fever held him in its grip. He had spoken of murder, betrayal, pain and heartbreak. Such things belonged to the white man's world. They had no place here.

She began to walk along the riverbank and Dan fell into step beside her. They made their way slowly along the banks, skirting the low brush that grew to the very edge of the water.

The clouds had blown over, revealing the golden full moon. Thin ribbons of moonlight danced across the waves and touched the shore with a luminous light.

"Your people are far from their hunting grounds," Dan said, hoping to keep the conversation impersonal.

"The buffalo herds have thinned. We are forced to travel new routes."

"Your tribe is smaller than I remembered."

"Many of our people have died. Others left for the reservations."

He heard the edge to her voice. "You make it sound like a hanging. Is life so bad on the reservation?"

She turned on him and he could see the fire in her eyes. "You ask such a foolish question? I will answer with a question. Tell me. Why have you come back here?"

"Texas is my home." He watched a strand of her hair lift on the breeze and then gently drift to her cheek. He curled his hand into a fist at his side to keep from reaching out to it. "I've missed it."

"You could have remained where you were. You had a warm bed? There was plenty of game?"

Her questions brought a frown to his lips as he thought of the teeming city of Boston. "The bed was warm. And there was more than enough to eat. But I couldn't stay."

"Why?" Her eyes flashed. "Did you miss the land of your birth? Did you realize that this was where your heart lay?"

He shrugged and said nothing.

Her voice lowered with passion. "It is the same for the Comanche. This land is home to us, as well. If we are sent away by your great chief, many will mourn their loss. Many, like Two Moons," she added softly, "would die of loneliness in a strange land."

"Two Moons is a strong chief. I doubt a move to the reservation would kill him."

"A great chief like my brother would lose his will for life," she whispered fiercely. "And that is worse than death itself. Something inside him would die. Something that sets him apart from other men."

Dan had no response for that. He knew she was right. Hadn't he found out for himself that there were some things worse than death? How would he have fared if he'd been forced to remain in Boston against his will?

"What about the rest of your people?" he asked softly. "What if the government decrees that all of you will be punished because of your brother's decision to remain free?"

"How will your chief punish us?" Morning Light whispered. The anger was evident in her tone. "Will he take away the blankets that cannot keep out the cold? Will he withhold the food and medicine promised us that we have never seen?"

This was the Morning Light Dan had remembered all these years. This fiery female whose eyes danced with a fierce flame, whose words lashed as surely as any whip. Not the woman who, in her brother's tepee, had lowered her gaze and assumed an air of humility. He could understand the anger that smoldered in her, even if he could not completely share it.

"What if the government sends troops after you?"

"Do you think we fear death?" Her hands clenched at her sides as she hissed, "We are prepared to die rather than give up the way of life that has sustained us since the time of our father's father, and his before him."

"If you don't fear what will happen to you, at least think about the children. And the old ones in the tribe who won't be strong enough to flee the wrath of the soldiers."

He saw the pain in her eyes before she turned away. Staring out over the river, she crossed her arms under her breasts and shivered.

With her voice barely more than a whisper, she said, "It is for the very young and the old ones that Two Moons makes this difficult choice. My brother is a good chief and a fair one. He knows that the old ones are pained by the loss of freedom to follow the buffalo. And he fears that the young will never know this same life. Soon, Two Moons has promised, he will call a council of all his chiefs. It will be for them to decide whether to accept the rule of the white man and take the last of our people to the reservation, or to continue our way of life as we have always known it in defiance of your great chief in Washington." Her voice lowered. "Know this. If Two Moons gives his word that the Comanche will live, or die, on the land of their fathers, it will be so. For you must know," she said, turning to face him in a gesture of defiance, "my brother does not lightly give his word."

He saw a tear squeeze from the corner of her eye and trail along her cheek. Without thinking, he lifted a hand and touched a finger to it.

He realized at once his mistake. At the mere touch of her he felt a jolt that left him shaken to the core.

"I hope you'll forgive the foolish words I spoke in anger," he whispered. "I respect your brother's word. And I certainly didn't mean to make you cry."

"I do not cry," she said in a tone of outrage.

"Of course not." His words warmed with unspoken laughter.

She slapped his hand away, catching him unawares. "Do you mock me?"

His smile vanished. His tone was low with feeling. "I may be guilty of many things, Morning Light. But not of that. I would never mock you."

She heard the change in his tone and felt a ripple of feeling along her spine. Fear? she wondered. Or—anticipation?

She saw the way his eyes narrowed as he studied her. A thrill shot through her as he lowered his head. She did not know whether to stay or run. And though she was filled with fear at what he might do, she found she could not escape. She was frozen to the spot.

He lifted a strand of her hair and watched as it sifted through his fingers. Soft. It was as soft as he'd imagined it would be. With a fingertip he traced the curve of her cheek and felt his throat go dry.

This was another mistake, he realized. He had no right to the thoughts that suddenly leaped into his mind to torment him. Thoughts that had nothing to do with Texas and survival.

"You'd better go back to your brother's tepee." His voice was gruff.

She was stung by the abruptness of his tone. "I will go when it pleases me."

Her nervousness had passed. She was in control once more. With a haughty lift of her chin, she said, "It is you who should return to your bed. I came to the river to be alone. I did not ask you here."

She turned away, intending to walk past him. She was unprepared for the strength in his grip as he closed a hand around her arm and pulled her toward him.

Her eyes widened as she was hauled roughly against him. She pressed her two hands to his chest to hold him at bay, but her strength was no match for his.

She looked up into his eyes and was surprised at the blaze of passion in them. A passion that both frightened and intrigued her.

"You will let me go." Her voice was low and breathless, and she blamed it on their struggle.

"When I'm good and ready." His blood was fueled by anger, Dan told himself. It was not caused by the woman in his arms.

He clutched her upper arms, his thumbs pressing into the softness of her flesh. As he dragged her closer, he lowered his head until his lips hovered a fraction above hers.

She felt his breath hot against her cheek and experienced a wild tremor of fear along her spine. It was unlike any fear she had ever known before. There was danger here. Everything about this man spoke of danger. But it was a danger that thrilled and fascinated her.

She saw his gaze narrow on her lips and tried to back away, but he held her fast. Alarmed, she ran a tongue over her lips and saw the way he watched the movement.

He was going to touch his mouth to hers. Her heart fluttered in her breast like a caged bird. "You must not." He heard her voice, low with feeling. "It is forbidden."

Her protests only made her more tempting. He drew her closer and felt a wave of heat as her breasts were pressed to his chest.

They stood staring at each other for long moments. Dan's eyes were narrowed in thought. Morning Light's eyes were wide with fear.

He wanted her. Sweet Jesus, Dan thought with a frown. Never in his life had he wanted to touch, to taste, as he did this minute. He had already broken so many rules, what would it matter if he broke one more? But her words had had the desired effect. He had no right to take what she did not willingly offer.

He studied the way she looked in the moonlight. Her hair drifted over one shoulder and spilled across her breast. Her upturned face was so lovely he longed to press his lips to her eyebrow, her temple, the curve of her cheek.

He saw the way her lips trembled as his gaze burned over her. She could feel his kiss as surely as if they were already sharing it. He felt scalded by the heat. It was as if he had already pressed his mouth to hers.

And then he knew.

"I didn't dream that kiss, did I?"

She stiffened in his arms and tried to draw away, but he held her firmly against him. His thumbs were no longer bruising as they made lazy circles on the soft flesh of her upper arms.

"What is a kiss?"

His eyes narrowed. "The pressing of two mouths together." He drew her fractionally closer, than lowered his head and touched his lips to hers. "Like this."

Heat poured between them, searing them with its intensity.

He lifted his head. "I didn't dream it, did I?"

She shook her head, unable to speak over the fear that constricted her throat.

He lowered his head and again brushed his lips over hers. The heat continued to build.

She sighed as his hands continued to weave their magic, moving along her spine, drawing her against the length of him.

Her hands, which she had kept firmly between them, now seemed to have a will of their own as they curled into the front of his shirt, drawing him even closer. A tiny fist seemed to tighten deep inside her, and the blood roared in her temples.

Dan was stunned by the rush of emotions unleashed by the simple touch of her lips. He knew he had to step back from this woman or be consumed by the flames that leaped between them. Still he lingered, unwilling to break contact.

How sweet the fragrance that drifted from her. How warm the breath that kissed his cheek. One taste of her lips would never be enough. Now that he had sipped this healing nectar, he wanted more. So much more. Calling upon all his willpower, he lifted his head.

He knew he must walk away now, before they were both burned.

He stared down at the woman who stood so close he could feel her heartbeat inside his own chest. Her lashes were lowered, veiling her look. Suddenly they swept up and he was staring into her eyes. Eyes that revealed her confusion. Never before had she had to battle such conflicting emotions.

He took a step back, needing to break contact. His hands curled into fists at his sides. "I'll leave you to your privacy."

Morning Light stood very still, hoping he would not see how affected she had been by his kiss. As if to prove her point, she rubbed the back of her hand across her lips, to erase his touch.

Instead of lingering by the water's edge, she turned toward the camp. "I…" She struggled to get the words out. "I must return to my brother's tepee. I will be missed."

As she moved through the grass, damp with dew, she prayed her trembling legs would not fail her. Her heart beat an unsteady rhythm in her chest. So this was what the white man called a kiss.

For many years now she had carried an image in her heart. An image of a sweet, gentle healer. She had even allowed herself to think about—kissing him. Never, in her wildest dreams, had she imagined such tumultuous feelings as those they had just shared.

This was not the shy, awkward boy she remembered. This was a man. A man whose touch had been far from gentle. She was aware of the effort it had cost him to hold his passion in check. A passion that frightened her. Yet she could not deny that his simple touch had set her aflame. What magic did he possess, that he could cause this weakness in her? Was he not, after all, her enemy?

Dan watched until she disappeared inside her brother's tepee. Then he reached into his pocket and rolled another cigarette. As he held a match to the tip, he noted that his hand was trembling. With a savage oath he turned and strode along the banks of the river.

If he went back to the tepee now, he would never be able to stop thinking about the woman who slept mere inches from him. He would be better to sleep here under the stars.

As he rolled himself into the buffalo robe and settled his back against a log, the fragrance of evergreen and wildflower still clung to him, clouding his thoughts.

Chapter Five

Dan awakened to the sound of children laughing. For long moments he lay in the buffalo robe and struggled to recall where he was. For so long now, he had heard only the sounds of sickness and pain; women moaning in childbirth; parents weeping for their dying children; the elderly, alone and feeble, crying out for help. In the cramped dispensary near Boston Harbor, laughter had been a rare and wonderful gift.

Sudden memory washed over him. He was no longer in Boston. He was in Texas, in the Comanche camp. Names filled his mind. Little Bear. Two Moons. His pulse raced as one name pushed aside all the others. Morning Light.

He opened his eyes and found three little children peering at him. One was Runs With The Wind, the other two were girls of six or seven. When they realized that he was awake, they ran away and took shelter behind a stand of trees. From there they continued to watch him. The girls' giggles trilled on the morning air.

He saw them peering out from behind the trees as he sauntered down to the river and washed. Pulling on his boots, he returned to find his bedroll placed neatly beside the log. He glanced around and saw Little Bear disappearing into her father's tepee. Everything in the bedroll had been cleaned and neatly replaced. Apparently the child had appointed herself his guardian angel.

Dropping his shirt over the branch of a tree, he lathered his face and began shaving. In the small, chipped looking glass, he watched as the three crept closer. Their puzzled looks brought a grin to his face.

In Comanche he heard one of the girls whisper, "Pale Wolf skins himself."

It was all he could do to keep from laughing aloud.

When they were directly behind him, he pretended not to notice as he finished shaving and wiped the lather from his face. Without turning, he said, "It wasn't skin I removed, only the hair from my face." He turned. "There's no blood. See?"

The three jumped as if burned. One girl shrieked, "He is a white devil with eyes in the back of his head." They began to beat a hasty retreat.

Shaking with laughter, he heard a voice telling them gently to return to camp. A moment later he saw Morning Light's image in the mirror.

She had been reluctant to return to this place by the river. But her brother had commanded it. She blamed her unsteady breathing on the hurried walk. It was not, she told herself firmly, the memory of last night's encounter.

The young woman studied Dan's broad shoulders a moment before meeting his glance in the mirror. Instantly she felt a rush of heat and fought to keep her tone impersonal.

"My brother sends his wishes that you will join him at his tepee for a morning meal."

He turned and reached for his shirt. As he pulled it on and began to button it, Morning Light's eyes followed every movement. How broad his shoulders. How strange the pale skin, darkened with a mat of dark hair that covered his chest. When he had been recovering from his wounds, she had been unaware of him as a man. He had been merely an injury that needed caring for. But now he was a strong, healthy man. Very much a man.

When he tucked his shirt into the waistband of his pants, she looked up to find his gaze locked on her. She knew her cheeks must be flaming.

"Tell Two Moons that I would be honored."

She nodded and hurried away, relieved to escape his probing stare.

Dan's thoughts were in turmoil as he put away his supplies and folded the buffalo robe over his arm.

The feelings that had surfaced were not the result of his encounter with Morning Light, he told himself firmly. He was simply restless. He'd been here long enough. His wounds were healing nicely. In another day or two it would be time to move on.

As he strode toward the tepee of the chief, he was once again aware of the many emotions from those who watched him. The braves stopped talking as he passed. Some made no move to veil their hostility. Some merely watched out of curiosity. Others, following Crooked Tree's example, called out a greeting or smiled as he passed. Some women gathered the smaller children close, as if to protect them from this intimidating stranger, while others held their infants aloft, as if to secure his benediction. The older children stared boldly as he approached, then quickly ducked their heads when his gaze challenged theirs.

Inside the tepee, Two Moons reclined on a folded buffalo robe. Beside him was Ishatai, The Coyote. The two were engaged in quiet conversation. When Dan entered, Two Moons looked up in greeting.

"My sister told me that your sleep was disturbed. Did you find rest by the water?"

"I was comfortable enough."

Dan glanced at Morning Light, who knelt to place a wooden bowl in front of her brother. He saw the way her cheeks flamed.

He held out the buffalo robe that he had folded over his arm. "Thanks for letting me use this."

"It is a gift. You will face many cold nights on your journeys. Let the buffalo robe be a reminder of our gratitude for your kindness to Little Bear."

"Thank you." Dan was touched by the chief's generosity.

"You will sit beside me," Two Moons said, patting the hides that had been placed on the ground.

Dan sat and watched as Morning Light placed before them a mush made of buffalo marrow mixed with crushed mesquite beans. He tasted it and was surprised to learn that it was sweet and delicious. Along with that there was deer and rabbit, roasted over the fire, and a bowl of grapes.

When Morning Light took her place next to her brother, his little son, Runs With The Wind, crept up shyly and sat beside her. Once again Dan noted in those few halting steps the boy's pronounced limp.

"When do you leave our camp?" Ishatai asked.

Dan watched as Morning Light urged the little boy to eat. It was plain that she adored Runs With The Wind and was as concerned as any mother.

"Soon. In a day or two if I'm strong enough."

At his reply, Morning Light's hand paused in mid-air and she glanced up. Seeing his gaze on her, she quickly returned her attention to the boy.

"That is good. That your wounds are healing," Ishatai hastily added. He began to relax. Soon this white man would be gone from their camp. He had been uneasy since the arrival of this intruder. And he did not like the way the white man looked at Morning Light. Nor the way she watched him when she thought no one was looking.

"You are not yet strong enough to sit a horse," the chief said sternly.

"I'll be fine. My strength returns more each day."

"You are eager to leave the camp of the Comanche."

"It isn't that. It's just—" Dan deliberately kept his gaze from straying to Morning Light "—time for me to leave."

"You have been gone too long from this land. Much has changed." Two Moons signaled his sister to remove the food. "The land has changed. As have the people."

"It looks like little has changed in your camp. You seem to live as you always did."

That fanned the flames of Ishatai's anger. The young brave snarled, "We are the only ones left who fight for the old ways. Nothing is as it was. Our people are sent to lands not of our choosing. Your iron horse speeds across our hunting grounds. The buffalo are being slaughtered by armies of hunters who roam our land."

Two Moons remained silent, watching the reaction between these two young bulls.

"Soon," Ishatai said with venom, "there will be no more buffalo for the Comanche to hunt."

"I read in a newspaper in Boston that the government promised you food, shelter and medicine."

Ishatai gave a snort of disgust. "This paper-that-talks has lied to you. Just as your great chief lied to the Comanche."

"What lies are you talking about?"

"Everything that was promised was a lie." Ishatai's voice rose with anger. "All white men lie to the Comanche."

Two Moons touched a hand to the young brave's arm to still his words. "Soon you will have your chance to speak to the council. Until then you would be wise to keep your thoughts to yourself."

Reluctantly getting to his feet, Two Moons beckoned Dan. "You will forgive Ishatai's anger when you see. Come."

Dan followed him from the tent. The people watched as they made their way through the camp.

Several tepees stood at the edge of the camp, isolated from the others. Two Moons drew open the flap of the first and waited until Dan entered, then followed him inside.

"This is Sings In The Forest."

An old woman lay wrapped in buffalo robes.

"When the buffalo herds thinned, she and her family left our people and journeyed to the reservation to accept the blankets the white man had promised," Two Moons said.

"These are the blankets," Ishatai said. With a look of contempt he held up several coarse, shabby pieces of fabric.

Dan felt a wave of disgust. The flimsy blankets would never keep out the chill of winter.

"She returned to our camp when she discovered that she had the white man's sickness."

Dan had heard about the illnesses that were sweeping the Indian reservations. Measles, whooping cough, cholera. The Indians, who had never before been exposed to such things, had no immunity with which to fight them. Sometimes entire tribes were wiped out.

Dan's first thought was cholera. But when he examined the woman he found the telltale blotches on her skin. "Measles." He glanced up. "Have any of the others been sick?"

"Two of her children. One died on the reservation. The other died before they were able to reach our camp."

"No one must come near Sings In the Forest," Dan said sternly. "Or your entire tribe could be infected. Any who have come in contact with her must be kept away from the others." He led them away from the tepee.

"We will not abandon our sick. The People take care of their own," the chief said just as sternly as he stepped outside.

"You don't understand, Two Moons. The sickness will spread."

"Then who will see to this woman's needs?"

Dan sighed. He really had no choice. "I'll stay and care for her."

"Why will you not get this sickness like the Comanche?"

"Because I have been exposed to it for years. But this sickness is new to your people. You have no way to fight it."

The chief's gaze narrowed. "The Comanche have always fought their own battles."

Dan swallowed back a smile. The years had not changed this proud man. "Are there any more who are sick?"

"There are more," Ishatai said, pointing to the other tepees that were isolated from the camp. "All carry the white man's sickness."

"You have medicine to fight these?" Two Moons asked softly as they made their way back to his tepee.

"I wish I did. For many of these sicknesses, the only medicine is the person's own body." Dan ignored the weariness that taxed his energy. "I will look at your people and do what I can."

"That is all I ask."

As they stepped into the chief's tepee, Dan said, "I don't want to offend your medicine woman." Turning to Morning Light, he said, "Would you like to come with me as I visit the tepees of the sick?"

The chief's sister pushed aside her food and stood. "I want no part of the white man's medicine."

"I understand your impatience, my sister," Two Moons said, choosing his words carefully. "But I cannot accept your behavior to one who is a guest in my tepee. You will go to a quiet place and pray to the great spirit for a more loving heart."

"If I go, I will pray also to the great spirit to lead our people to a land that is free from the tyranny of the white man and his great chief who lies to the People."

Two Moons and Morning Light faced each other in ominous silence. Only Ishatai seemed unaffected by her words. In fact, though he tried to show no emotion, he was pleased that she had given warning to this intruder that she would not be misled by him.

It was Two Moons who finally broke the strained silence. "Morning Light, you will go with our visitor to the tepees of the sick."

With a sigh of reluctance the young woman nodded and led Dan from her brother's tepee. It was obvious to all that she accepted this chore reluctantly. She would have preferred to remain behind.

Dan and Morning Light walked from the last tepee and squinted against the light. They were surprised to note that the sun was already high in the sky as they made their way to the banks of the river. The day had fled while they had gone from tepee to tepee visiting the sick.

Dan watched as she knelt and filled a small buffalo horn with water. Before taking a sip, she offered it to him. He drank gratefully, then returned it to her.

He lifted his hat to wipe the sweat from his brow. "I see now why you're so angry about the lack of medicine," he muttered. "I hadn't expected so many to be sick. If Two Moons isn't careful, everyone in this camp could become infected."

She said nothing. But he could read the anguish in her eyes.

"I don't have much medicine with me, but I'll do what I can. And when I'm strong enough to ride, I'll find a town where I can buy more medicine for your people."

Her tone was harsh. "It is not necessary to say that."

He glanced at her in surprise. "What do you mean?"

She struggled to control her anger. "You need not make such promises. We are not your responsibility."

"I know that. Why are you so angry?"

"I am not angry. I am weary. Weary of empty promises." She began to turn away. "Do not offer gifts you do not intend to bring."

He caught her by the shoulder and forced her to turn back.

"Damn it, Morning Light. This isn't an idle promise. I told you I'd get the medicine and I will."

She stared coldly at the offending hand, then up into his face. "I have heard the promises before. From your missionaries, who taught us your language and promised us peace between your people and my people. And from your great chief, who promised us food and medicine, as well as safety from your soldiers." Her voice lowered. "Your missionaries taught us that it was wrong to make false promises."

He heard the pain beneath her haughty words, and understood her fears. How many lies must these people endure? How many broken promises?

He bit down on the anger that surfaced. "Like your brother, I don't lightly give my word. I'll do everything I can to see that your people get the medicine they need."

She refused to meet his eyes. She could not allow herself to trust this man.

A sudden breeze caught her hair and flailed it across her face. Without thinking, he lifted his hand. He saw her eyes darken with sudden feeling. Abruptly he dropped his hand. He had no right to touch her. But the urge to crush her against him was so strong he was forced to curl his hand into a fist and hold it firmly by his side.

His voice was gruff. "I'd better find your brother and tell him what sicknesses I've found among your people."

Morning Light watched him walk away and felt a tug of disappointment. She had not wanted to exchange harsh words with him. But it seemed to happen more often than she intended.

Throughout the morning, as he had examined the sick, she had been constantly surprised by his gentle manner. With just a few easy questions he had pried information from people who were unwilling to trust him. And when he had touched them, she had watched his big hands probe with such infinite care. The same hands, she realized, that so deftly handled a gun.

The thought of those hands touching her, caressing her, caused strange little tremors deep inside her. Such thoughts were alien to her. Especially since they involved this man, who was so different from anyone else she had ever known.

Soon, she reminded herself, he would leave their camp as quickly and mysteriously as he had arrived. Still, she could not erase the thought of his hands. Hands that held a healing touch. Hands that lingered at her cheek.

The mere thought of his touch had the blood pounding in her temples and her heartbeat racing.

She sighed and scolded herself for such foolish thoughts. Walking to the banks of the river, she stood and watched as Runs With The Wind limped along beside the other children. His obvious joy made her heart feel lighter. But as her thoughts drifted once more to Pale Wolf, her smile faded.

Though he had shown a gentleness with the sick, he was kind, it seemed, to everyone except her. With her, his voice was always gruff. His touch, too, was not the same with her. There was a carefully coiled tension in him whenever he touched her. As though, she thought, he was struggling with an evil spirit within him.

She reminded herself that she had no right to the thoughts that played through her mind. She and Pale Wolf came from two different worlds. He was a white man, an educated man who had returned to the land of his people with dark secrets in his heart. And she was the sister of a great Comanche chief, who had vowed to keep his people free from the white man's domination.

She must be on her guard around this man. He seemed to possess some magical power that caused her to forget who she was when she was in his arms.

She would be relieved when this white man was gone, she told herself. Then she could get on with her life as it had been before his unexpected arrival. She much preferred a night of blissful sleep to the unsettling feelings his mere touch aroused.

She crossed her arms under her breasts and kicked at a pebble embedded in the sand. Again, she found herself thinking about the kiss they had shared. And the feelings that had poured through her at his simple touch.

Chapter Six

"Morning Light said that you brought great comfort to our sick." The chief walked through the camp, with Dan at his side.

"Did she?" Dan had no idea why that should please him. She had been cool and correct with him throughout the entire day. But she had rejected all attempts at anything that even faintly resembled friendship. In fact, she made no secret of the fact that she resented having to accompany him. "As I explained to your sister, I'll try to get more medicine when I'm strong enough to ride to a town. It may take a while, but I'll see to it."

Two Moons smiled, displaying white even teeth. "Did Morning Light grow angry at your promise?"

Dan chuckled, thinking of the way she'd bristled like a cat tossed into a barrel of rainwater. "How did you know?"

The chief's smile faded as they reached his tepee. "Like all of my people, she is weary of the white man's empty promises." His voice lowered. "Morning Light refuses to put her trust in you, or in any white man, for fear of being betrayed again."

Dan turned to him. "I'm sorry. Sorry about the lies and the sickness and the way you've been treated in the past. But I give you my word, I'll see that you get the medicine you need."

Two Moons studied Dan's weary features and decided to withhold judgment. Perhaps this white man was different from the others; perhaps not. "You have pushed your body beyond its limits, Pale Wolf. Your wounds are not fully healed. Now you must rest."

"In a while." Dan paused beside the folded buffalo robe and waited until the chief was seated. Then he sat beside him. "How did so many of your people get these sicknesses?"

For a moment Two Moons didn't meet his gaze. When he did, his voice was strangely subdued. "I once trusted your great chief in Washington. When the buffalo herds grew thin, many of the People went to the reservation. Some went willingly. Others were forced." He looked up and Dan saw the smoldering anger in his eyes. "When some managed to return, I learned what had happened to my people. Many had died. Those who lived were cold, hungry, sick." His voice deepened with passion. "I was the cause of their pain. I trusted your great chief in Washington. He betrayed that trust."

Dan felt a slow, simmering anger building deep inside at the injustice of it.

Pressing a hand over his eyes, he said wearily, "Someone has to convey to the men in Washington what is really happening here. As soon as I'm strong enough to ride, I'll go to the Indian agent and learn why my government has failed to live up to its promises."

The chief's look was grave. "I do not think it wise to go to him." When Dan said nothing he said tiredly, "We will speak no more of it now. You must rest, Pale Wolf, and regain your strength. Come. We will eat."

The chief led the way as Dan followed him from the tepee.

In the distance the sun dipped below the mountains, casting the land in a red glow. Shadows lengthened, softening the harsh landscape.

Morning Light and Runs With The Wind were laughing together as they worked. Several plump quail were roasting over a fire. On a large, flat rock Morning Light pounded wild berries and pecans into a paste and mixed it with dried buffalo meat, then laid it out to dry after cutting a piece for the little boy.

"Smells good," Dan muttered, coming up behind them.

"You would like some pemmican?"

He nodded and she handed him a piece. Dan hadn't expected it to be so delicious. Now he understood why the children were often seen eating this thing the white men called Indian bread.

As Morning Light moved about, she felt Dan's gaze following her and her cheeks grew hot.

How different he looked with his face clean shaven. Without the dark bristly beard to mask his features, she was even more aware of the finely chiseled nose, the perfectly sculpted mouth, the defiant thrust of his chin. A chin, she noted, that had a small indentation. But it was his eyes that held her. Eyes that could convey cold fury, as they had when he had listened to the litany of cruelties endured by the people who had returned from the reservation. Eyes that could show such tenderness and compassion as they had when he examined the old ones, whose suffering had been the greatest.

She glanced up and found him watching her. Heat flooded her cheeks. Needing something to do, she reached for the iron kettle sitting on the fire. Distracted by thoughts of the one who sat beside her brother, she failed to notice that it was red-hot. With a cry of pain she dropped it, spilling its contents into the flames.

With a feeling of dread Dan leaped up and raced to her side.

"I need water," he shouted to Runs With The Wind.

The chief's little son filled a bowl and hurried to stand beside them while Dan lifted Morning Light's hand for his examination.

Already the flesh was puckered and swelling with angry blisters.

Two Moons looked on with concern.

"It is nothing," Morning Light whispered, feeling mortified by her carelessness. She could not stop the tears that flowed freely down her cheeks.

As she tried to pull her hand away, Dan's grip tightened. "First you will sit," he said through gritted teeth, forcing her down upon one of the folded buffalo robes. "And now you will hold your hand in here—" he placed the bowl of water beside her and plunged her hand into it "—until I can find something that will soothe your burns."

She watched as he strode to his saddlebags, which he had deposited inside the chief's tepee. Opening the black bag, he rummaged through until he produced a small vial. Removing the stopper, he began to spread the slippery substance over her hand. Within minutes the pain had subsided.

Morning Light looked up at him with a dazed expression. "You are truly of the spirit world, for you have magic in your hands."

She studied the vial with great interest. But her mistrust of this white man would not permit her to speak the questions that burned within her.

"There's nothing mystical about this," Dan said with a reassuring smile. "In Boston I had great success healing burns with this ointment. The recipe was given me by an old woman who wandered about the countryside healing her neighbors."

Seeing the way the chief's sister studied the vial, he said softly, "I boiled thorn apple leaves in fresh hog's lard. If you'd like, I'll show you how to make it."

"The old one taught me the ways of the People. I do not need the white man's tricks."

Very gently Dan brushed the tears from Morning Light's face. Instantly she lowered her head to avoid meeting his gaze. She knew her cheeks were flaming and she could not bear to reveal her emotions in front of this man.

"I burned our food," she muttered awkwardly.

"It does not matter," the chief said. He salvaged what was left of their meal and began to parcel it out.

Dan hesitated a moment, unwilling to leave Morning Light's side, yet aware that his presence beside her made her extremely uncomfortable. He walked to the fire and busied himself beside Two Moons.

When the food was ready, Dan took the seat beside Morning Light. She watched as he tore a strip of tender meat from the bone and lifted it to her lips. A tiny thrill shot through her and she forced herself to accept his offering. But even as she chewed her food and kept her gaze firmly fixed on the ground, she could still feel his hands upon her, so big and yet so gentle. She shivered. What was happening to her? Why was she allowing herself to be drawn to this man?

In her heart she knew that she must fight this attraction. What she was feeling for this man was wrong. She was the sister of Two Moons, the great Comanche chief.

She closed her eyes to keep from looking at the source of her temptation. The pain in her hand had faded until it was nothing more than a dull ache. She felt ashamed that she had brought this on herself by becoming careless for a moment. A moment when she had been distracted by the very man who now crowded her thoughts.

It seemed too much effort to open her eyes again. The lids were so heavy. Her head nodded and she snuggled into the warmth that seemed to surround her. She felt herself drifting on a cloud. And then she was bundled into the softness of a buffalo robe. Content, she slept.

Morning Light awoke and lay very still. She could not recall walking to her brother's tepee. Nor could she remember crawling into her buffalo robe. Suddenly she was overcome with shame as it dawned on her. The warmth that had surrounded her had been arms. Pale Wolf's strong arms. She remembered the big hands, so strong, so gentle, lifting her as easily as if she weighed nothing at all. And she remembered the rough, scratchy collar of his shirt. And the scent of him that she had drawn deeply into her lungs as she had pressed her lips to his throat. She felt the warmth wash over her as she remembered his hands gently drawing the buffalo robe around her. And the deep sound of his voice murmuring words to her. Words she could no longer recall.

She sat up and glanced at the sleeping figures gathered around the hot coals of the fire. Two Moons lay on a mound of buffalo robes. Runs With The Wind lay in the bend of his father's arm.

Morning Light glanced at the pallet where Pale Wolf should be sleeping. It was empty.

Tossing back her buffalo robe, she got to her feet and made her way soundlessly from the tepee.

The night was still. Not a breath of air stirred the leaves of the trees. The moon was obscured behind a bank of clouds.

As she approached the river she saw him. Leaning against the trunk of a tree, he was motionless, staring at the stars. In his hand was a cigarette. As he lifted it to his lips, she saw the tip glowing red in the darkness. She watched as a stream of smoke dissipated into the night air.

Her mouth felt dry. Her heart had suddenly begun to beat wildly. What was it about this man that the mere sight of him could cause such feelings?

For long minutes she watched him, unwilling to reveal her presence. Then, recalling his reaction the last time she had come upon him unexpectedly, she deliberately stepped on a twig to announce her arrival. She watched as his head came up sharply. His hand, she noted, went instantly to the gun at his waist. He whirled, then froze.

"I did not want to cause you alarm," she said, watching the way his hand slid away from his pistol.

He waited until she moved closer. "How does your hand feel?"

She flexed it and he saw her wince. "It—no longer causes me pain."

"I'll bet." He caught her hand in his and lifted it, palm up, for his inspection. "You don't lie very well."

Even by the pale light of the stars the extent of her injury was evident. "I'll get more salve."

"No."

She tried to stop him but he brushed past her. Minutes later he returned with the vial. As he spread the precious ointment over her palm, she felt her hand tremble. She found herself praying that he couldn't detect the tiny tremors she sought to hide. Within minutes the soothing ointment began to take effect.

"Better?" he asked.

She nodded, afraid to trust her voice. He was so close. And he continued to hold her hand between both of his.

"We're quite a pair." A hint of laughter warmed his voice. "I get myself shot, you get yourself burned."

Sometimes, when he smiled like this, she found herself less afraid of him. Praying to the spirits for courage, she removed her hand from his and asked, "Why do you leave the tepee in the dark of the night and come to the water alone?"

Dan's smile faded. How could he explain the feelings he had experienced when he awoke and found her asleep so near him? He needed only to reach out a hand and feel her there, just inches away from him in the darkness. It had been the sweetest torment to lie there, watching her while she slept.

"I couldn't sleep." He turned toward the river and she walked along beside him. "I didn't want to wake the others, so I came out here to walk. And think."

"You are eager to leave here and join your people?" She held her breath at his reply.

He shrugged. "I'm just glad to be alive. There were times when I thought I wouldn't make it."

"There were many times when I thought you had joined the spirit world." She hesitated, then added, "You were reluctant to return to us. I thought perhaps you did not want to walk among the living any longer."

"Maybe I didn't." He was silent for long minutes while they stood on the banks of the river and studied the still, dark waters. He turned to her. "But I'm glad you brought me back."

"I did not do it, Pale Wolf," she said solemnly. "It was you who brought yourself back from the spirit world."

"Maybe it was because I caught a glimpse of what awaited me here."

There was no smile in his voice now. His tone was low, gruff.

Morning Light felt a shiver along her spine and blamed it on the chill of the night. The frown was back on his face, she noted. It must be because of her. Whenever he was alone with her, he seemed angry about something.

"I did not mean to intrude on your solitude," she said, turning away. "I will leave you to your thoughts."

"You didn't intrude." His hand snaked out, stopping her in midstride. His voice lowered. "And I don't want you to go."

Her heart began thudding in her chest. She should not have come here. There was about this man a hint of danger that frightened her even while it fascinated her.

Dan stared at the woman whose eyes had widened in surprise. He was itching to kiss her. He desperately wanted to taste her lips again.

His voice was low, seductive. "Sometimes, when I look at you, I still can't believe I'm here with you. After all these years..." He let the rest of his words trail off.

His hand continued to grasp her arm. His thumb moved slowly, lazily around the soft flesh of her upper arm.

"I must..." she swallowed "...get back to my brother's tepee."

"And I must..." his eyes darkened "...kiss you." He gave her no time to protest.

Bending his head, he covered her mouth with his in a searing kiss.

He felt the jolt and thrilled to it. This time he'd been expecting it, but still the intensity of it caught him by surprise. Such heat. Such fire whenever they touched.

As his lips moved slowly, intimately over hers, he savored the wild, exotic taste of her. The fragrance of evergreen and wildflowers filled him until he was drowning in the taste of her, the smell of her.

His arms came around her, pinning her to the length of him. "I've been so hungry for this." With a low murmur he took the kiss deeper.

Morning Light held herself stiffly in his arms, fighting the feelings that washed over her. She was achingly aware of the powerful body pressed to hers. Of the hands that molded her to him without effort.

Of the thighs pressed to hers, alerting her to his arousal.

Suddenly the night seemed to take on a magic of its own. The clouds vanished, leaving the moon glowing softly in the night sky. A million bright stars lit the velvet canopy. The softest breeze whispered past, cooling their heated flesh.

For Morning Light everything seemed new and fresh and wonderful. All her senses sharpened as his lips moved over hers. She was suddenly aware of the sounds in the night. From far off came the mournful wail of a coyote. In the camp a baby cried. From another tepee came the low, husky sound of a woman's laughter. And the answering sound of a man's voice, deep, subdued. A night bird cried overhead.

She was aware of the warmth of his breath as his lips roamed her cheek, her eyelid, her temple. And as his lips returned to claim hers, she tasted the sharp tang of tobacco. He smelled faintly of horses and leather, scents that were as familiar to her as the smells of the earth around them and the river beside them.

Dan plunged both hands into her hair, drawing her head back. His eyes, as he stared into hers, smoldered with desire. She could feel the carefully coiled tension in him as he lowered his head and plundered her mouth once more.

With one hand still cupping her head, his other hand roamed her back, drawing her closer, until her wild heartbeat could be felt inside his own chest. He wanted her. How he wanted to take her here, now. The longer he kissed her, the stronger grew the need. And though he cursed and called himself every kind of a fool, it was already too late. Though he knew better than to tempt himself with this woman, he had slipped beyond reason. He was drowning in the wild, sweet taste of her. Nothing would do except to have her. All of her.

He felt the thundering of her heartbeat and the way her breath caught in her throat. He knew he had to end this. Still, tempting himself further, he lingered over her lips, drawing out the moment. Then, with an ache of regret, he lifted his head.

Morning Light stood very still, feeling the earth tilting at a dangerous angle. "You must not touch me again. It is—"

"Forbidden," he said quickly. He touched his index finger to her lips and slowly traced their outline, all the while watching her eyes. "I will remember from now on."

She took a step back and stood very straight, praying her legs wouldn't buckle.

"I must . . ."

"Go back to your brother's tepee." He caught her hand in his and lifted it to his lips. Very gently he placed a kiss in the palm of her burned hand and closed her fingers over it. His gesture caused a flood of feelings that nearly swamped her.

She swallowed, then turned and fled.

Dan watched until she disappeared inside the darkened shelter. He would speak with Two Moons in the morning. There was no way he could go on sleeping in the chief's tepee. The thought of lying so close to Morning Light and not touching her was becoming intolerable.

Chapter Seven

"Where will you sleep?" Two Moons demanded.

Dan kept his tone deliberately bland. He had no intention of giving even a hint of the way he felt about sleeping in the same tepee with Morning Light.

"Under the stars. Along the banks of the river." Dan folded the buffalo robe over his arm and reached down for his saddle.

"You will continue to eat with us?"

Dan smiled. He'd learned that eating was a gesture of hospitality among the Comanche. Whenever a guest arrived, he was fed at once. "As long as you allow me to supply some of the game."

"You are our guest."

"Not anymore. Unless I can share the work, I'll become a burden. Is it agreed?"

Reluctantly the chief nodded.

As Dan walked from the tepee, Two Moons asked quietly, "It is not because of the harsh words spoken by my sister?"

"No," Dan was quick to reply.

It was obvious to the chief that Dan was covering up something.

"Morning Light is young and impatient, and she has not yet learned that the hatred and injustice of a few powerful men is not shared by all your people. Or mine."

Dan wondered if that lesson was ever really learned. In the so-called civilized East, or here in the untamed West, the cruelty inflicted by the powerful against the weak was the same.

Balancing the saddle on his shoulder, he turned toward the chief. "I've intruded on your family long enough. I'm grateful for all that you and the others have done. But my wounds are healed enough to allow me to take care of myself."

As he made his way to the river, Morning Light's gaze followed him. But when she saw her brother watching her, she lowered her head and began to tend the fire.

"Your chief told me you've been caring for my horse." Dan paused before the tepee of Little Bear and her family.

"Pale Wolf." With a shriek of joy the girl gave him a wide smile, revealing a dimple in her cheek. "You honor us with your visit."

At her words, both her parents appeared at the entrance of the tepee and greeted Dan.

"You will eat with us," Crooked Tree said, while his wife, Winter Bird, hurried to the fire where a kettle of deer meat simmered.

"I just ate," Dan protested.

"You will eat again." Crooked Tree offered Dan a buffalo robe on which to recline.

Dan sat, knowing it was impossible to refuse. He had no choice but to accept the kind hospitality of these people. When he was comfortably seated, the others gathered around the fire. Wooden bowls of steaming meat were passed around, as well as a dish of dried pumpkin drizzled with honey.

"You're a lucky man, Crooked Tree," Dan said, savoring the meal. Now that his wounds were healing, his appetite was sharper than ever. "Winter Bird is a fine cook."

"That is one reason I took her for my woman," the brave said, glancing fondly at his wife.

Winter Bird refused to sit, hovering instead while she saw to the needs of their honored guest.

"You told me it was because she was the prettiest maiden in your village," Little Bear said to her father.

"That also." Crooked Tree shot a grin at Dan, then gathered his daughter close and ruffled her hair.

Dan sat back, enjoying himself. He liked these people. In many respects, they reminded him of his sister, Jessie, and her husband, Cole. There had been an easy, good-natured bantering between them that he'd loved.

He was relieved to see that Little Bear seemed to have recovered from her ordeal at the hands of the buffalo hunters. But he wondered if the unseen wounds had healed as well.

"You are worried about your horse?" Crooked Tree asked.

"Not worried. I just realized that I hadn't seen him since I came here. Where do you keep him?" Dan glanced around the spotless area that surrounded their tepee.

"He is safe. My daughter has been caring for him since you returned her to us." Crooked Tree glanced lovingly at the girl who had chosen to sit beside Dan. Her hero worship was evident in her eyes. "Little Bear has always loved the care of the horses."

Since coming here Dan had learned that the Comanche prided themselves on their horses, treating them with great care. They were excellent horsemen and considered a fine horse to be their greatest treasure.

"The horses are in a secret place," Little Bear said. "If you would like, I will take you there now."

"In a while," Crooked Tree said. "You must allow our guest to fill his stomach first."

"I couldn't eat another thing." Dan smiled at her mother and offered his hand to her father. "Thank you for your kindness."

"You will come again, Pale Wolf," Crooked Tree said, clasping Dan's outstretched hand. "When we can sit and smoke and talk."

Dan nodded. "I'd like that."

With a secret smile Little Bear led him along the banks of the river toward a stand of trees that formed a thick wall. Between two trees the girl had strung a rope. Tied to the rope were over a dozen horses. Spotting his, Dan approached and ran a hand along the animal's smooth flank.

"His coat is sleek, his belly full." Dan lifted the horse's hoof, then another and another, until all four hooves were checked for cracks or infection. "He shows no trace of the tough journey he was forced to endure." Dan turned to Little Bear. "You've done a fine job of caring for him. He's in good shape. I'm grateful."

"You do not check the others?" the girl asked.

"Why would I check those horses?"

"They are yours."

Dan looked at her in surprise. "What are you saying? How can they be mine?"

"They belonged to the buffalo hunters. You took them with you when you helped me escape their camp."

"You mean you never turned them loose?" He paused, struggling to remember. "When I no longer heard their hoofbeats, I just assumed you'd let go of the rope."

"You were gravely wounded, Pale Wolf. You drifted to the spirit world, where you could not hear even my voice at times." The girl's smile grew and her eyes sparkled at the joy of giving him a surprise. "To my people, you are a very wealthy man. Only the chief has more ponies than Pale Wolf. You can buy any woman in our village."

Dan placed a hand beneath her chin and lifted her impish face for his inspection. "And what makes you think I would be interested in buying a woman?"

With the innocence of the young she said, "I have seen a look on your face, Pale Wolf. It is a look that my father sometimes has when he watches my mother. And when she sees that look, she blushes."

Dan shook his head. "Are little girls born with such foolishness? Or are they taught by their mothers?"

"Foolish?" Little Bear pulled herself up on the back of one of the horses, so that her face was even with Dan's. Looking him straight in the eye, she said softly, "I have seen that look, Pale Wolf, when you watch Morning Light."

She gave a delighted laugh when she saw his mouth drop open in surprise.

Lying low over the horse's neck, she slipped the tether loose and plunged her hands into its thick mane. "Examine your horses, Pale Wolf," she called. "They will make a fine bride's gift."

With a slight nudge of her skinny knees, the horse took off at a trot. Dan watched as the girl urged him into a run. As they skimmed across the flat stretch of land in a fluid movement, it looked as if the girl and the horse were one.

Marveling over Little Bear's skill, Dan watched until she disappeared over a rise. Then he turned toward the horses that had suddenly become his property. Stolen property. He had no use for them. But he knew of someone who would enjoy his newly acquired wealth. He went in search of Crooked Tree.

"All of our people talk of your generous gift to my brother and to Crooked Tree." Morning Light stirred the ashes and added a log to the fire, taking care to see that the rough bark didn't tear the tender flesh of her hand. The burn had nearly healed, thanks to Dan's dwindling supply of ointment.

"I had no claim on those horses." He watched the way her hips swayed as she moved around the fire. It gave him such pleasure to watch her. Too much pleasure. He had to constantly remind himself to keep his distance. "It was Little Bear who brought them with us. It should be her family that benefits from their use. I gave the rest of the horses to your brother to thank him for his hospitality."

Dan watched as the chief strode toward them, carrying his little son on his shoulders. Lowering his voice, Dan asked, "How long has Runs With The Wind had that limp?"

"Since his birth. He was crushed beneath the hooves of a horse. An evil spirit entered his body and took shelter in his leg. Our medicine man did all in his power to free Runs With The Wind from the spirit. He even went to the sacred tepee and prayed to the great spirit."

Dan knew what she meant. In his youth he had seen Comanche shamans use peyote cactus, which produced hallucinations. Often while in this hypnotic state they communed with the spirits of their dead. For many it was a deeply religious experience.

"But as the boy grew," she added, "we could see that the evil spirit still sleeps within him." Her voice lowered. "When Runs With The Wind struggled to take his first steps, it was the first time I ever saw my brother weep."

"I'd like to examine the boy," Dan said softly.

"No." Morning Light's head came up sharply.

At Dan's narrow look she glanced toward her brother before hastening to add, "You must never speak of the boy's evil spirit. It would add to my brother's grief."

"Do you really believe that by not speaking of it, Two Moons will forget about his son's problem?"

She shook her head. "How could he ever forget?"

"Do you think that by not speaking about it, the evil spirit will one day leave the boy's body?"

She remained silent.

Dan studied her bowed head. "I see. And what will happen if I examine the boy?"

In halting tones she whispered, "You might wake the spirit and it will take over the rest of his body as well." She looked up and he could read the anguish in her eyes. "My brother has already buried his wife. He could not bear to lose his only son also. Please, Pale Wolf. Do not touch the boy and incur the wrath of the sleeping spirit.''

Dan tossed his cigarette into the fire and strode away, deep in thought. So much for the trust she had placed in his healing powers. If only, he mused, he could perform a few miracles.

The first miracle occurred the next morning. Dan stood in front of the small looking glass that he had hung on a tree branch. As he worked the straight razor across his morning stubble, he heard the sound of voices raised. Rinsing off the lather that clung to his face, he grabbed a shirt and began hurrying toward the Comanche camp. Before he reached the clearing he heard the familiar voice of Sings In The Forest, the old woman who had been near death with measles.

"The spots are gone from my flesh," she shrieked, waking the entire camp. "The evil spirits are gone from me."

As the people filed from their tepees, many still wrapped in their buffalo robes, they gathered around the jubilant old woman.

"Look," she called, holding out her arms. Lifting her skirts she displayed her legs, which had been covered with red blotches. "Pale Wolf has strong medicine. The spirits fear him. They have all fled."

Amid much laughing and cheering, she was led to the tepee of the chief, where she again proclaimed herself healed. After seeing the old woman's arms and legs, Morning Light found herself watching Dan more closely as he moved through the camp.

The second miracle occurred two days later. Dan had pulled himself into the saddle and forced himself, despite the pain and stiffness in his back, to ride several miles alongside Little Bear. By the time they returned to the camp, he was clenching his teeth against the pain. But at least he had bagged a deer and several rabbits. That would be a small payment indeed for the hospitality shown by Two Moons and his family.

Morning Light watched as Dan slid from the saddle. She saw the way he moved in a slow, stiff gait and knew instantly that he had pushed himself beyond the limits of his endurance.

With a frown knitting her brow, she started toward him.

"You should not have gone riding with Little Bear. I told you your wounds were not yet healed. And they will never heal if you continue to do these things. You are not yet ready to leave us, Pale Wolf."

The fierceness with which she spoke those words brought him unexpected pleasure. With a hint of laughter touching his lips, he questioned, "You don't want me to think about leaving?"

Instantly she lowered her head to hide her feelings. With a shrug of her shoulders, she whispered, "What you do is of no concern to me."

"And that's why you get so mad at me? Because you don't care what I do?"

"You mock me?" Her eyes blazed.

He couldn't hold back the laughter. Touching a hand to her cheek, he said, "It's called teasing, Morning Light. I just like teasing you."

"I do not understand this teasing." She grew silent, contemplating this new word.

"When someone likes someone, they often tease. Just to see the other's temper flare a little. But they don't do it to really cause a temper. They just do it to—tease."

Before he could say more, the chief approached, surrounded by many people from their camp. In the middle of the group was an old man, who dropped to the ground and sat cross-legged, resting his head in his hands. He moaned as he swayed back and forth.

"What's wrong?" Dan asked in alarm, thinking the old man had been seriously injured.

"This is Running Elk. For many days he has been suffering with pain and our medicine has not helped. He is afraid he might have the white man's sickness, and that would mean that he would have to leave his wife alone. She is old and he cannot leave her." The chief said softly to Dan, "The pain is too much to hide any longer. And so he has come to you."

"Where is your pain?" Dan asked.

The old man continued to hold his head while he rocked back and forth.

Two Moons issued a sharp command. At the sound of his voice the old man obediently stopped his moaning to open his mouth and point. A quick examination showed Dan that one of the old man's teeth had become infected.

"Can you stop his pain?" the chief asked.

Dan nodded. "Make him comfortable on a buffalo robe. I'll get my supplies."

When Dan returned, most of the Comanche in camp had gathered around to watch.

From his black bag he removed a small vial that had once contained laudanum. He held it up to the light. It was now empty. Shaking his head, he removed a bottle of whiskey from his saddlebags and thought

about the supplies that had once been available to him
in Boston. Laudanum, sulfuric ether, chloroform. He
shrugged away such thoughts. The whiskey would
have to do. Along with it he withdrew a pair of pliers.
Uncorking the whiskey, he handed it to the old man.

"Drink," Dan said softly.

The man took a small swallow, and made a face. "It
burns like fire."

When he started to hand it back, Dan shook his
head. "Drink more," he said.

With a quizzical glance at Dan, the old man lifted
the bottle and took a long swallow. Dan waited, hoping the alcohol would begin to take effect. Within a
few minutes Running Elk lifted the bottle and took
another healthy swallow, and then another.

Satisfied, Dan took the bottle from the old man's
hands and motioned for him to open his mouth. It
took only a minute for Dan to locate and yank the offending tooth. The old man gave a yelp of pain, then
stopped his cries as Dan held up the bottle and motioned for Running Elk to drink again. This time the
whiskey cleansed and soothed the bleeding gum before it disappeared down the man's throat.

Running Elk pressed a hand to his face, then looked
up at Dan in wonder. The pain, which had been driving him half-mad, was slowly dissipating. In its place
was a strange numbness.

When Dan offered Running Elk his tooth, the old
man accepted it like a trophy. As he walked through
the assembled, he held the tooth aloft for all to see. On
his face was a smile of pure delight.

Within minutes the entire camp had followed the old man to his tepee, where he sat and displayed the tooth that had caused him such suffering.

Several times more, Dan stopped by the old man's tepee and urged him to hold the whiskey in his mouth for several minutes before swallowing.

By nightfall, the legend of Pale Wolf was being repeated beside every campfire.

Chapter Eight

Thad Conway tied his dusty horse and crossed the patch of sun-baked earth that separated the military fort from the rest of the buildings at Fort Elliot.

"Morning, sir."

Thad knew the boy behind the desk had to be a new recruit. He could tell by the crisp uniform and the eager smile on his face. Most of the officers were holdovers from the War Between the States, whose experiences on the battlefields had left them bitter and cynical. Men who still bore the grim reminders of what war was really like.

"Name's Thad Conway. I'd like to see your commanding officer."

"That would be Captain Peters."

The boy knocked on a door, then disappeared inside. A minute later he returned. "The captain will see you."

Thad crossed the room and stepped into a cramped office that smelled of whiskey and cigars. He'd been in saloons that smelled better.

"What can I do for you?" the captain asked, without looking up from the map he was studying.

Thad waited a minute, hoping the captain would give him the courtesy of at least a cursory glance. He studied the thin dark hair carefully combed over a bald spot. Then his gaze moved over the hunched shoulders, the pudgy finger tapping a pencil with agitated rhythm.

"I was told at Fort Cobb that a doctor passed through this territory about a month ago and stayed on through an outbreak of cholera."

"Could be. What's it to you?"

Thad leaned over the desk, planting his hands squarely on the map. The captain's head came up sharply. He found himself staring into eyes that pierced him with a look of cold fury.

"I have reason to believe that doctor was my brother. I've come a long way to find out." Thad thought about the hundreds of miles he'd traveled and the few facts he'd been able to gather. "What can you tell me about him?"

The captain studied the man before him. He was lean and rangy, well over six feet tall, with sun-bronzed skin and the corded muscles of a man who knew hard work. His pale hair spilled over a wide forehead. For a moment he felt the jolt of recognition. The similarity was there in the eyes. They held a fire that few men could match. He had no doubt this man was brother to the doctor who'd gone without sleep for days while he nursed the sick of the fort.

"He was as tall as you. But his eyes were green and his hair was dark."

Thad straightened. It was the same description he'd been given at every stop. It had to be Dan.

"Did he say where he was headed?"

"No. Just left one night without a word."

"Thanks," Thad said, turning away.

"Just a minute." The captain opened a drawer.

Thad turned. With a surly grunt the captain held up a piece of paper. "If he's your brother, you'll be interested in this. It just came with yesterday's post."

Thad took a step closer and stopped. The paper was a wanted poster. On it was a rough sketch of a man with dark shaggy hair. Thad studied the picture for several minutes, trying to reconcile the face of this stranger with the memory he'd carried of his brother all these years. Finally he read the caption. "A thousand-dollar reward for the capture of Doctor Daniel Conway, wanted for murder in Boston, Massachusetts."

The words were like a blow to the midsection. For a minute, Thad read and reread the words until they were burned into his mind. Then he crushed the poster in his hand and let it drop to the floor as he spun toward the door. Before he could yank it open, the captain's words stopped him.

"I'll remind you that if you find your brother, you have a duty to turn him in to the proper authorities. Or you'll be considered a wanted criminal as well."

Without a word Thad opened the door and strode out, slamming the door behind him.

"Goodbye, sir," the young recruit called.

Thad's eyes narrowed. He was only a couple of years older than the lad. But in the past few moments, he'd aged considerably. After today, he'd never feel young and carefree again.

"You must wake, Pale Wolf."

Morning Light's urgent tones penetrated Dan's sleep-drugged mind. Instantly alert, he sat up and tossed aside the buffalo robe. His hand went to the pistol that lay by his side. "What is it? What's wrong?"

"Nothing is wrong." Morning Light realized instantly her mistake. She should not have come here. She had been so concerned about her brother's son, she had forgotten how isolated was this place Pale Wolf had chosen for his camp. She had forgotten also how erratic her heartbeat became whenever she got too close to this man.

"I would speak with you before my brother awakens." She struggled to avoid staring at Dan's hair-roughened chest, so unlike that of any of the braves.

His eyes narrowed. Something must be terribly wrong in the Comanche camp to bring her here at such an hour. "What about?"

"Runs With The Wind."

"He's sick?" He started to rise.

She placed a hand on his shoulder to still his movements. "No. Nothing is wrong."

The breath he had been holding came out in a slow hiss of air. He leaned on one elbow and studied her as she knelt beside him. A mist had settled over the river during the night. Now, as the sun hovered on the horizon, it created a soft, hazy glow. Morning Light, her hair swirling forward across one breast, appeared pale and ethereal, with a halo of light surrounding her. Her eyes were wide and pleading.

"I came to ask that you use your medicine to drive away the spirit that sleeps within the child."

This was finally beginning to make sense. She had witnessed the cures of the others, and now she was seeking a miracle for her nephew. But why had she chosen such an hour to approach him?

"I want you to understand—" his gaze held hers "—that I can make no promises. I will examine his foot. But I might be helpless to undo what was done at birth."

Morning Light nodded. "I ask only that you keep the evil spirit from taking over Runs With The Wind's entire body."

Of that he had no fear. "I give you my word," Dan said.

"Also," she cautioned softly, "Two Moons must not know of this. This must be our secret."

So that was the reason for her early-morning visit.

She saw the frown line that appeared between Dan's brows. "I don't like keeping secrets from the chief. The boy is his son. He has a right to know that I've examined Runs With The Wind's leg."

"Please," she said pleadingly. "You do not know the pain that has been caused my brother. There must be no more pain."

Dan placed his hand over hers in a gesture of acquiescence. Didn't she understand that he could deny her nothing? Especially when she appeared to him in the morning mist like an angel.

"All right," he said softly. "It will be our secret. For now."

"Thank you, Pale Wolf."

As she started to stand he caught her wrist, stilling her movements. Her eyes widened in surprise as she was forced to continue to kneel beside him. Her throat went dry.

His tone was low, ominous. "The others are asleep?"

His voice seemed suddenly deeper, more dangerous.

She swallowed and tried to speak, but no words came out. She nodded her head.

He could feel the pulse at her wrist beating an unsteady tattoo against his fingers. He didn't know why, but it gave him a perverse sense of pleasure to know that he made her nervous. Maybe that cool sense of detachment she usually showed him was merely a pose.

"Then you won't be missed if you don't return soon?"

"I . . ." She struggled to pull her hand free, but he tightened his grip. "Pale Wolf, what are you doing?"

He gave one tug and she found herself sprawled across the solid wall of his chest.

For a moment she was speechless as her hands came in contact with the springy mat of hair on his chest. His eyes looked heavy lidded and dangerous. His lips were mere inches from hers.

She was engulfed in a wave of heat as his arms came around her, pinning her to the length of him.

She saw his eyes narrow as his gaze roamed her face before settling on her lips. She thought her heart would leap from her throat as he cupped her head with his hand and drew her slowly down to his waiting lips.

For a moment it was the merest brushing of mouth to mouth. His lips skimmed hers, nibbling, tasting, teasing, until her mouth softened and her lips parted on a sigh.

Her whole body seemed to grow slack. Slowly her hands, which she had tried to keep firmly between them, began to move across his chest, tingling as her fingertips came in contact with his naked flesh.

She felt her nipples harden as they pressed against him. She should flee, she scolded herself. Now, while she still had her wits about her. She felt his arms tighten their grasp as he suddenly rolled her over on the buffalo robe until she was pinned beneath his hard, firm body. And then all thought was swept away as his mouth covered hers in a hot, hungry kiss.

His lips were no longer gentle, but demanding. His mouth moved over hers with practiced ease until he heard her little moan of pleasure.

He plunged his hands into her hair and rained kisses along her exposed throat to the little hollow between her neck and shoulder. She moved in his arms and gave herself up to the feelings his touch unleashed.

She was hungry for his mouth. She moaned and clutched at his head until his lips returned to hers. He lingered over her lips, savoring the wild, sweet taste of her. And all the while his hands worked their magic, touching, caressing, seducing.

They both knew they had to end this now, before they crossed the line into madness. And yet neither was willing to give up this intense pleasure.

When his fingers reached for the laces that held together the bodice of her buckskin gown, she stiffened. Struggling through the mists that had begun to cloud her will, she pushed him away.

"I must go. Already the morning is upon us. Please, Pale Wolf."

He knew the wisdom of her words. And still he lingered over her lips a moment longer before lifting his head and breaking contact. With great reluctance, he let his hands fall to his sides.

While she got to her feet and smoothed her skirts, she was painfully aware of Dan, lying very still, watching through narrowed eyes.

She ran in her haste to return to her brother's tepee before she was missed. While she rolled her buffalo robe and began to prepare the morning fire, she struggled with the wild beating of her heart. Wild. Indeed, there was something wild and primitive about the feelings Pale Wolf aroused in her. Feelings unlike any she had ever known.

She must never allow herself to forget for even a moment that it is dangerous to rouse a sleeping wolf.

Runs With The Wind lay quietly on the buffalo robe while Dan poked and prodded and studied him from every angle. While he was being examined, the little boy watched the man's eyes, searching for a clue to his thoughts. But the green eyes, so different from any Runs With The Wind had ever seen before, gave away nothing.

If the man's eyes were indifferent, his hands were not. His touch was easy and gentle. As he probed, his fingertips soothed away the fears the boy had experienced when he had first arrived at the secluded camp of Pale Wolf. The little boy was no longer afraid; merely puzzled.

He had already accepted the fact that a spirit dwelled within him. Though it took tremendous effort, he had learned to run and play and keep up with the other children. And when he fell behind, they did not mock him. They, too, knew about the spirit.

At last, the examination completed, Dan reached down and lifted the boy.

For one brief instant Dan was a boy again, lifting his little brother from the dirt where he had fallen. Thad. It had been a long time since he had allowed himself to think about the brother he had left behind when he had gone off to Boston to study. Their parting had been too painful. The boy had clung to him, begging Dan to stay a few more years, until Thad was old enough to go with him.

Thad would be a man now. Dan's heart contracted painfully. A stranger.

For a moment longer he hugged Runs With The Wind to his chest, feeling all the old stirrings of love for his family that he had long cherished. How he had missed them. How desperately at times he had longed for their love and comfort in that strange place.

Maybe, more than any of them, it had been Thad who had made Dan yearn for the knowledge to be a doctor. Thad, so young and helpless without a mother's love, had often burned with mysterious fevers in his childhood. And Dan, with a growing frustration, had vowed to find a way to cure all his ills.

How simple it had all seemed then. An education in Boston, he'd thought, would equip him to cure everything. With a wave of his black bag, he would ride across the West, erasing all pain and illness. What bitter irony. The more he learned, the more he realized how little he knew.

Morning Light, watching in silence, saw a look of pain cross Dan's face before he handed the little boy over to her arms.

"Take him to play with the other children," Dan said wearily. "He's had enough serious business for one day."

"The spirit . . . ?" she began, but Dan cut her off abruptly.

"We'll talk later, Morning Light. When Runs With The Wind is sleeping."

She felt fear clutch at her heart and turned away, hugging the boy to her breast. She had defied her own brother, the chief. She prayed that any punishment for her boldness would be upon her, and not upon this innocent.

Two Moons watched as his sister tossed and turned in her buffalo robe. His son, resting in the crook of his arm, was sound asleep. But Morning Light could not get comfortable. She seemed troubled in her mind.

He suspected that it might have something to do with Pale Wolf. His suspicions grew when, a short time later, he saw his sister throw off her covering and make her way silently from the tepee.

It was not his way to follow Morning Light, for that would be an insult. But he would pray to the spirits for her guidance. She was treading a narrow, dangerous path.

Dan was waiting by the river. Morning Light saw his darkened figure hunched on a fallen log. He could have been carved from stone, except for the occasional movement of his hand as he lifted the cigarette to his lips. The red tip flared for a moment in the darkness, then arced as he tossed the cigarette into the water.

He sat staring at the moon. In profile his handsome features were marred only by the frown that furrowed his brow.

His thoughts were as dark as the night that surrounded him. What had he done? Why had he insisted upon examining the boy? Now he had raised Morning Light's hopes, only to have to dash them.

Miracles, he thought, curling his hand into a fist. He'd hoped for miracles to persuade her. What a cruel joke. Sings In The Forest had survived her bout with measles. Running Elk's pain had disappeared as soon as his tooth had been pulled. But neither had been miraculous cures. Now he needed a real miracle. And he had been around long enough to know that such things were not to be.

"You have spoken with the spirit?" Morning Light asked softly.

Dan whirled.

As always, the sight of her took his breath away. The fawn-colored dress revealed the soft contours of her slender body. The laces at the bodice exposed the shadowed cleft between her breasts. Her tiny waist was accentuated by a beaded belt that held a small pouch. Tucked into the waistband was a knife. The blade caught and reflected the light of the moon. Her softly rounded hips swayed as she walked closer. On her feet were moccasins that cushioned and silenced each step.

Her hair fell to below her waist in a veil of dark silk. Several strands had drifted forward to kiss her cheeks. He longed to catch the strands and watch them sift through his fingers. But he had no right. And so he kept his hands stiffly at his sides.

She saw the look on his face and felt the fear once again clutch at her heart.

"What has the spirit told you, Pale Wolf?"

"Only that I'm a fool." He gave a bitter laugh. "And a poor excuse for a doctor."

"What are you saying?"

"I can't help Runs With The Wind."

Her eyes widened. "You have angered the spirit within him?" She let out a cry and brought her hand to her mouth. "What have I done? The spirit will now take over his body, as it took over the body of his mother."

"No." Dan gripped her by both shoulders to still her words. In low, measured tones he said, "There is no evil spirit. He's not doomed to die. But the horse's hooves crushed the tiny bones and muscle and sinew. They've fused together. If I had better skills. If I had the proper equipment. If..." He shrugged, and his tone hardened. "There's nothing I can do to change what has been done to him. But he won't have to suffer a life of pain and agony, Morning Light. He can run and play and ride a pony."

"The spirit that stole his voice and withered his leg will now choke the life from him."

"No. I promise you. It won't happen."

He saw the tears that shimmered in her eyes. She blinked quickly, but her eyes filled again. "But you are the healer. I saw you drive the evil spirits from the others. Why can you not do the same for Runs With The Wind?"

"I wish I could. You'll never know how badly I wish that."

"And his voice?"

Dan shrugged. He had examined the boy's tongue, mouth and throat. He could find nothing physically wrong. But he could not explain why the boy didn't speak. "I don't know. I just don't know. Maybe it was the pain of the accident. I can't even guess what he went through."

She pushed away from him and drew her arms around herself as if to ward off a sudden chill. "I must go back to my brother's tepee and stay close to his son."

"I promise you, Morning Light, nothing terrible will happen to him because of my examination."

She wouldn't meet his gaze. He knew, in that moment, that she didn't believe him. Once again, in her mind, she had been betrayed by a white man.

"I must go," she whispered. "And keep watch."

With a muttered oath he watched as she ran through the darkness toward the fires of the Comanche camp. Then he returned to the log where he continued his troubled, silent contemplation of the stars.

Chapter Nine

"A party of braves will hunt this day for game,"
Two Moons said. "Will you join them, Pale Wolf?"

"No." Dan left his breakfast untouched and
watched as Morning Light moved around the fire.
Each time he saw her, he felt the need for her. And
each time he was forced to fight the same battle. "It's
time I moved on."

His words brought a reaction from everyone seated
around the fire. For long minutes there was only silence as they studied him in surprise.

Dan felt Morning Light's gaze boring into him.

Too many thoughts tumbled through her mind,
leaving her dazed. He had said nothing last night. Was
that why he was so somber while he stared out over the
waters of the river? Had he already known then? Yet
he had chosen to say nothing to her. She felt a rush of
anger. The kisses they had shared had meant nothing
to this man. He would ride out of her life as quickly as
he had appeared.

Dan forced himself to turn away from her when the
chief asked, "Where will you go?"

"I thought I'd ride to the reservation and speak with
the Indian agent."

He'd had plenty of time to think this through. All night he had paced the banks of the river, waging a terrible battle with himself. A part of him longed to stay here. He had found a measure of peace with these people. He genuinely cared about them. What was even more rewarding, many of them had begun to show similar feelings for him. They were slowly becoming the family he had left behind so many years ago. Here he would be needed. He could use his skills in healing in the way he'd always intended. And, of course, there was Morning Light. Though he tried to deny it, she had become important to him. But it was time to go. He had run out of excuses to stay.

Ishatai stood up, his eyes blazing with anger. To the chief he said, "This man knows that we are renegades."

"To the white man we are renegades," Two Moons said sternly. "We know that we are merely living as we always did. Besides, tonight I meet with my council. I will decide, after I hear the words they speak from their hearts, whether we will continue our life as we knew it or go to the land set aside for us by the white chief in Washington."

"There is another choice," Ishatai said angrily. "We can join with the Kiowa Apache to fight the white soldiers."

Two Moons stiffened. "I do not forget the cowards who attacked in the night. Theirs is a futile dream. They will be hunted until they are destroyed."

Unnerved, Ishatai deflected attention back to Dan. "This man knows our hunting grounds. He will tell the Indian agent about our camp. The soldiers will come for us."

"You're wrong." Dan saw the mistrust in Morning Light's eyes. This brave's words had awakened her own dark terrors. Dan wished he could find a way to calm her fears. "I need medicine. The Indian agent should have a supply. While I'm there I intend to issue a complaint about the poor quality of blankets given to your people."

"Complaint?" Ishatai hissed, "He is one of your kind. He will persuade you that we are not worthy of anything more than the white man's castoffs. And once he has your confidence, he will ask where we hide and you will tell him. Besides," he cried, "how can you mention the blankets without telling him where you saw these blankets? He will force you to admit that you were with our people."

The chief laid a hand on Ishatai's arm to silence him. When he turned to Dan, his look became grave. "My people have a right to be afraid. We break the white man's treaty by remaining free. But I believe you when you say you will not disclose our camp. Still, you should not go, Pale Wolf. I do not trust this man sent by your great chief in Washington."

"Neither do I. That's why I have to go. I need to see this man. To see for myself why he isn't doing his job."

Ishatai, who remained standing beside the chief, could not hide his fury at Dan's pronouncement. He would never trust this white man. But at least he would be rid of this intruder. He turned to study the chief's sister. Seeing the bleak look in her eyes, his smile faded slightly. She would forget this white man in time. Ishatai was a patient man. One day he would be chief of the Comanche. The sister of the great chief, Two

Moons, would be a worthy woman to stand at the side of the new chief.

"When do you leave?" the chief demanded.

"As soon as I've finished eating."

"So soon."

"I have a lot of miles to cover."

Morning Light had remained silent throughout this entire exchange. Without a word she lifted a buffalo paunch and hurried away to the river. When she returned, there was no trace of the tears she had shed in private.

Dan saddled his horse and tied his black bag and bedroll behind.

Many of the Comanche gathered around to bid him goodbye. The women stood back shyly while the men came forward to say a word or offer their hands in friendship. Many of the children touched his medical bag with a sort of reverence. All knew of the healing power contained in that bag.

Sings In The Forest kissed his hand. Running Elk proudly displayed his tooth, which now hung on a leather strip around his neck. Little Bear and her parents thanked him profusely for saving her life and returning her to her people. Crooked Tree added his gratitude for the gift of six horses.

Little Bear surprised him by throwing her arms around his neck and hugging him fiercely. "My Pale Wolf. You will return soon to us."

"I'm afraid not," he said. "My home lies a long way from here."

"That does not matter," she said solemnly. "I saw you in my dream, last night. You will leave us. But you will return soon." She placed a hand on his and added,

"You must beware, Pale Wolf. There are men who would harm you."

At the girl's words, Morning Light, standing nearby, brought a hand to her trembling lips and turned away. Dan watched but was helpless to stop her as she fled.

Crooked Tree chimed in, "Do not take Little Bear's dreams lightly, Pale Wolf. She sees things the rest of us cannot. It is her *puka.*"

Seeing that Dan didn't understand the Comanche word, he explained, "Her power, her medicine, is the gift of seeing the future in dreams. That is her *puka.*"

"Then I hope you see only happiness in your dreams," Dan said.

Ishatai was not among those who had gathered to bid Dan goodbye. It was plain that he had no words to speak to the white intruder.

Two Moons, holding his little son, offered his hand to Dan. Dan tousled the boy's hair and gravely shook hands with Two Moons.

Both were surprised when the little boy clutched the front of Dan's shirt, as if urging him to stay.

The chief cast a puzzled glance toward Dan, then drew his son close to his heart. For a moment neither man spoke. It was Dan who finally broke the silence.

"I should have told you, Two Moons. I examined your son's leg," Dan explained. "But I know of no medicine to heal it."

"When did you do this thing?" The chief's voice was low with anger.

"Yesterday. By the river."

The chief looked into Dan's eyes and saw the truth before he even asked the question. "Did my sister know of this? Did she help you?"

"She did. But it was at my insistence."

"This was a serious thing that you did. Did not Morning Light tell you that I would be displeased?"

"Yes. I know how much you love your son. I didn't do this to bring harm. I merely wanted to see if there was anything I could do to heal him."

"Did you think to do what even our great medicine man could not do?" When Dan said nothing, he added, "I could have told you that there is no medicine that will remove the spirit from Runs With The Wind."

Dan made no response. He saw the chief's frown suddenly deepen as a new thought intruded.

"Did you speak with Morning Light about this last night while we slept?"

"Yes."

"That would explain her uneasiness." He fixed Dan with a piercing look. "I thought, when she went to you... that you had taken Morning Light for your woman."

Dan's gaze met his. "I was tempted to."

"But you did not."

"No."

The chief studied Dan for a long, silent moment. The true test of a brave was his strength in moments of temptation. This man would make a fine Comanche brave.

He offered his hand. "May the great spirit keep you safe, Pale Wolf."

"And you, Two Moons."

He made his way to the river and glanced around, hoping for a chance to be alone for a moment with Morning Light. But she was nowhere to be seen.

Many of the women and children splashed in the shallows, where the women washed the clothes and the children made a game of chasing minnows into shore. But there was no sign of the one he sought.

He felt a sudden rush of frustration. She was giving him no chance to exchange words, to explain his decision. He gave vent to his anger as he tightened the cinch and tied his bedroll. It was better this way. What, after all, could he say to her? With a clench of his jaw, Dan pulled himself into the saddle and urged his horse into a trot.

As he disappeared over a rise, a figure emerged from behind a tree and stood alone by the banks of the river watching. Then she lowered her head and made her way to the tepee of the chief.

A hundred miles or more lay between the Comanche camp and the reservation. A hundred miles of broiling sun and bitterly cold nights. A hundred miles of desolate land, broken here and there by drab little towns that seemed to have sprung up overnight. In every town, it seemed, there was a saloon crowded with bearded men who carried the now-familiar large-bore, long-range buffalo rifles in the boots of their saddles. They carried, too, a thirst for cheap whiskey and a chance to forget the rigors of the trail. The saloon girls were kept busy. Their purses jingled with coins.

Dan thought he would welcome the chance for a hot bath and a soft bed. But the sounds of a tinny piano and raucous laughter and gunshots in the night soon soured him on the rewards of civilization. He found himself yearning for the peaceful murmur of a river and the scent of a fresh breeze beneath a canopy of stars. Most of all, he found himself missing Morning Light. The touch of her hand. The husky sound of her voice. The quickening of his heartbeat whenever she was near.

Dan leaned a hip against the windowsill of the room above the saloon and watched as the first light of dawn streaked the sky. He could wait no longer. Pulling on his boots and strapping on his holster, he strode to the door. Today, before nightfall, he'd reach the reservation. And meet, firsthand, the man sent by Washington to see to the peaceful settlement of the Indian nations.

Lemuel Rollins settled his considerable bulk behind his desk and studied the man who had demanded this meeting. The stranger was tall and lean, and moved with a steady, deliberate gait. But beneath the man's studied casualness, Rollins detected a carefully coiled tension. The lower part of his face was covered with a dark beard. But it was his eyes that held Rollins. Eyes as hard as flint. Probably another buffalo hunter, Rollins thought, leaning back. He'd see how much money this one would offer for the privilege of trespassing on Indian territory.

At twelve years old Lemuel Rollins had turned his back on the hard-scrabble farm in Missouri and the father whose drunken rages had left him with a patchwork of scars across his body. He'd drifted across the country, doing anything he could for a bed and a meal. A chance to soldier during the War Between the States had given him his first taste of fairly regular pay and he'd discovered he liked it. What he liked even more was the feeling of power he had when he looked down the barrel of a rifle and found a man quivering with fear. Let his father try to beat him now, he thought with a blaze of fury. Let any man try to beat him, ever again.

After the war, when most of the troops had returned to their homes and their farms, he'd stayed on in the army until a particularly brutal brawl with a drunken captain had him banished to an outpost along the Texas-Mexican border. Here he'd had his first contact with Indians. Within two years he had gained a reputation for dealing quickly and efficiently with a people who had once roamed this land without interference. Whenever a tribe of Indians became a 'problem,' Lemuel Rollins was dispatched. No one questioned his methods. Only the results mattered. Soon his fame spread even to Washington, where his name was offered as Indian agent.

Lemuel Rollins liked this even better than his old army job. Not only did he have power of life or death over the Indians, but a new kind of power, as well. There was money to be made. A great deal of money, if he played his cards right. He had found his gold mine, at the expense of the very people he'd been hired to serve.

"I didn't catch your name."

"Dan Conway."

"You a buffalo hunter?"

Dan shook his head. "I'm a doctor."

Rollins folded his hands over his stomach. "Didn't send for a doctor. Nobody's sick here. At least not anybody who counts."

Apparently the raging sickness on the reservation held no interest for the Indian agent appointed by Washington.

"I was told the government supplied you with medicine for the Indians."

Rollins nodded. "So what?"

"I'm in need of a few supplies." Dan watched the man's eyes. They had narrowed perceptibly.

"You willing to pay?"

"I heard the medicine was free."

"It's supposed to be free if it goes to the Indians. Only problem is, those savages would rather chew cactus and get crazy on peyote than accept the white man's medicine." Rollins's eyes suddenly hardened. "You weren't thinking of taking medicine to those heathens, were you?"

Dan paused for only a moment. He'd see what this man's game was. "There are a lot of people who need medicine out here."

Rollins leaned forward. "That's what I thought. You're one of them buffalo hunters, aren't you?"

When Dan said nothing, he went on, "You must be with Quent Barker's buffalo hunters. I heard he found some doctor to save his life out on the reservation."

His words stunned Dan. So the tougher-than-nails trail boss had lived. But how was it that Rollins knew about the buffalo hunters? And if he knew, why hadn't he ordered them off the Comanche land? The answer came to him instantly. Cal's words that day echoed in his mind. "We got some friends in high places."

So this was why the Indian agent was so determined to round up the last holdouts and force them on to reservations. He was working with the buffalo hunters.

"Did Barker send you here?" Without waiting for Dan's reply, Lemuel Rollins added, "Hell, what do you need?"

Dan kept his tone bland. "I'll take anything you have. Sulfuric ether, chloroform, laudanum, quinine."

"You can have all you want. Come on." Rollins pushed back his chair and lumbered to his feet. Taking a key from his pocket, he hollered, "Yancy. Get in here before I kick your lazy hide all the way to Oklahoma Territory."

An old man wearing the uniform of an Indian scout hobbled in and paused when he saw Dan. Hair like bleached corn silk spilled over his wide forehead. From a lifetime under a Texas sun, the old man's face was tanned and wrinkled like aged leather. Despite his years, his blue eyes sparkled with the curiosity of a child.

"We're going to sell some medicine," Rollins said. To Dan he added, "Just be sure to let your boss know he owes me plenty." He unlocked a door.

Yancy held a match to the wick in a lantern, then held it high.

Dan followed the two men into a back room, where wooden shelves were stocked to the ceiling with supplies.

"What's all this?"

"Huh." Rollins gave a grunt of laughter. "We call these things blankets." He picked up one of the flimsy blankets Dan had seen in the Comanche camp and unfolded it, then tossed it aside. "It's too good for those savages. Of course," he added slyly, "I keep the good things for people with money."

They all glanced up at the sound of approaching hoofbeats.

Hurrying to the door, Lemuel Rollins said importantly, "As you can see, I'm a busy man. Got a lot of people who need me. Help yourself to what you want while I take care of this. Yancy, you see that he gets what he needs. And make a list. His boss still owes me for the last—favor." He tossed the key to the old scout and added, "Lock up and bring the key back to me."

When the door closed behind them, Dan opened several crates and studied the contents in silence. Beside him, the old man merely watched.

The first boxes were filled with good, sturdy blankets. Dan glanced up in surprise, and found the old man watching him closely.

"These don't look like the blankets given to the Indians," Dan said, keeping his voice devoid of emotion.

The old man shrugged.

Ripping open several more crates, he discovered ammunition. Holding it up to the lantern, he said, "This wouldn't do the Indians much good. I haven't seen any Comanche hunting buffalo with long-range rifles." He met the old man's sullen look. "Have you?"

Yancy spit a mouthful of tobacco, missing Dan's boot by mere inches. "Can't say as I have."

"What's going on here, Yancy?"

"You look like a smart fellow. I bet you'll figure it out."

On the top shelf Dan found sealed crates containing vials of precious medicine. Just as he began to sort through them, he heard the rumble of voices from the other room and froze. One of them had sounded familiar. He'd heard that voice before. He felt the hair on the back of his neck begin to rise. Rushing across the room, he opened the door a crack and peered at the scene in Lemuel Rollins's office. A jolt of recognition shot through him at the sight of Cal, the man who had forced Dan to accompany him to the buffalo hunters' camp. Beside him, with his arms crossed over his chest, was the trail boss, Quent Barker. He was very much alive.

Both men looked stunned as Lemuel Rollins was saying, "Your doctor is in the back room right now, picking up supplies for your men."

"What do you mean, 'our doctor'?" Cal shouted.

Before he could hear any more of their conversation, Dan threw the bolt on the door and began stuffing vials of medicine into his pockets. As he did, he looked around for another way out and realized there was none.

He glanced at the old man who still held the lantern aloft. Yancy was watching him without emotion.

Trapped. Dan muttered a savage oath. He was trapped in a storage room, and the only escape was through a door filled with men who would never let him walk away from here alive.

Chapter Ten

Dan heard the rumble of voices from the other room. And a moment later he saw the door shudder as a log was rammed against it again and again.

He spun around toward the man holding the lantern, expecting to see him reaching for his gun. Yancy stood quietly, watching. His face showed no emotion. For the moment, he seemed unwilling to lift a hand against Dan. But Dan had no idea how long that would last. At any moment the old scout could decide to join forces with the others in the battle. But at least, for now, Dan could concentrate on the matter at hand.

He had no way of knowing how many men were outside that door. But since he had spotted Cal and Quent, he figured the rest of the buffalo hunters were here, as well. A dozen men or more.

He began piling crates against the door until the pounding was muffled. Then, certain that it would take a while to break through, he began to prowl the room, searching for a way to escape. It was a solid building, made of logs and sealed with pitch. Solid and impenetrable. And there was no other door.

"Thought you were one of them." Yancy motioned toward the door.

"Do they sound like my friends?" Dan gave a bitter laugh. "They've sworn to kill me."

"That so?" Yancy's features became animated. "Looks like you'll be needing a way out." He spat a wad of tobacco on the floor.

Dan's eyes narrowed suspiciously. "Are you saying you'd help me?"

"Could be." Yancy faced him, holding the lantern high so he could see Dan's eyes. He'd always been able to tell a lot by a man's eyes. "Why do they want you?"

"We didn't meet under friendly circumstances. They took me by gunpoint to their camp and forced me to save the life of their trail boss."

"You say you saved his life. You sure he didn't die?"

Dan shook his head. "He's out there waiting to kill me."

"Funny way to thank a man for saving his life. What'd you do to make them so mad?"

"I—left before they were ready to let me go." Dan's tone hardened. "And I took a little Comanche girl they'd stolen for their—pleasure, and returned her to her people."

"That so?" Yancy eyed him more carefully, beginning to like what he saw. And heard. "Is that all?"

"I helped myself to all their horses while I was leaving. Gave them to the chief and the girl's father."

A smile started on the old man's lips, then spread to his eyes. "That'd do it." He glanced up as the door began to splinter. A man's fingers could be seen clawing at the rough boards. "Come on. We'd better get out of here before they break clean through."

"We?" Dan's eyes narrowed. "Aren't you going to stay and watch the fun?"

"Nah. I'd rather be part of it. Besides, anything I can do against Lemuel Rollins, I'll do gladly. I've watched that man cheat the Indians and line his own pockets since he came here. So if you don't mind company, I'd like to go along for the ride."

"What are we going to do? Fly?"

Yancy grinned. "I thought we'd crawl."

He pushed away several crates and lifted a small trapdoor in the floor. Leaning down, he dropped the lantern, illuminating a tunnel. "This'll take us to just beyond the wall of the fort." He motioned for Dan to go first, then carefully spread a couple of blankets over the trapdoor and slowly lowered it.

As they began to crawl along the narrow tunnel, they heard the sounds of voices raised in anger. From the banging and cursing, they knew that crates were being tossed aside in search of the two men.

By the time Lemuel Rollins and the buffalo hunters discovered the trapdoor, Dan and Yancy had escaped through the tunnel and were safely hidden in one of the hundreds of caverns that dotted the barren landscape beyond the fort.

After dark Yancy slipped away. At first Dan thought the old man had simply abandoned the adventure. An hour later he returned leading their horses.

"How did you manage this?" Dan bent to examine his horse and found the black medical bag still tied behind the saddle.

"I knew which corral they'd be in. I've been around that old fort for a long time now. Too long."

Yancy watched while Dan removed a piece of paper and began to write furiously. When he was done, he folded the paper and wrote a name on the outside.

"Where're we headed now?" Yancy asked as Dan pulled himself into the saddle.

"You might not want to join me when you hear where I'm going." Dan's recently healed wounds ached. His stomach was empty. His body was stiff from the long crawl and the time spent crammed into a narrow cave. But though he longed for a hot meal and a soft bed, he knew he couldn't rest until he warned Two Moons and the Comanche about the dangers that awaited them at the reservation. They had convened a council on the day Dan had left their camp. By now they could be halfway here.

Whatever dangers they faced by breaking the laws set by Washington, they faced even greater peril at the hands of an unscrupulous man like Lemuel Rollins. There was no doubt in Dan's mind that the very man sent by Washington to see to the needs of the Indian was in league with the armies of buffalo hunters that freely roamed the Comanche territory.

"I'm heading for the camp of Two Moons. The Comanche are not feeling very friendly toward white men these days."

Yancy grinned. "Used to have a wife. Part Comanche. Nine Fingers Lil. More woman than I've ever met in all my years on this earth."

"What happened to her?"

"She died giving birth to my only son." For a moment Yancy's eyes clouded. Then he spat a wad of tobacco and pulled himself into the saddle. "Think I'd like to try out a few Comanche phrases again." His lips split into a wide, engaging grin. "Course, they're probably all swear words. Old Lil sure did work up a head of steam when she was mad."

"You didn't mind?"

"Hell, I liked her even more when she got mad. She was one fine woman, my Lil. And besides," he added with a laugh, "there was always the making up afterward."

Dan joined in the laughter as he urged his horse into a run. Maybe the journey wouldn't seem quite so long with someone like Yancy to keep him company.

They rode hard for three days, from sunup until long after darkness settled over the land, stopping only long enough to catch a few hours of sleep.

Once along the trail, Dan slipped into a small outpost and asked the man to send the letter by the next stage. The man agreed.

On the second night, as Dan and Yancy lay in the bedrolls beside a fire, Dan rolled a cigarette and lit it.

Yancy leaned his head against his saddle and said, "You seem more at ease tonight. Figure we outran those buffalo hunters?"

Dan shrugged. "I wasn't too worried about them. It's the Comanche that had me worried. I guess I figured we'd find the entire Comanche nation thundering toward the reservation. But the more miles we go, the more certain I am that the council must have agreed with Two Moons that they should resist the law."

"That means their tribe will be considered renegades by the army. That'll give Lemuel Rollins an excuse to send the troops after them."

"I know." Dan blew out a stream of smoke and cradled his head on his arm. "But at least, for the moment, they're free."

"Free." Yancy gave a snort of disgust. "Did you see the towns and settlements that've sprung up across

Texas? Hell, don't you know the Comanche will never be free again?''

Ishatai's words rang in Dan's mind. Aloud he said, "An angry young brave told me that the train already steams across his hunting grounds."

Yancy nodded, keeping his eyes on the stars. "Pretty soon we'll be able to travel from the East to the West in two weeks or less. All those little stockyards along the route will gradually become big, important cities to rival the ones in the East." He chuckled. "When I was just a pup, I could ride all day and never see another human. After the War Between the States, farmers in the South headed west to try their hand at ranching. Now we're seeing farmers who can't farm, joining up with scum like Barker to slaughter the buffalo. And if that's not bad enough, ever since gold was discovered in California, we've got all those speculators whispering that there's gold in the Indians' sacred mountains." He muttered a savage oath and rolled to his side, pulling his blanket over his head. "Makes a man start thinking about moving on. But hell, I've been all the way to the ocean in California, and there's nothing that stirs my heart like Texas. Guess it's just in my blood."

Within minutes Dan heard the old man snoring loudly.

While he finished his cigarette, he thought about what Yancy had said. Civilization was already on its way west. There would be no stopping the stampede of men hungry for more. More land. More gold. The simple way of life the Comanche sought was gone forever.

* * *

Dan recognized the river and slowed his pace. Behind him, Yancy reined in his mount.

"What's wrong?" he asked, seeing the frown line between Dan's brows.

"This is the river. This is where the Comanche camp should be." Dan glanced around, searching for any trace of the tepees that had once been here, of the ponies that had trod these grasses. The ground had been swept clean of any sign of habitation. "How could a tribe of this size just disappear?"

"If you're Comanche, it's easy," Yancy said, sliding from the saddle. He picked up a horse dropping hidden among the grass and crumbled it between his fingers. "Looks like they've been gone four or five days."

"They could be anywhere by now."

"Not just anywhere," Yancy interjected. "If you want to find Comanche, just look for buffalo."

Dan shot him a hopeful glance. "Do you think you can track them?"

Yancy spat a wad of tobacco and pulled himself into the saddle. "I could track a bird that hopped aboard a freight car and rode the rails from here to Kansas City if I wanted to."

They set off at an easy pace, with Yancy in the lead.

Dusk was settling over the land. Deep purple shadows cast the distant peaks of the Rocky Mountains in a soft haze. The horsemen followed the meandering trail of the Rio Grande, near the border between Texas and Mexico.

Yancy had noticed, as they drew near the river, that Dan had grown very quiet. He hadn't spoken in over an hour. On his face was a strange, almost haunted look.

The old man wisely kept his silence, sensing that Dan was visiting some pleasant old memories.

Dan thought of the little sod shack in which he'd lived with his pa and sister and little brother, here on the banks of the Rio Grande. Jessie had kept the place as neat and clean as a palace. Her enthusiasm was contagious. It was Jessie who had kept the family together after the death of their mother. And Jessie who'd been driven to find their father when he'd been imprisoned in an Abilene jail.

Without realizing it, Dan's gaze scanned the rocks and brush, searching for the marker his pa had put over his mother's grave. It had long ago disappeared. But he knew. Without finding the exact spot, Dan knew that his mother had been buried nearby. He could feel her presence here. He smiled, remembering. What an extraordinary creature she'd been, to leave her friends and family behind and travel beside her young husband to this unknown wilderness. Though her life had ended far too soon, she had found love and happiness, and pride in her three children. Dan glanced at the river. He hoped she'd found peace, as well.

Yancy saw the pensive look. "Something on your mind?"

Dan was startled out of his reverie. "I was just remembering, Yancy. I grew up here. In a little sod shack. My mother is buried somewhere nearby."

"God's country," Yancy murmured. "I wouldn't mind being laid to rest along the banks of the Rio Grande myself someday." His eyes twinkled. "Course,

I hope it's not someday soon. I still got a lot left I want to do.''

As they topped a rise, he pointed and said with a trace of pride, ''Told you I'd find your Comanche.''

Nestled among the trees was a cluster of tepees, barely visible in the fading light. As they approached, Dan caught the aroma of deer meat roasting over a fire. And trilling on the breeze was the sound of a child's laughter.

It was Little Bear who spotted the horsemen, and, recognizing Dan, let out a cry before racing to meet him. Within minutes he had slipped from the saddle and caught her, tossing her high in the air before gathering her into his arms.

''I knew you would return to us, Pale Wolf. Did I not tell you so?''

He couldn't speak. For some strange reason his heart seemed filled to overflowing.

The others filed from their tepees and gathered around, smiling, shouting words of greeting. And in their midst stood Morning Light, her eyes wide, her mouth open in surprise.

Over the head of the little girl in his arms, Dan's gaze met and held Morning Light's, and Dan felt as he had the first time he'd fallen from a horse and had all the breath knocked from his lungs. His chest felt tight. His throat was constricted.

''You have brought a stranger to our camp.'' The sea of greeters parted and Two Moons strode through their midst until he reached Dan.

''This is Yancy,'' Dan said, still holding Little Bear in his arms. ''He helped me out of a little trouble. And when I found your old camp empty, he helped me track you here.''

The old man slid from the saddle and offered his hand to the chief. "I come in peace and friendship," he said in Comanche.

Two Moons accepted his handshake and studied the man closely. "How is it that you know our tongue?"

"My wife was Comanche," Yancy said in English.

"Was she a good wife?"

"The best. I still miss her."

Two Moons studied him for a moment longer, then nodded. "Come." The chief led Dan and Yancy toward his tepee. Little Bear, released from Dan's arms, walked proudly beside him. "We will eat. Then, when you are refreshed, we will talk."

While he ate, Dan watched Morning Light as she prepared their food and took her place beside her brother and his son.

Dan ate without tasting any of the food. The voices speaking around him never penetrated his mind. He was aware of but one thing. It had been a lifetime since he had felt at home anywhere. But it occurred to Dan, as he glanced around the campfire at the smiling, friendly faces and listened to the murmur of familiar voices that he felt more at home here with Morning Light and the Comanche than he had in many years.

Chapter Eleven

"You are certain? This man sent by your great chief in Washington, knows about the white hunters who kill the buffalo on the land set aside for the Comanche?"

Dan nodded. "There is no doubt in my mind. The man was willing to sell me any medicine I needed, when he thought I worked for Quent Barker."

"And this Barker is the same buffalo hunter who stole Little Bear?"

"Yes."

Dan saw the anger smoldering in the chief's eyes before he turned away.

Two Moons turned toward Yancy. "You say this man Rollins is evil. Why does the great chief in Washington not order him to be removed from his position of power over the Indian?"

Yancy examined his hands for a minute, before meeting the chief's grave look. "Maybe the president doesn't know this man is no good. Maybe he just doesn't care. Hell. Texas is a long way from Washington. I think most of those Easterners look at all Texans as savages."

Dan was reminded of his own experiences at school. When he had first arrived he'd been treated as an outcast. His rough clothes, his manner of speech, his lack of formal education had set him apart from all the others. It had been Dr. Zachery Dowd who had finally recognized the zeal, the burning need to be a doctor, beneath the Texan's rough exterior. Under his tutelage Dan had lost many of the rough edges and attained the polish needed to succeed in a city like Boston. Dan frowned. But even Dr. Zachery Dowd could not completely eliminate his own prejudice. It had erupted into a bitter argument before Dan left for Texas.

Dan's frown grew as he became lost in dark, brooding thoughts. He had tasted the inhumanity of those who could not accept people who were different from themselves. Even greater would be the cruelty against the Indian, whose language and customs set him apart from the white man.

Two Moons turned a grave look on Dan. "I had hoped, before the snows come, to persuade my council to accept the white man's law. I know that if we continue to remain free, the soldiers will come for us. But if I lead my people to the reservation, I may be leading them to a much harsher life—and death—at the hands of this man Rollins."

Dan nodded, but before he could speak, Ishatai, who had been listening attentively, got to his feet and pointed an accusing finger at Dan and Yancy. "How do you know that they have not led the soldiers to our camp? They could be, at this very moment, circling our camp, preparing to attack. These men should not be trusted."

Two Moons said quietly, "Pale Wolf has proved his friendship to the Comanche. Did he not visit the tepees of our sick? He would not knowingly bring trouble to our people."

"I do not trust him. Hear me," the young brave said. "One day this man will bring death and destruction to our people." Ishatai shot an angry look at Dan before stalking away.

The others had grown silent. Once again the seeds of distrust had been planted. Dan and Yancy could feel the silent questions of the others.

In the same quiet tone he always used, Two Moons said, "You will rest now. It has been a long journey. We will speak of this again in the morning."

Within minutes the others had scattered. Fires were banked. Buffalo robes were laid out in tepees in preparation for sleep.

Yawning, Yancy set his bedroll beside the fire. After seeing to his horse, the old man was soon asleep.

Dan preferred to set his bedroll near the banks of the stream that skirted their encampment. With his saddle as a pillow, he lay in the darkness, listening to the sounds of the night.

The moon was a silver crescent in the darkness, surrounded by a million twinkling stars. Dan thought he had never seen a night so perfect.

The rustling of dried grass alerted him to someone's approach. It was obvious that his night visitor had not wanted to surprise him. Dan lay perfectly still, waiting, his hand on the pistol at his side. Suddenly one shadow separated itself from the others and moved near. He let out the breath he'd been unconsciously holding when he recognized the spill of long, dark hair and the graceful sway of skirts.

For a moment she hesitated, afraid that he was already asleep. Seeing her reluctance to draw nearer, he leaned up on one elbow.

"Morning Light?"

At the sound of his voice she felt a little shiver of apprehension, then, before she could lose her courage, she forced herself to walk to his side.

"I would speak with you."

Dan watched her kneel beside him and felt his throat go dry. If it was possible, she was even more beautiful than he'd remembered. The rush of desire was swift and unexpected.

"You should not have returned to the People," she whispered.

"You don't want me here?"

"Ishatai says that your presence here will bring the soldiers."

Dan remained silent.

"Ishatai says that this man Yancy works for your great chief in Washington, and that he will return to the reservation and repeat all that he has seen and heard in our camp."

Dan went very still, watching her as she spoke.

"Ishatai says that you will make bad medicine and all our people will become too weak to hunt the buffalo or fight the soldiers."

Did she know what the sound of her voice did to him? The low, almost husky tones whispered over his senses, arousing him far more than any music. He itched to touch her. Instead, very slowly, Dan rolled a cigarette and held a match to the tip. For a moment the light flared, illuminating her features, showing the confusion in her eyes. Then the light was extinguished, and only the red glare of his cigarette remained.

He drew deeply, then exhaled. "Does Ishatai say anything more?"

"Only that you would not have come back to us unless you intended harm to our people."

Very deliberately he leaned his back against his saddle and rested his head on his arm. He exhaled and watched her through a haze of smoke.

"Ishatai says that—"

"What do you say, Morning Light?"

She hesitated for a moment, studying the man who reminded her of a panther about to strike. This was a mistake. She should not have permitted herself to come this close to him again. She started to get to her feet. In one easy motion he tossed aside the cigarette and clamped his hand on her wrist, holding her still.

His eyes narrowed. "I'm not interested in what Ishatai thinks about my return. What do you think, Morning Light?"

"I think—" she ran her tongue over her dry lips "—that you are not like the others."

She felt his fingers relax their grasp. But he didn't release her.

"What makes you think I'm different from any of the other white men?"

Her voice lowered. "I have tasted the cruelty of such men. They speak with their guns."

He wondered just how much she'd endured in the years that he was in Boston. He really knew nothing about her. But he wanted to. Suddenly he wanted to know everything about her. What she thought. What she dreamed of. How she would taste, early in the morning, after a night of being thoroughly loved. The thought was like a blow to his midsection.

He drew her fractionally closer and watched as her hair swirled forward to stream across her breasts. "How do you know Ishatai is wrong? Maybe I've come here to set a trap for your people."

Her eyes narrowed. Her nostrils flared. "If you ever brought harm to my people, Pale Wolf, I would not go to the great spirit until my knife found your heart."

He caught a handful of her hair and tugged until her face was mere inches from his. "I don't doubt it. I remember another time when you nearly killed me because I was trying to help you."

He saw the look that came into her eyes and knew that she was remembering that fateful struggle in their youth when he'd been determined to remove the bullet that festered in her shoulder. A bullet, he suddenly recalled, fired by a white man.

In a softer tone he added, "I give you my word, Morning Light, I'm still trying to help you."

She glared at the hand that imprisoned her. "Is this how you help me?"

"No." A hint of warmth touched his words as he drew her head down until her lips hovered just above his. "I do this for the pure pleasure of it."

She felt his breath, warm and tempting, a moment before his lips claimed hers. For a moment their lips merely brushed, nibbling, tasting. It occurred to her that she should resist. But then, as his arms came around her, drawing her firmly against his chest, she became lost in the kiss. She no longer had the ability to think, only feel.

Waves of feeling washed over her, leaving her flushed and breathless. She wondered if it was the same for him. But surely a man such as Pale Wolf would never be overwhelmed by such feelings.

At first she kept her fists between them, acting as a barrier. But as he lingered over her lips, she could not stop her hands from sliding upward until they were entwined around his neck. His strong hands moved over her, molding her to the length of him. She thrilled to the touch of his hands along her body.

Her breasts were flattened against his chest. Her hips rested against his, making her achingly aware of his arousal.

For a moment he cupped her face with his hands and drew her head back, staring deeply into her eyes. This time there was no fear, no smoldering anger. In those wide dark eyes he could read a mixture of surprise and pleasure. And the beginning of awakening desire.

"Oh, yes." Again she felt the warmth of his breath as he muttered, "So much pleasure."

With one fluid movement he rolled them both over, until she found herself lying beneath him. Before she could catch her breath, he covered her mouth with his.

Wave after wave of feeling threatened to swamp her as his mouth moved over hers. He lingered over her lips, kissing her slowly, thoroughly, until she moaned and opened her mouth to his probing tongue.

At his leisure he explored the sweetness of her mouth, savoring the exotic taste of her. As he took the kiss deeper his hand moved along the slope of her hips to her slender waist, then upward across her rib cage to the curve of her breast.

She flinched at his touch and he felt the wild thundering of her heartbeat beneath his palm. Its erratic rhythm matched his own as his thumb teased her nipple until it hardened. She gasped as he brought his fingers to the rawhide laces at her bodice and untied them. As the laces fell away and the bodice parted, she caught her breath at the look of passion that glazed his eyes when he lifted his head to study her.

She had thought she could resist him. Now she knew that she could not. Her body cried out for more of his fiery touches.

With a moan of impatience she reached up and ran her fingers through his hair, drawing his head down to her. His breath was unsteady as he brought his lips to her breast. As his mouth closed over her erect nipple, her body seemed alive with feelings. With his lips, his fingertips, he awakened needs she had never even known existed, until she was caught up in a need stronger than any she had ever experienced.

Dan felt her complete surrender and thrilled to it. As she clung desperately to him, he filled himself with the taste, the touch, the scent of her. How sweet she was. How wild. Beneath the very proper face she showed the world was a seething, slumbering passion that had awaited only his touch to be released.

He lifted his head and studied her as she clung desperately to him. Her head was thrown back, displaying her long column of throat and the soft swell of her breasts. Her chest rose and fell with each shuddering breath. Her hair spilled across his arms in a wild tangle. Her eyes, heavy lidded with passion, watched as he lowered his mouth to hers.

He knew he had to end this or betray all those who trusted him to be strong. But the lure of those lips was more than he could resist. He had to taste, to touch, a moment longer.

As his lips moved over hers, he felt the compelling throb of desire. It would be so easy to take what he so desperately wanted. One step more and they would both tumble over the precipice and plunge into a world of exquisite pleasure. One step. One touch. One word. And he could have it all. But by taking, he would lose everything.

He hesitated, feeling the thundering of his pulse and hers.

Very deliberately he lifted his head. Her lips were moist and swollen from his kisses. The bodice of her gown gaped open, exposing the swell of her breasts. Her skirt was tangled around her thighs, revealing her shapely legs.

He wanted her.

Her breathing was as ragged as his. He had taken her too far, too fast.

He stood, then helped her to her feet. For a moment she swayed and he held her until she pushed away from his arms.

Without a word she gathered the remnants of her bodice together, holding the rawhide laces in her other hand.

"You..." She swallowed and wondered why her throat was so dry. Forcing the words from between clenched teeth, she whispered, "You should not have come back."

"I'm here, Morning Light. I don't know how long I'll be here, but for now, I'm here. Get used to it. Now return to your brother's tepee. Before I do something we'll both regret."

She turned away and kept her head high as she made her way in the darkness toward the tepee. When she disappeared, Dan rolled another cigarette. In the flare of the match, his eyes were narrowed in thought. He leaned a hand against the gnarled trunk of a tree and lifted his head to the night sky. Overhead a million stars blazed in the midnight blackness. It was the same sky he had seen in Boston, he realized. But here in the Texas wilderness it seemed far more vast, far more magnificent. Or was it only because of the magnificent woman it sheltered?

From his position behind a stand of trees, a lone figure continued to watch until Dan finished his cigarette and rolled himself into his bedroll. Then the figure melted into the shadows and disappeared.

Chapter Twelve

"Morning, Yancy," Dan called. "What've you got there?"

The old man had balanced a sturdy pine sapling across two huge rocks and was busily scraping off the excess branches and bark.

"Sings In The Forest needs new lodge poles for her tepee. Thought I'd lend a hand."

They had been in the Comanche camp for several days, and Yancy had surprised everyone with his many talents. He could sharpen a blade or fashion an arrow from scraps of wood and animal bone. He could plug a leak in a bucket or tan a hide better than most women. There was no chore he wouldn't tackle. And though many men in the Comanche camp scorned him for doing women's work, they were forced to secretly admire his skill.

"Sings In The Forest lost her husband a couple of years ago," the old man commented as he worked. "Afterward her daughter's husband saw to her food and shelter. But he wanted to try life on the reservation, so she was forced to leave her people and accompany her family there. That's when the entire family was wiped out by sickness. Now she's alone, and has to turn to the tribe for all her needs." He spat a stream of tobacco juice. "Just don't do for a body to feel useless and dependent."

Dan watched as Yancy's blade smoothed and shaped the wood. "What's the difference if you do the chores for her or the others in camp do them?"

"I don't make her feel useless. She finds ways to repay my favors. Yesterday I caught two rabbits. Sings In The Forest cooked 'em for me. The day before, I caught a deer. She made me a feast. Best meal I've had in years, since Lil died. And the hides she's tanning will provide her with a deerskin jacket and me with a pair of moccasins lined with rabbit fur. Now that's what I call payment in full."

Dan admired the old man's logic. Still, he remarked with a frown, "I know how private these people are. They never talk about themselves. How did you get Sings In The Forest to confide in you about her husband's death and her daughter's illness?"

Yancy shifted the wad of tobacco to the other side of his mouth and grinned. "I don't know why, Doc, but people have always liked talking to me. Maybe it's 'cause I enjoy listening. I've learned a lot about these people and why they're on the run. And I think I know what makes their chief tick, and why his sister is so suspicious of all white men."

At that, Dan's head came up sharply. Yancy bent to his work with a grin. He'd seen Dan's reaction. He now had his undivided attention.

"What've you heard?" Dan asked.

"This tribe suffered a massacre at the hands of a band of soldiers. At least Sings In The Forest says they were soldiers. I'm wondering if they weren't a band of deserters.''

Dan was silent as Yancy shifted the tobacco around his mouth and continued. ''The chief's wife was shot before she could deliver her baby. The boy was taken from her dead body by the old women of the tribe. But before they could get him to safety, they were all trampled, including the boy. That's why his foot is twisted like that.''

''Morning Light only told me that he'd been run over by a horse. She never explained that it was a white soldier's horse.''

''Speaking of the chief's sister,'' Yancy went on, ''she was about to be married to a great warrior when he was shot down and died in her arms. Just about every family lost someone before it was over. They never even had time to mourn their dead before they were forced to run. They've been running ever since.''

Dan thought about the pain he'd seen in Morning Light's eyes. And of her fear and hatred of the white man. At least now he understood.

''Heard something else, Doc. About that young brave,'' Yancy said, pointing to Ishatai, who pulled himself onto his pony's back and led a group of braves on a scouting mission. ''He hasn't had much to say to me, but I've heard what he's been telling the others.'' Yancy glanced up and met Dan's dark gaze. ''It's mostly about you, and none of it's good.'' He lowered his voice. ''Sounds to me like he's got a personal grudge against you. Did the two of you have a run-in about something?''

''No.'' Dan shrugged. ''I think he just mistrusts all whites, like the rest of his people.''

"Maybe." Yancy went back to his work. "But if I was you, I'd keep a sharp watch over my shoulder, or you might find his knife planted squarely in your back."

"Thanks, Yancy. I'll keep that in mind."

Dan made his way to the tepee of Two Moons. Outside, Morning Light was preparing a midday meal over the fire. When she saw Dan she felt her cheeks grow hot and blamed it on the flames. Since his first night back at their camp, she had studiously avoided him. It would not do to allow this man to get too close again. She had already had a taste of his magic. There was no other way to explain his power over her. Even One Who Will Lead, whose death still brought a mist to her eyes, had never made her burn for his touch as this man did. There was a spirit within Pale Wolf, a dark spirit that took over her will and robbed her of the strength to resist.

"You are here, Pale Wolf," the chief called out. "Sit and eat."

"Thank you." Dan greeted the chief and his sister, and noted the two bright spots of color on Morning Light's cheeks before she lowered her head. He noticed far too many things about her. And now that Yancy had told him of her past, he was even more aware of her.

He turned to the chief. "You sent for me?"

Two Moons nodded. "Each day my braves ride out in search of the herds of buffalo. Each day they return with no sign of the great herds." His voice lowered. "If we kill no buffalo before the winter comes upon us, the People will not survive. We are called by others the meat eaters, or the buffalo eaters. But it is much more than nourishment we get from the sacred buffalo.''

"I've heard the braves talking," Dan said. "I know they're concerned."

Two Moons nodded his head. "They fear the spirits have deserted us."

"There's still plenty of time left before the winter comes. Time to slaughter the animals and tan the hides."

"Time." The chief's look became grave. "For the Comanche there is little time." He glanced up at Dan. "My dreams are troubled, Pale Wolf. Who will lead the People through the perils they must face?"

"You've done a fine job so far. Why can't you continue to lead them?"

Two Moons gazed at the distant peaks of the mountains, ringed by tufts of clouds. "Already I have heard the call of the great spirit. My time here grows shorter. And I must choose the one who will follow."

Dan was silent for a moment, digesting what the chief implied. He knew how much faith the Comanche put in their *puka* or power. Despite the fact that Two Moons was still a young, healthy man, he would prepare himself for the death foretold in his dream.

"Crooked Tree is a fine brave. And the people respect him. They would follow his leadership."

"Crooked Tree has not the heart for it." Two Moons touched a hand to his chest. "The fire does not burn within him."

"If you want fire, there is Ishatai."

Two Moons nodded. "There is much fire in his heart. But he is young, and his hatred of the white man could cloud his mind. He is reckless and headstrong. He could lead the People into a battle they could not win.''

''Then I guess you'll have to look for someone who possesses the best of both Crooked Tree and Ishatai.''

Two Moons grew quiet. He believed he knew such a man. But the man was not one of them. At least not by reason of birth. But in his heart . . .

His thoughts were somber as his sister began to clear away the remains of their meal. He could not help but notice the way the man beside him watched every movement she made. Nor could he ignore the way Morning Light's movements seemed stiff and awkward in this man's presence. She deliberately kept her gaze averted. As if, he realized, she dared not allow herself to look upon the white man. Could it be she feared that her eyes might mirror her feelings? Feelings she strove to keep safely locked in her heart?

Noting the sudden silence, Dan got to his feet. ''I promised Yancy I'd give him a hand.''

The chief nodded. As Dan walked away, he continued watching. It was obvious that there were strong feelings between this man and his sister. He would watch. And wait. And keep his own counsel.

Seeing Yancy struggling under the weight of the pole, Dan stripped off his shirt and offered to help. In the heat of late afternoon they lashed the four foundation poles together with thongs of buffalo hide and set them upright. When the butt ends were pulled out and evenly spaced, they added the rest of the poles, until there were two dozen. Then they draped them with the hides that bore the intricate scrollwork that Sings In The Forest had learned from her mother and her mother's mother.

"The door has to face the rising sun," Yancy explained as he covered the flap with an extra pelt.

With a weight at the bottom, it was self-closing.

Dan marveled at the cleverness of the Comanche dwelling. It was cool in summer, warm in winter, and easily raised or lowered in minutes.

Soon the new tepee had been erected, bringing cries of pleasure from Sings In The Forest and a cluster of her friends. The women's faces were wreathed in smiles as they admired the handiwork of the foreigners.

"You will sit. I will make you food," the old woman said.

Yancy's mouth was already watering at the thought of her fine cooking.

Dan picked up his shirt. "I'm afraid I haven't worked up the appetite that Yancy has. I'll leave him to enjoy his meal. He's earned it."

Slipping his arms through the sleeves of his shirt, he made his way through the camp, then paused when he reached the heavy undergrowth along the banks of the stream.

The sun had already dipped below the foothills of the Rockies, bathing the land in a soft twilight haze. At first, as Dan peered through the tangle of trees and vines that grew to the water's edge, he saw only the ripples on the stream. Then, as he stood watching, Morning Light broke the surface and began swimming. When her feet could touch the bottom, she began walking slowly toward shore.

He watched, mesmerized, as her wet dark hair fanned out around her on the water. Her face was upturned, her gaze fastened on the gathering shadows of evening. She had not as yet seen him.

He knew he should walk away and allow her the privacy she sought. But he stood rooted to the spot, unable to turn away from the vision that teased and taunted him as she slowly advanced toward him.

The water swirled around her shoulders, concealing all but the soft swell of her breasts and the darkened cleft between them. He held his breath as she took several more steps, until the water seemed to slip away, revealing her narrow waist, her softly rounded hips, her long, shapely legs. God in heaven. She was the most stunning creature he'd ever seen.

Suddenly he stepped from his place of concealment. She whirled to face him.

On her face was a look of surprise mingled with anger. "You have no right to be here."

"Don't you think I know that? This isn't something I planned. It just happened."

She began to back up, but he strode forward, unmindful of the water that spilled over his boots.

"It is not right for a man to see a woman other than his own. You must leave."

His pulse quickened. "It's true that I didn't plan this, Morning Light." With the back of his hand he stroked the wet tangles that caressed her cheeks. "But now that I'm here, don't ask me to just walk away."

Morning Light felt the thrill of anticipation that jolted through her at his simple touch. She was afraid. Afraid of the passions that simmered in this man. Passions that awakened something deep inside her that she had thought long dead. And she was afraid, also, of his carefully coiled tension, of his anger, of his strength. She must hold him at a distance. Or she would be lost.

"You will go now. Or..."

"Or what?" His voice was dangerously soft. "Will I feel the wrath of your brother if I touch you like this?" He moved the back of his hand along her cheek.

She struggled to hold herself perfectly still. Despite her struggle, she could not stop the involuntary movement as her face moved to his touch like a kitten being stroked.

His eyes narrowed. His voice was little more than a whisper. "Could anyone blame me for wanting to taste your lips like this?" With his hand beneath her chin, he lowered his face to hers and lightly brushed his lips over hers.

Her stomach muscles contracted violently. She felt the fire begin, low and deep.

"Such cool, tempting lips," he muttered against her mouth.

She trembled and his hands clutched her shoulders, as his lips continued weaving their magic. She swayed and his arms came around her, drawing her firmly against him. With a sigh she clutched blindly at his waist, no longer able to deny the fire that blazed out of control.

"How I want you." The words were murmured inside her mouth as he plunged his hands into her hair and drew her head back.

His kisses became more demanding, plundering her mouth until she was trembling and breathless. And still he continued to kiss her. Long, drugging kisses that took her higher than she'd ever been.

His need for her was staggering. He could hear the wild thundering of their heartbeats. And the ragged tempo of their breathing.

"You must go. Now," she cried urgently as she pushed herself roughly from his arms.

Dan was surprised at the venom in her tone. "One day you won't send me away."

Mustering all of his willpower, he strode from the stream and made his way to his own camp.

Morning Light waited until he was gone before striding from the stream. As she reached for her dress swinging on the branch of a tree, she heard the sound of horses splashing in the stream.

She lifted her head and turned toward the sound. Suddenly she froze.

The voices were not Comanche.

In one swift motion she clutched her dress in front of her and pressed herself into the shelter of the foliage.

Peering through the branches of a tree, she watched as two white men slipped from their saddles and surveyed the Comanche camp.

"That's them, Billy."

"There's more of 'em than I expected."

"You afraid of a few tomahawks?"

"Nah," the gangly youth said, touching a hand to the pistol at his waist. "Long as I got this, I ain't afraid of no Indian."

"Let's go tell Rollins where they're hiding. If he dispatches the army fast enough, they'll be off our hunting grounds in a couple of days. And Barker will have that buffalo herd to himself."

As the two pulled themselves into the saddle and turned their mounts, Cal's eyes suddenly narrowed. He squinted against the light reflecting off the water, and a grin split his lips.

"But before we go riding all the way back to the fort, I think I'll just have me some fun with a little squaw."

"You crazy?" Billy called.

"Maybe." Cal nudged his horse forward and slid from the saddle. "Maybe I've just been in this god-forsaken wilderness for too long." He pushed aside the branches of the trees and caught Morning Light roughly by the arm. She held her dress in front of her. "But this looks like a squaw to me."

His grunt of crude laughter was followed by a shriek of pain as her hand lifted high and the dress fell away, revealing a knife. By twisting sharply Cal was able to deflect her blow. The blade of her knife landed in his shoulder instead of his heart.

His hand curled into a fist and he landed a blow to her jaw. But when he bent to lift her to her feet, he found himself holding a wildcat. With a grunt of pain he grappled with her until Billy joined him.

Morning Light found herself facing the two men. She saw the naked hunger in their eyes and felt the cold thread of fear along her spine. If she had to, she would fight to the death. But as the men's hands roughly caught and pinned her, she realized that death would be far better than what they had in mind.

It took both men to subdue her. With her hands and feet bound, she was tossed over Cal's saddle.

Pulling himself up behind her, he tossed a rough saddle blanket over her and shouted, "Come on, Billy. I think we've earned the right to a little fun."

Numb with pain, Morning Light squeezed her eyes shut as the horses plunged into the water and climbed the bank on the other side of the stream. The forest was cool and dark as it closed around them.

Chapter Thirteen

Dan strode along the banks of the stream, berating himself for his latest bout of foolishness. The woman was like a fever in his blood. But now that he knew a little about her past, he realized why she didn't return his passion.

She was no longer the young, innocent maiden he'd met when he was little more than a boy. She was a woman who had loved deeply and had been deprived of that love. The things that had been done to her and her people were unspeakable. She would never be able to forget that the crimes had been committed by white men. There was no doubt in Dan's mind that every time she looked at him, Morning Light was reminded of the pain she had suffered at the hands of men like him.

He knelt by the edge of the stream and scooped water into his hands to splash on his face. As he did, he thought he heard a strange sound. A cry perhaps? Or merely the laughter of a child? He glanced around, then, seeing no one, scooped more water. He heard it again. Standing, he wiped the water from his eyes and peered through the trees. Though he could see nothing unusual, he felt the hairs on the back of his neck rise.

Creeping silently along the banks of the river, he retraced his steps until he came to the place where he had last seen Morning Light. The stream was empty. The water sparkled in the late-afternoon sunlight. She had most probably returned to camp.

He turned, about to retreat, when his gaze centered on something lying in the rushes that grew near the banks. He moved closer and picked up Morning Light's dress.

Something was very wrong. She would never have returned to camp without her clothes.

On the opposite bank he thought he saw a movement. But when he blinked and looked again he could see nothing but the swaying of the grass and the ripple of the leaves in the trees.

With Morning Light's dress still clutched in a death grip in his hand, he raced to where he kept his horse tethered, knowing he was wasting precious minutes. Pulling himself into the saddle, he splashed across the stream and entered the forest.

He was a man who had always trusted his instincts. And this time, every fiber of his body told him that Morning Light was in grave peril.

Cal and Billy whipped their horses until they were safely away from the Comanche camp. Then they slowed their mounts to an easy trot.

''Where're we headed?'' the boy asked.

''Somewhere secluded,'' Cal said with a laugh.

''What if the Comanche follow us?''

''Who's going to miss one little squaw?''

Billy shrugged. "No one, I guess. But those Indians make me nervous."

"Everything makes you nervous, boy." Cal grinned. "You're probably scared of women too."

"Am not."

"Bet you ain't even had a woman before."

"Have too. I had one of Rose Woodling's whores last time we were in Kansas City."

"Yeah?" Cal looked at the boy with new respect. "Well, that was a warm and willing body. This'll be a whole new kind of thrill. I'll have to show you how to treat an unwilling squaw."

Morning Light wondered if she would suffocate beneath the heavy horse blanket that had been tossed carelessly over her. Despite the heat of the day, a trickle of fear inched along her spine, leaving her cold and clammy. But at least she was hidden from view. With every jarring movement of the horse, she scissored her feet, struggling against the ropes that cut into her flesh until she bled. She lifted her bound hands to her teeth and began to bite at the ropes that cut into her wrists.

If these men took her to the fort, she would be defenseless. But if they stopped before reaching the fort, she would have a fighting chance. Though she was unarmed, she had her fists, her teeth, her fingernails. She would bite and claw and scratch. But she would never submit.

If only she had not sent Pale Wolf away, she thought with a growing feeling of desolation. Had he been there with her, this never would have happened.

She must not dwell on that now. She must keep her wits about her and wait for her chance to escape these vicious dogs.

"We'll make camp beneath those buttes," Cal announced. "We can take turns keeping watch while the other has some fun with the squaw."

Morning Light gave a last desperate bite at the ropes and felt them begin to unravel. The first faint flicker of hope burned in her heart. She would find a way. She would escape.

Dan saw the dust rise up far ahead of him and urged his horse into a run. Topping a rise, he squinted against the sunlight glinting off the rocks below. There were two riders. One of them had something slung over his saddle. Though it was covered by a blanket, he felt his throat go dry. He had no doubt that the blanket concealed Morning Light. And though he could detect little movement, he knew she was alive. These man would never carry off a dead Indian. But the thought that she might be wounded filled him with a sense of outrage.

He rode parallel to them, keeping them always in his sights. Suddenly they dipped into a dry wash, disappearing from view. With a feeling of desperation he nudged his horse into a run.

"This is far enough." Before his horse even came to a halt, Cal slid to the ground and hauled the blanket-clad figure from his saddle.

Morning Light slumped to the dirt and clasped the filthy blanket to her. Beneath it, she frantically worked her feet free. She watched through narrowed eyes as Billy carefully circled the campsite.

"What's wrong with her?" Billy asked in a fearful tone as he dismounted.

"What do you mean?"

"She just stares at me and chews at her ropes like an animal."

"That's the way of the Comanches. They don't talk to none 'cept their own kind, which suits me just fine. I don't want no jabbering woman."

"Do you think she knows what we're saying?"

Cal shrugged. "What does it matter? She knows what we want. You start a fire, boy. I'm going to have some fun."

As Billy turned away, Cal leaned down and yanked the blanket from Morning Light's grasp. He was unprepared for the handful of sand she tossed in his eyes. Blinded for a moment, he let out a howl of protest and rubbed his eyes. In an instant Morning Light scrambled to her feet and began to run.

With tears coursing down his face, Cal raced after her and dragged her to the ground. She sank her teeth into his hand and he gave a cry of rage before lifting his hand and slamming his pistol against her temple, hitting her so hard it snapped her head to one side. Blood oozed from the cut, and for a moment she was too dazed to move.

His pistol crashed into her temple again. Stars danced before her eyes, and she saw flashes of bright lights as the ground seemed to tilt out of control. Dizzying feelings spun through her, leaving her gasping for breath. If she lost consciousness now, all would be lost.

Gathering all her strength, she struggled to scramble away and nearly broke free, but Cal's hand shot out, catching her by the ankle.

"You going to help me, boy?" he shouted hoarsely. "Or do I have to fight this squaw by myself?"

When there was no reply, he turned his head and saw Billy lying in a heap in the dirt. Directly behind his left ear Cal heard the click of a pistol and felt the cold steel pressed to his flesh. A calm, icy voice whispered, "You move a muscle, you're dead."

Reflexively he lifted his gun, but a booted foot smashed his hand into the dirt. He gave a shriek of pain when he felt the bones snap. His gun fell harmlessly to the sand.

Morning Light looked up to see Dan standing over them. But on his face was a look she had never seen before. His features were contorted with rage.

He saw the blood that streamed down her face. "God in heaven, what have they done to you?"

With a savage oath he knelt beside her for a moment, then turned on the man who had inflicted such pain.

He caught Cal by the front of his shirt and dragged him to his feet.

Cal clutched his broken hand to his chest and whimpered.

"You're worse than an animal," Dan said through clenched teeth. "You don't deserve to live."

Behind him, Billy cowered as he saw Cal reach for the pistol hidden at the back of his waist. The damned fool was going to get them both killed.

In a voice low with fury Dan said, "I once took a vow to do all in my power to save lives, but I swear to you, if either of you ever cross my path again, I'll kill you."

Morning Light gave a low moan. Instantly Dan was beside her, cradling her in his arms.

What happened next left Billy gasping. Cal drew the gun from his waist and aimed it at Dan's head. Before he could fire, Dan turned and the sound of gun-fire echoed through the towering buttes that ringed their camp. Cal stood a moment, his pistol still aimed. Then he crumpled into the dirt.

Billy never looked back as he raced to his horse and thundered across the desert toward the safety of the fort.

In the eerie silence that followed, Dan carried Morning Light to a shaded place beneath the buttes. Wrapping her in a blanket, he used water from his canteen to bathe her wounds. And as the sun dipped below the mountains, he kept watch as she fell into a fitful sleep and fought the demons that tormented her.

Moaning softly, Morning Light struggled up through layers of pain and suffocating heat. The pain seemed concentrated in her head and when she turned to one side it crashed upon her in waves.

The men. Cal and Billy. She could feel their hands, pressing her down, holding her, soiling her. Clawing against them, she tossed aside the heavy blanket and lay, bathed in sweat, taking in great gulps of air.

She fought the arms that held her and the hands that brushed her damp hair from her cheek. And with a cry of anguish she surfaced.

Her lids flickered, then lifted. Stars blazed in a darkened sky. The night air was cool and refreshing. She breathed it in, then slowly exhaled as a familiar face swam into her line of vision.

"Pale Wolf. Where are the men who...?"

"One is dead, the other gone. You're safe."

Safe. She shivered. Instantly his arms were around her, drawing the blanket over her shoulders.

"You need to rest now, little one. In the morning we'll return to your people."

She closed her eyes, savoring the feeling of being held in his arms. She was weary. So weary. Yet, even as she drifted on a cloud of contentment, something, some important fact, seemed to hover at the very edge of her consciousness. She tried to brush it aside. Pale Wolf was right. She needed sleep. But it would not come. There was something she must do.

Her eyelids snapped open. "Pale Wolf."

"Hush, Morning Light." His words were soft, his touch soothing. "You're safe with me. I'll keep watch through the night. Sleep."

"There is something...." As she struggled to remember, it all became suddenly clear. "Oh, Pale Wolf." She pushed herself free of his arms and struggled to stand. The pain seemed to envelop her, but she refused to give in to it.

When she realized that she was naked, she gathered the blanket around her. "We cannot linger here. We must warn the others."

"Warn them of what?"

"Those men. They were not merely looking for a woman. They were here to find our camp and report back to the fort." Her voice became a cry of desperation. "The one who escaped will send the soldiers. We will be slaughtered, once again. We must reach them in time." Tears flooded her eyes and she was powerless to stop them.

From his saddlebag Dan removed her dress and discreetly folded the blanket while she eased the garment over her head and smoothed it over her waist and hips. When she turned to him, the fear in her eyes added to his fury and frustration.

"Are you strong enough to ride?"

"I must."

He nodded. In a tone devoid of emotion he said, "Don't worry, Morning Light. We'll make it back in time. By dawn we can manage to put enough distance between us and those animals to elude them."

Us. She fastened on that single word. "You ride with us?" she asked.

Her question caught him off guard. He had no business here. She had made that abundantly clear. And yet he couldn't leave these people. Not yet.

He paused, but only for a moment. In his heart, the decision had already been made.

He nodded. "Maybe your people will have need of a healer."

"We have long had need of a healer, Pale Wolf. But I do not think even you can heal the wounds inflicted on my people by your people."

He lifted her easily into his arms before mounting. Holding her gently against his chest, he murmured, "Tell me when you need to stop."

She nodded and drew her arms around his waist. With her cheek resting against his shoulder, he paused a moment, staring at the peaceful beauty of the Comanche land. It was hard to believe that in such a tranquil setting, men like Cal and Billy and Quent Barker could inflict such horrors.

Morning Light's words echoed through his mind, taunting him. My people. Your people. He felt a wave of revulsion.

He nudged his horse into a walk and glanced down at the woman in his arms. Her eyes were closed. He urged the horse into a trot, then a full run, but she never cried out or issued a sound of protest.

He'd never known such strength. It was one more reason why he had to stay, even though she gave him no encouragement.

He called himself every kind of fool.

Did he really believe two people could bridge the wide chasm that lay between them?

Chapter Fourteen

"We anger the spirits of darkness," Running Elk said to the chief as he and his elderly wife dismantled their tepee. "We should not ride until the spirit of light has chased away the spirit of darkness."

"We go now. Before the soldiers have time to find us."

"Ishatai was right," one of the old ones said as he passed the chief. "By permitting the white men in our camp, we have brought the displeasure of the spirits. The soldiers hunt us. And the buffalo we seek elude us. It is the punishment we must expect for arousing the anger of the spirits."

Two Moons made no reply. But the words of his people were unsettling. He knew their fears. Did he not share them? But he believed in his heart that if the spirits were angry, it was not the fault of Pale Wolf and Yancy. Had not Pale Wolf risked his own life for that of the People? Was that not proof enough that his heart was pure?

Two Moons watched as Ishatai and a group of young braves leaped onto their ponies. With their heads lifted at a proud angle, they passed by with all of their goods loaded onto their horses.

A frown touched the chief's face as he watched the disjointed procession. Sleepy children were handed over to the old ones, who were forced to ride on a travois loaded with household goods. Some of the women rode behind their husbands. Many others walked alongside their older children.

When the long column of people and horses topped a rise, Two Moons turned for a last glimpse of their encampment. This had been a peaceful place, a place of much game. He had hoped to keep his people here until the sacred buffalo returned.

His feelings of unease grew. Since the treaty with the great chief in Washington, nothing was as it had been. The land was overrun with men who took pleasure in inflicting pain upon the People. Many suffered from mysterious sicknesses. And now even the buffalo did not return. But worst of all, his sister had nearly been violated by the white buffalo hunters.

He felt an overwhelming sense of relief. Had it not been for Pale Wolf. . .

He thought of the terror he had experienced when his sister had disappeared, along with Pale Wolf. His first thought had been that she had gone with the white man to his people. But he had instantly dismissed such a thought. Both Pale Wolf and Morning Light were too honorable to leave without his blessing. Fearing the worst, he had sent out a party of his finest braves. But it was not until Pale Wolf had returned to their camp, holding the wounded Morning Light in his arms, that they had learned what had really happened.

When they were alone, Pale Wolf had admitted that it was two of the men from the white buffalo hunters' camp who had stolen Morning Light. Two Moons regretted that Pale Wolf had not carried the scalps of the two on his belt. He sighed. It was not the way of this white man. Still, Pale Wolf had saved Morning Light's honor and her life. For that, the chief of the Comanche would be forever grateful. He would find a way to pay this debt.

The spirits must indeed be angry. Two women had fallen into the hands of the enemy. Two Moons felt a tremor of apprehension. Often, such anger could only be appeased by sacrificial offerings. He did not mind if it meant that he must be the one to be sacrificed. But he prayed it would not be one of the innocent ones who must pay the supreme price.

For many days they journeyed, leaving the high country behind, and moving into the plains. Riders fanned out in all directions, to watch for the buffalo hunters and soldiers that they knew would be tracking them. So far they had managed to elude them. But they all knew that it was only a matter of time. There were so many soldiers. And so few Comanche left free.

Though the Comanche traveled the familiar trails of their ancestors, they found no trace of the great buffalo herds.

When they stopped to make camp each night, Dan was surprised at the ease with which families came together to laugh and talk, to eat and relax around the fire. In the brief hours of late afternoon, the air was filled with the sound of children playing and women laughing and chatting. The Comanche seemed to take hardship in their stride. Despite the rigors of the trail, they were happy and content.

Dan found Yancy seated outside the tepee of Sings In The Forest. On the old man's feet was a pair of sturdy, new moccasins.

"Seems like I always know where to find you these days, Yancy."

The old scout looked up from the block of wood he was whittling and said with a grin, "There isn't anything Sings In The Forest can't do." He wriggled his feet to show off his ornate moccasins. "She can make chicory leaves taste better'n coffee. And she fixes the best rabbit stew in all of Texas. Can you blame me?"

"I'm beginning to wonder if those are her only talents that keep you here."

Yancy chuckled. "I'm not denying she's a mighty fine woman, Doc. I might be persuaded to unhitch my wagon and stay a spell."

Dan heard the older man's easy rumble of laughter and grinned.

"What about you?" Yancy asked. "What keeps you here, Doc?"

Dan shrugged. "I'd like to stay as long as I'm some use."

"Your decision to stay wouldn't have anything to do with the chief's pretty sister, would it?"

Dan squinted up into the fading light. "I didn't think it was so obvious."

"A man would have to be blind." Yancy shot him a glance before returning his attention to the block of wood. "I've seen the way you two look at each other sometimes. Enough to scorch my beard if I got too close."

Dan grinned and changed the subject. While they talked, Sings In The Forest brought them two steaming cups, then retreated to her tepee.

Yancy winked as he took a long drink. "See what I mean about her chicory?"

Dan drank the hot liquid and leaned back, completely relaxed. "What are you making?"

Yancy shrugged. "Whatever catches my fancy. I guess I've whittled just about everything you can think of."

As the two men talked, Runs With The Wind and several of the other children sidled up to watch as the old man's fingers and knife flew over the block of wood until it transformed into a pony. With the tip of the knife he cut fine lines into the mane and tail until they looked as delicate as horsehair.

When he held it up, the children giggled and clapped in appreciation.

Seeing the look of yearning in the eyes of the chief's little son, Yancy held it out to him.

"Here, Runs With The Wind. Now you have a pony just like your pa's."

The boy's eyes went wide with surprise. With a look of near reverence he ran a hand over the smooth wood, then limped off, with the other children in tow, to show it to his father.

"Runs With The Wind," Yancy mused aloud. "Odd kind of name to give a boy who can barely walk. But the Comanche always give strongest names to the weakest children in hopes they'll gain strength from their names."

"His affliction seems to cause more pain to those who love him than to the boy himself."

"That's because the chief broke an old taboo Doc."

"What do you mean?"

"Look around you. Have you noticed any other children with deformities?"

At Dan's shocked look, Yancy said, "It's just their way. They believe a deformity in an infant means evil spirits. Rather than allow those evil spirits into their camp, they take a deformed infant out on the plains where he's left to die."

"Would they do that to Runs With The Wind?" Dan asked. "Or is he protected because his father is the chief?"

Yancy shrugged. "If enough evil began visiting these people, they might just decide that it's because of the boy. Then there'd be no saving him."

Deep in his own thoughts, Dan watched until Runs With The Wind disappeared into his father's tepee. Then, with a strange light in his eyes, he turned to the old man. "You say you can make anything?"

Yancy shrugged. "Just about."

"And Sings In The Forest . . . could she make another pair of those tall moccasins, only smaller?"

"Of course, but . . ."

"Listen a minute, Yancy, while I think aloud." Dan leaned close. "I've examined the boy and learned there's nothing I can do as a doctor to help him walk without that limp. But there may still be a way he can walk and run with the other children."

"I'd like to see that," Yancy said softly.

Very quickly Dan outlined his plan. When he was finished, Yancy thought about it a minute, then nodded. "Hell, why not? It doesn't sound that tough."

"Want to give it a try?"

Yancy grinned and picked up another block of wood. "Sure. I'll give a holler when I have something worth looking at, Doc." He glanced up as another thought struck. "What about the boy's voice? Think you can restore that?"

Dan shook his head. "That would take a miracle. And I'm fresh out of those."

He drained his cup and got to his feet. As he strode toward his camp fire, he heard the laughter of the children. The sound made his heart feel lighter than it had in a long time.

Morning Light topped a rise and halted in mid-stride.

Riding directly toward her was the one man she had managed to avoid for several days. She glanced around in desperation, but there was nowhere to hide. Lifting her chin, she forced herself to face him.

Dan slid from the saddle. "You're far from camp."

"Not so far." Nervously she fingered the beaded belt at her waist.

Dan noted that she had tucked a knife into her waistband and another in her moccasin.

"Why do you ride here, Pale Wolf?"

"I've been searching for water. There's none to be found. And from the looks of this grass, we won't find any nearby. This area's suffering a terrible drought."

She nodded at his words and stared out at the sea of prairie grass. Lowering her gaze, she studied the green plants that reached barely to her ankles. Always before the grass was waist high. Stooping, she picked a clump of grass and held it in her hand. The sand at the base of the fragile roots crumbled and blew away in a puff of dust.

Morning Light's heart was troubled. Since she was a little girl this had been the route of the great buffalo herds.

"Ishatai has said that the spirits are angry."

"And you think that caused the drought?"

She averted her gaze. "Since the time of my father and his father before him, there has always been grass for the buffalo. Now the grass dies. And the buffalo comes no more."

She turned to gaze down on the encampment. Lazy curls of smoke drifted from the cooking fires. Even from so great a distance, the sounds of children's laughter drifted on the breeze.

"It's my fault. I angered the spirits."

"How?"

"By permitting you to rouse the spirit within Runs With The Wind."

Dan reached a hand to her shoulder. "Morning Light..."

"No." She twisted free of his touch and faced him, her eyes wide, her hands lifted as though to keep him away. "You must never again touch me."

He was startled by her violent reaction. His eyes narrowed. "Are you saying that you also anger the spirits by allowing me to touch you?"

She lowered her head, avoiding his eyes. There was magic in his eyes, his touch, that weakened her resolve. "Ishatai warned me. I have brought great pain to my people by not heeding his words."

"Morning Light." His voice was low, patient. "You and I didn't cause this drought, or chase away the buffalo, or bring the soldiers down upon the camp."

"The words are so easy for you." She took a step away, to make certain he could not reach a hand to her. She wanted no more temptation. "But Ishatai's words frighten me. I am..."

The words froze on her lips as he took a menacing step toward her. "What you are is the most beautiful, beguiling creature I've ever seen." He touched a hand to her shoulder and moved his fingertips seductively along the slope of her upper arm. While his fingertips skimmed her flesh, his gaze narrowed as he stared down into eyes that had gone wide with fear.

He lifted his hands to cup her face. His breath was warm against her cheek as he lowered his face to hers.

Her heart began thundering in her chest. Her throat went dry. And though she struggled to deny it, she ached to feel his lips on hers.

"And every time I'm near you, I want you." His lips brushed hers, sending icy needles along her spine. He plunged his hands into her hair and drew her head back while his lips plundered her mouth.

The thought of taking her here in the grass drove him to the brink of madness. For days he had been taunted by the sight of the cuts and bruises at her temple. Taunted because she would not allow him near her. And now he knew why. Ishatai's threats had fueled her fears.

For long moments he lingered over her lips, savoring the sweetness of her taste. Then, summoning all his strength, he lifted his head and took a step back. "Now tell me you didn't want that as much as I did." His tone was low, almost savage.

For long moments they stood facing each other, their gazes locked, their breathing labored.

"The words of Ishatai still sound in my mind. I cannot forget." Lifting her head proudly, she rubbed the back of her hand across her mouth, as if to erase the taste and touch of him. "Leave me now. Go," she shouted when he continued to watch her without emotion.

He clamped his mouth shut on the words he wanted to speak. Pulling himself into the saddle, he turned his mount toward the camp below.

When she was certain he couldn't hear, she lifted her gaze heavenward and whispered, "I will heed the words of Ishatai. I have been unfaithful to the spirit of One Who Will Lead. Now I must repent my evil actions. And I must stray no more."

Morning Light watched until Dan reached the camp and tied his horse. She saw him turn and glance her way. Dropping to her knees in the stunted grass, she felt tears burn her eyes. Even from so great a distance he could touch her with but a single glance.

She must never let him see the power he held over her. The words of Ishatai still rang in her ears. Words that condemned her to a lifetime of pain if she let the pale wolf into her heart. But the spirits knew what she would not admit, even to herself. She wanted him. Every bit as desperately as he wanted her.

Lemuel Rollins was seething with anger. The young lieutenant and his eager patrol had been dispatched to subdue a tribe of renegade Comanche. Instead of the battle they'd anticipated, they had encountered only a vast, empty wasteland that stretched clear to the Rocky Mountains. They had returned with nothing to show for their efforts except dust-stained uniforms and tired horses.

Lieutenant Hall shook the dust from his hat and entered the Indian agent's office. "We followed the directions given to us by Billy. The Indians weren't there, sir. We spent the next two days searching for them, but never even found a trace."

From his position in the corner of the room, the young buffalo hunter held his silence. Billy knew that he must never reveal the fact that he and Cal had stolen a woman from the Comanche camp. He figured he'd been lucky to escape with his life. If Quent Barker discovered what they'd done, he'd have Billy's hide.

"Looks like you sent a boy to do a man's job," Quent Barker hissed as he stood at the window and watched the last of the patrol parade through the gates of the fort.

Lumbering to his feet, Rollins let loose a stream of vicious oaths. "What kind of damn fool can lose an entire tribe of Comanche?"

"We didn't lose them, sir, we just never found them." The young lieutenant turned to Quent Barker. "Maybe your man gave us the wrong directions."

Barker glanced over the army officer's head to catch the angry denial in Billy's eye. "Maybe. But my man has been riding these trails a lot longer than you."

Lieutenant Hall flushed. He had been at the fort less than two weeks. This had been his first real assignment. And he had failed. Miserably. "If the scout you'd promised me—"

"Don't you ever mention Yancy's name again," Rollins shouted. "You heard my orders about that deserter. He's to be shot on sight."

A roar went up from the men outside and Lieutenant Hall rushed to the door. While the others watched, two men rolled around in the dirt, fists flailing, blood pouring from their faces.

At a sharp command from their officer, several men stepped in to break up the fight.

Lieutenant Hall groaned inwardly as he stepped between the two men and assigned them extra duty. He could be in for a long night if these fights continued to break out all over the fort.

In Lemuel Rollins's office, Quent Barker and his men stocked up on extra ammunition before taking their leave. When Rollins tallied the money due, Barker merely laughed.

"If you want to be paid, I'll expect more than bullets for our guns. You offered protection for me and my men, Rollins. Protection from the Comanche." His eyes narrowed. "Cal paid with his life because of those heathen Indians. How many more men should I risk?" Without waiting for a reply, he added, "When you deliver, you'll get paid. And not before." An evil light suddenly glinted in his eyes. "Oh, by the way. There's one more thing I might have forgotten to tell you. Billy told me that he spotted that doctor among the Comanche." His smile grew. "You remember. The one who stole your supplies—and your scout."

Rollins's jaw dropped. "Dan Conway?" His eyes narrowed to tiny slits. "Why the hell didn't you tell me this sooner?"

"It was going to be your little bonus when your men brought them in. But since they can't even carry out a simple order, I figured I'd let you in on our little secret now so you'd know what you missed out on." Quent Barker and his men strode from the room.

As they left, Lemuel Rollins stood at the window, staring at the vast expanse of barren land that stretched as far as the eye could see. Somewhere out there was a band of renegades that had just cost him plenty. And a doctor that had made him look like a fool in front of the entire fort. Tomorrow he'd take that snot-nosed lieutenant by the ear and show him how a real soldier did his job.

Chapter Fifteen

The walls of the fort shimmered and swam in the distance. Thad Conway pulled the brim of his hat lower, to shield the burning sun from his eyes, and continued to slow his pace. Several miles back his horse had come up lame, and Thad was forced to lead him. Considering the heat of the day, most men would have ridden the animal until it dropped. But Thad had always taken as much care with horses as most folks would take with a baby. The stifling heat, the broiling sun that turned a man's flesh to parched leather, the loneliness of the desolate land, had all been a part of Thad's existence from birth. Texas was all he knew. And all he cared to know. His family, his horses, his land owned his heart. He needed nothing more.

Right now the fate of his family occupied his mind more than his horse. He'd been trailing Dan for too long now. Each time he got close, Dan seemed to slip away. This time, he vowed, he'd take any chance, no matter how slim, to find his brother.

The wanted posters made no sense to Thad. The brother he knew and loved would never be able to kill a man without provocation. From somewhere in the back of his mind came the thought that he hadn't seen his brother for many years. And people change. He brushed the thought aside. Something must have gone very wrong in Dan's life to keep him away. There was no other logical explanation for his mysterious actions.

By late afternoon Thad passed through the gates of the fort. It was bustling and busy, he noted. Several soldiers patrolled the outer perimeter. Over a dozen men stood watch atop the walls. Because of the heat of the day, most people usually stayed inside their homes until dusk. But long lines of soldiers hurried around, loading pack animals. Adding to the noise was the steady ring of hammer against steel as the blacksmith worked outside the stable.

Thad led his horse toward the sound. The smith looked up in surprise.

"I'd like to stable my horse for a couple of hours while I apply a poultice to his hoof," Thad said.

The smith shrugged. "The stall is free. Oats and water will be fifty cents."

Thad pulled some coins from his pocket and handed them to the blacksmith, then led his horse to an empty stall and began to work on the animal's hoof. While he worked, he noted that the blacksmith and an assistant never slowed their pace as they formed several horseshoes and repaired an assortment of guns and rifles. Though Thad had spent time in half a dozen forts across Texas, the people here seemed by far the busiest.

A short time later he emerged from the stable and made his way to the military commander's office. Inside, an aide looked up from a desk littered with papers. It occurred to Thad that all the aides had begun to look the same, as did all the desks and offices and forts.

"I'd like to see your commanding officer." Even the words exchanged had become the same.

"Lieutenant Hall is busy preparing his men for a dangerous patrol, sir. I don't think he could make time for you right now."

Thad swallowed back his laugh. This was nothing new.

"How about the Indian agent? I was told that he was actually the man in charge of the fort."

The young soldier bristled. "That would be Lemuel Rollins."

The way the young aide said his name, Thad had no doubt that Lemuel Rollins was not a man he liked. And from what he'd heard at nearby forts, he was not alone.

"Is he in?"

"Yes, sir. But he's busy, too. He's going to lead…ride with the patrol." At the slip of his tongue, the aide's face grew nearly as red as his hair.

That confirmed what Thad had heard. "Tell him I'll only take a minute of his time."

The aide left the room, then returned quickly. "Through that door."

Thad had to duck his head as he entered Rollins's office. He stood a moment, taking the measure of the man behind the desk. He didn't like what he saw.

"What do you need?" Rollins asked without preamble.

Thad deliberately took his time lowering himself into a chair and stretching out his legs in front of him. "I'm looking for a doctor who's been reported passing through the territory."

Rollins's gaze darted to the poster lying with several other papers atop his desk. After it had arrived, he didn't know what had made him more furious: the fact that a man wanted for murder had pulled a fast one on him, or the fact that he had missed collecting the reward being offered for the notorious doctor.

The look on Rollins's face wasn't missed by Thad, who was watching him carefully. The wanted poster had obviously preceded him. And the Indian agent was deciding whether or not to admit what he knew.

"You a bounty hunter?"

For several seconds Thad sat motionless, watching the man behind the desk. Then he gave a slight shrug of his shoulders, and the corners of his lips turned up in a half smile. "Let's just say I'd like to find this doctor."

Rollins made a quick assessment of his own. Of course this stranger was a bounty hunter. It was there in those cold, calculating eyes, in the way he sat, loose and easy, even though his hand rested just above the gun at his waist.

Lemuel Rollins shifted uncomfortably. He didn't like working with professional gunmen. But he wanted Dan Conway. And Yancy, if the old coot was still alive. His mouth almost watered at the thought of what he'd do to them. The two had made him look like a fool in front of the entire fort. For that, they would pay dearly.

"What makes you think the man you're trailing has come this way?" Rollins knew none of the men in this fort had talked. He'd vowed to kill anyone who told about his humiliation at the doctor's hands.

"I've been on his trail for a long time now. I think I'm getting close."

Rollins picked up a cigar from the desk, a gift from a grateful buffalo hunter, and held a match to the tip. As an afterthought he offered one to Thad, who declined. Through a haze of smoke, he watched Thad's eyes as he said, "Sorry. I haven't seen your doctor. But we're leaving for patrol tomorrow. Feel free to join us if you think it might help."

"Who are you hunting?"

"Comanche. Renegades."

Thad got to his feet. "Thanks for the offer. I'll think it over and let you know in the morning."

"We leave at dawn."

When the door closed behind him, Thad made his way to the stable. He didn't need a room. He'd sleep in the stall with his horse. And maybe, between now and dawn, he'd find out what Lemuel Rollins was hiding behind those shifty eyes.

At the chief's command, the Comanche continued their trek across the plains. For days they traveled the routes of their ancestors, seeking the sacred buffalo that sustained their lives.

Each evening, as they made camp, Ishatai became more vocal about the reasons for their misfortunes.

"It is the presence of the white men," he told a cluster of braves. "They were sent by evil spirits to destroy the People."

The young men nodded and grumbled among themselves. Crooked Tree, overhearing his remarks, lifted a hand for silence.

"How can Pale Wolf be sent by evil spirits when he saved the life of my daughter? Without him, Little Bear would still be in the camp of the white buffalo hunters."

At his words, several of the men hung their heads and drifted away from the group, ashamed that they had allowed themselves to be swayed by the hot-headed young brave. But instead of being silenced by the words of Crooked Tree, Ishatai grew even more impassioned.

"Does the white man cure the strange sicknesses that have come upon our people? Or is he the one who brought these sicknesses, so that he could appear to be a medicine man?" Seeing that he now had the interest of many, Ishatai leaped upon a rock and faced the crowd. "Hear me. The People have survived from the time of the first moon in the sky. We have no need of the white man's medicine. We must crush the skull of the white man beneath our heel. Only then will the sacred buffalo reveal itself to us."

On the fringe of the group, Two Moons stood alone, frowning as he heard the words spoken by the brash young brave. This time Ishatai had gone too far. Unless he recanted his words, he would be called before the council.

Whenever he had a spare moment, Yancy worked on Dan's project, carving, shaping and smoothing. Sings In The Forest worked at his side, fashioning a pair of hide moccasins softer than anything Yancy had ever touched. When Yancy had taken the woman into his confidence, she had been eager to help. Now the two had become co-conspirators, whispering as they worked, sharing secret smiles.

"You are hungry?" Sings In The Forest asked softly.

"Nah. I'd rather work a while longer."

"You will tell me when you wish to eat."

Yancy nodded and continued whittling. The sun had long ago drifted behind the banks of mountains. Stars winked in a velvet sky. Light and shadow played over his hands as he worked. Suddenly the wonderful aroma of rabbit stew had his stomach rumbling. He looked up to see Sings In The Forest watching him.

"You would like to eat now?"

He grinned. "I guess I just needed to be reminded." He set down the wood he'd been carving and accepted a wooden bowl from her hands.

A short time later he leaned back and sipped a cup of strong, hot chicory. "Sings In The Forest, there's just not much more a man could want."

He saw the mysterious smile that touched her lips. "I think there are other hungers in you, Yancy." Firelight played over her face as she got to her feet and made her way to her tepee. Turning, she said in English, "But like your hunger for food, you need sometimes to be reminded."

As the meaning of her words washed over him, Yancy went very still. For long minutes he sat, watching her silhouette as she moved about inside the tepee. It was plain that she was preparing two buffalo robes, side by side.

When he saw her lie down, he banked the fire and entered the tepee.

"You were right." His voice was little more than a gruff whisper. "I've got a powerful hunger, Sings In The Forest."

"Come," she said, patting the buffalo robe beside her. "We will feed each other."

Little Bear awoke crying. Her father and mother gathered her close and tried to comfort her. But she clung to them, her thin, almost womanly body racked with tremors.

"Can you tell us what frightens you?" Winter Bird asked.

Little Bear shook her head and continued to cling to them. Over her head her parents exchanged worried looks. This was not like the dreams she had suffered when she had first been returned to them. Then, in halting whispers, she had confided the horrors she had experienced at the hands of the white buffalo hunters. Her father had been filled with a hatred unlike any he had ever before known. Even now, the thought of what his child had endured sent a surge of blood-lust racing through his veins. Winter Bird, in her quiet, gentle way, had absorbed all her daughter's pain. And slowly, tenderly, had led Little Bear back toward the sunny, laughing child she had once been.

But this was different. The girl seemed too terrified to speak. While scalding tears rolled down her cheeks, she clung to her parents as if to life itself.

"What is it?" Winter Bird whispered. "Your father and I cannot rest until you tell us what has happened."

"It came to me in a dream." Her words were choked and halting.

"What came to you?"

"The spirit of death." She covered her face with her hands. Her words were muffled. "He came in the form of a buffalo. There was much rejoicing among the People. But when we tried to kill him, he took off his mask and his robe, and we saw that he had tricked us. He..." she was weeping now, harder, and her voice was choked with sobs " ... devoured us."

"All the People?"

She nodded, too overcome to speak.

Winter Bird gathered her daughter close and wrapped a buffalo robe around her thin shoulders. "You will sleep now, Little Bear. And when you awaken, you will have forgotten all about this dream."

The girl wiped her tears and fell asleep on her mother's lap, secure in the knowledge that her parents would keep watch through the night.

But Winter Bird stored the knowledge away in her heart. For despite her words meant to comfort, she knew that her daughter's *puka* was the gift of foretelling the future. If the dream was this horrible, how much more terrible would be the reality?

In the morning the Comanche moved out again. For two more days they traveled slowly. On the third day they came to a place of trees and water and small game.

"Here we will stay until the sacred buffalo come," Two Moons said solemnly.

Many of the People rejoiced, for they knew that their great chief possessed knowledge shared by the spirit world. Their ancestors had led them here, they whispered. Here they would be nourished once again, as the Buffalo Eaters had always been nourished, by the buffalo. They would wear the buffalo hides, eat its meat, drink its blood. And the cycle would begin anew.

Ishatai, passing the tepee of Crooked Tree, heard the cries of the young maiden, Little Bear, and paused to listen.

"It is as I saw in my dream. We must not stay here. For only death and destruction await us in this place."

"Hush," Crooked Tree commanded. "Do you think you know more than your chief?"

The girl bit down on her trembling lip and shook her head.

"Then you will speak no more of this dream. Go now," her father said sternly. "Tend to our horses."

Ishatai drew back and concealed himself behind a tree as the girl stepped from her father's tepee and made her way to the stream, where the horses had been tethered.

Following at a discreet distance, he watched as the girl sat down on the bank of the river and propped her chin in her hand. His mind was racing. He must think of a way to get her to reveal this dream that troubled her, for he was aware of her *puka* and intended to use it for his own advancement.

"I hoped I would find you here," he called, walking toward her.

Little Bear looked up in surprise. Never before had the fiery Ishatai sought her out.

"Do you look for Morning Light?" She had seen the way this warrior looked with naked desire at the sister of the chief when he thought no one was looking.

"It is you I seek. I know of your gift. I have come because I had a puzzling dream last night," he said, dropping to his knees beside her. "It would please me greatly if you would tell me what it meant."

Little Bear was too stunned to speak.

Seeing the flush on her cheeks, Ishatai's mind raced furiously before he finally spoke. "In my dream I saw a tree, withered and faded. From its dried-up roots I saw a sapling spring, young and fresh and green."

Catching the girl's hands in his, he said, "Can you tell me what all this means? Do you truly have the vision?"

Little Bear felt the heat of his hands burning into her flesh. Strong feelings swept through her. It was not fear she felt but something more like—dread. She chided herself for such foolish thoughts. Of all the braves in camp, Ishatai was the fiercest. She knew, from the whispers and giggles, that he sent many maidens' pulses racing. She should consider his request a great honor. She struggled to shake off the strange chill that gripped her.

Staring into his eyes, she said, "The tree represents one of the old ones among our people. Someone of great importance. The sapling is the one who will spring from his roots and become as important as the one who has withered."

"There was more to my dream." Ishatai tightened his grasp on her hands as he allowed his imagination to take over. He would weave a fine dream for her to interpret. "I saw a darkened sky, and two full moons fading to tiny slivers. Beneath the sky, on a hilltop, I heard a coyote howling. The coyote leaped up and touched the sky, and caught the slivers of moon in its teeth. And then, just before the dream faded, I saw the coyote racing across the sky and all the glittering stars were following."

Little Bear felt a shiver of fear at his words, for the coyote in a dream was always the cause of confusion. To the Comanche, the coyote was a trickster, a demigod, whose flesh, like that of the dog, was never eaten. Though many other tribes ate the flesh of those animals, the Comanche never did, though they occasionally wore their fur.

"The moons can only be our great chief, Two Moons. The coyote is you, Ishatai."

She felt his gaze burning into hers, demanding her to finish what she had started. But to do so would be to acknowledge her own dream. And she must not speak of it.

"What is it, Little Bear?" He gripped her hands so tightly she cried out. "What is it you will not tell me?"

"I cannot." She tried to pull away, but he held her fast.

"Are you saying that I will be the next leader of the People?"

She lowered her head, afraid he would read the truth in her eyes. If he had truly had this dream, her own dream became even more significant.

He caught her chin in his hand and forced her to look at him. "So. It is as I thought. Have you also had this dream, Little Bear?"

She shook her head. "Mine was of death."

The moment the words were out of her mouth she gave a little cry of alarm. "I vowed not to speak of it. What have I done?"

"So. You have seen the destruction of our people if they continue to follow Two Moons." His eyes narrowed. "But what if the People should follow a new leader? Could we then return to the strong, free way of life of our ancestors?"

When she said nothing, Ishatai got to his feet, drawing her up with him. He stared down at her with a tender, knowing smile. "Your secret is safe with me, Little Bear."

"You give me your word?" Her tone was pleading. "You will speak of it to no one?"

"You have the word of the one who will one day be your leader," he said, eyes flashing. "Now you will go and tend to your work. The words between us were never spoken."

Chapter Sixteen

There were hoots and shouts as a party of braves returned to camp with six elk. Amid much celebrating, the game was skinned and a feast was prepared. The People were eager to celebrate.

Dan had never seen the Comanche so relaxed and happy. Everyone in camp ate until their stomachs could hold no more. The men sat around a large fire, exchanging tales of earlier hunts and elaborating on stories of bravery. The women sat apart from the men, gossiping among themselves. Infants fell asleep on their mothers' laps. The older children played games until, subdued, they gathered around Yancy. Their eyes grew wide as his knife flew over a chunk of wood, transforming it into an eagle. When he had finished the carving, he presented it to a little girl, who ran off proudly to show her mother.

Yancy turned to Dan. "Sings In The Forest has finished the moccasins. And I've made the insert. When are you going to try them on Runs With The Wind?"

Hearing his son's name, Two Moons glanced up. "What is it you have made for my son?"

Yancy saw the hesitation in Dan's eyes and instantly regretted his impulsive words. But there was no turning back. "The doc asked me to whittle something special."

"You will show me."

Reluctantly Dan nodded. He had hoped to do this at some time when the others were away from camp, so that if his idea failed, no one would be the wiser. Now, he realized, an innocent little boy might have his hopes lifted, only to have them dashed once more. He set his jaw as Yancy got up and made his way to the tepee, then returned with a pair of small moccasins.

Two Moons eyed them suspiciously. "What is special about these?"

"The doc thinks they'll help your boy to walk without a limp."

The People had gone strangely silent. It was impolite to mention Runs With The Wind's infirmity. To do so was to insult their great chief.

The chief got to his feet and crossed his arms over his chest. His gaze pinned Dan. His voice seemed even more thunderous in the stillness. "You would risk rousing the spirit within him once more?"

"Yes." Dan stood and faced the chief. "I'd risk anything to help Runs With The Wind walk like the other children."

"Why must you taunt the spirits, Pale Wolf? Why can you not let them sleep? Are you so bold that you would risk their wrath?"

Dan said nothing in his defense. He would let his success or failure speak for itself.

Everyone turned toward the little boy, who stood peering from behind Morning Light's skirts. He looked at Dan, then turned his gaze toward his father.

For long moments the chief studied his son in silence. At last he spoke. "You will try these moccasins," Two Moons said sternly.

A murmur went up from the crowd. Would their chief risk waking the spirit within the boy?

As the little boy started to walk toward Yancy, Ishatai strode forward to stand between Dan and Two Moons. In a loud voice he cried, "Our chief grows old and weak. He would let the white man defy our spirits. I say it is time for the council to speak in one voice. It is time for a younger brave, one with the will to fight, to lead our people to victory over the whites who desecrate our holy ground and slaughter our sacred buffalo."

A ripple of hushed expectancy seemed to shudder through the crowd.

As if Ishatai had not even spoken, the chief moved past him. Showing no emotion, Two Moons pressed his hand on his son's shoulder. Softly he said, "You will do as Pale Wolf commands."

Dan hadn't expected such an emotional outburst from Ishatai or from the Comanche. It was plain that much more was riding on this than a little boy's ability to run and walk. The chief was now risking his ability to lead his people. Everything depended upon the outcome of this endeavor.

Still, Two Moons allowed none of the emotion churning within him to show on his handsome face.

"Sit," Dan said.

The boy sat very still while Dan slipped the moccasins on his feet. Inside the left one was Yancy's carving, an exact replica of the boy's left foot. Runs With

The Wind slid his foot neatly inside the insert. When he was helped to his feet, the insert added nearly two inches to his withered left foot, making both legs the same length. The tall moccasins, covering his thighs, completely concealed the insert.

"Does it hurt you?" Dan asked.

The little boy shook his head.

"Can you walk?"

Runs With The Wind took a tentative step and halted, glancing at his father. Two Moons nodded and the boy took another step, then another, until he crossed to his father. Six steps he had taken, but it was not plain whether or not he was limping. The little boy had moved slowly and awkwardly as he adjusted his weight to these new moccasins.

Dan held his breath. "Can you walk to me?"

The boy looked up at his father, then glanced at Morning Light, who stood a few feet away. She tried to give him an encouraging smile and found her lips trembling.

Dan held out his hands. "Come here, Runs With The Wind."

The boy crossed the distance between them, and this time there was no doubt. His rough, uneven gait was gone. Though he walked slowly, with much hesitation, there was no limp. Everyone in camp burst into spontaneous shouts of encouragement.

Dan leaned down and whispered, "Now you can run. Run and play with the others."

For a moment the boy merely stared at him, as if unable to comprehend. Then, with a smile, he turned and began to run through the camp, the other children streaming after him.

Morning Light could not stop the tears that spilled over and ran down her cheeks. In that moment she felt her heart nearly explode with gratitude and love. Love. The feeling overwhelmed her. Love. Love for her brother and his small son, who had been deprived of the beautiful Shining Star, who would have been so proud and happy at this moment. Love for her people, who rejoiced at the boy's sudden good fortune. And love for the man who had made this moment possible.

She went very still. She could no longer deny it. She loved this man who was not of her people. Loved him as she had never loved any other. As the crowd surged forward, she stood alone, buffeted by a storm of emotions that left her stunned and reeling.

Two Moons watched his son run through the camp. On his face was a look of pure joy. Since the day he had realized that his son would never walk like other children, he had prayed to the spirits to touch the boy. And now they had. Through the hands of this white medicine man.

Blinking back the mist that clouded his eyes, he strode into the crowd that had formed around Dan. As their chief pressed forward, the people fell back a few paces. Two Moons grasped Dan's hand in his. Taking a knife from his waist, he sliced across his finger and Dan's, and was pleased that the white man did not flinch. His eyes narrowed as he pressed their flesh together, mingling the blood. His words were husky with emotion. "From this day we are brothers. You need only ask and it is yours."

Over the heads of the crowd, Dan's gaze met Morning Light's. A slow, liquid warmth seemed to seep through her veins, heating her blood, bringing a flush to her cheeks. Her eyes softened in the way of a woman in love.

Dan watched as she stood alone, staring at him with that strange, haunted look in her eyes. This was indeed a proud and happy moment for him. Perhaps one of the happiest moments of his life. But the one thing that would have made it perfect was still being denied him. The woman stood apart from the others and merely watched. Nothing, it seemed, would break down those barriers between them.

Standing on the fringe of the crowd, Ishatai seemed thunderstruck. For a moment he was paralyzed. Pale Wolf's medicine was indeed potent, for it defied even the spirits. He was a man to be greatly feared. The brave glanced at those who had long listened to his words. Their gazes were now fastened on the white medicine man. As was Morning Light's. In her eyes he saw the look that could no longer be denied.

A sense of rage filled Ishatai. They had all lost their senses. He was the only one left who had not been taken in by the white man's tricks. He alone would have to show them what a bitter harvest they would reap.

With his face a mask of fury, Ishatai strode from the camp.

With his hand beneath his head, Dan lay in his bedroll and stared at the stars. Lifting a cigarette to his lips, he filled his lungs, then watched the stream of smoke dissipate into the night air.

All through the evening he'd watched Runs With The Wind playing with the other children. Though the boy had fallen several times, causing much fear among those who watched, he had always managed to pick himself up and continue the game. By the time Morning Light had finally led the boy to his father's tepee, Dan was convinced that he had done the right thing. With the help of Yancy's insert, the boy's limping gait had disappeared. If there was any lingering doubt, it vanished when Runs With The Wind had solemnly offered his hand to Dan before going off to his buffalo robe. The smile on the boy's face when he turned away had said it all.

Dan listened to the sounds in the camp. The celebration around the camp fire had finally ended. But from the murmurs and whispers coming from the tepees, and the playful looks that had been exchanged between husbands and wives as they had caught hands and hurried away, Dan knew they were engaging in more intimate festivities.

He felt an overwhelming sense of isolation, as sharp as any he'd experienced in Boston. Once again he was the loner, the outcast. Whether by accident or by design, he seemed destined to follow a path that most men would shun. A path that could lead to great rewards, or deep sorrow. Strange that on this night, when he had experienced such joy at his success, he should also feel such a sense of loneliness.

A shadow fell over him. In one swift movement he tossed aside his cigarette and brought his hand to the pistol at his waist. Seeing Morning Light, he let out a long, slow breath.

"Is something wrong?"

She shook her head and he found himself watching the way her hair followed the movement, drifting across her shoulders, spilling across her breasts. He longed to fill his hands with her hair. Instead he lay very still, watching her.

"No one is sick?"

"No one." Her voice was hesitant, breathless.

"Then why have you come?" To torment me, he thought. To rob me of sleep for another night.

She dropped to her knees beside him. "There were so many around you this night. I wanted to be alone when I express to you how I feel. Your cleverness has given my brother back his son. My heart overflows with joy."

When Dan remained silent, she felt her first moment of fear. She had not thought this through. She had merely given in to the compulsion to come to him, to speak the words that were in her heart.

She ran the tip of her tongue across her dry lips to moisten them. "I know now that Ishatai's words were false. Your presence among the People does not anger the spirits."

"How can you be certain?"

"You caused the spirit to flee the boy's body. Only one with strong medicine can do such a thing."

He itched to touch her. Instead he curled his hands into fists at his sides.

He saw the shiver that passed through her. "The night air is cool. You should return to your brother's tepee."

"I would stay here with you."

He tensed. He knew he must have misunderstood. After all, her words had been hardly more than a whisper.

His tone was stiff and formal. "I'm tired, Morning Light. It's been a long day. I have no time for sparring."

"Sparring?" She did not understand this word. "I will not go." Tentatively she touched a hand to his shoulder and felt him flinch. "You cannot force me to go, Pale Wolf."

At her touch his muscles contracted violently. He sat up and glanced at her, then away. It hurt too much to look at her. For suddenly he had realized why she came. She had come to pay a debt for her brother.

He looked beyond her to the stars that glittered in the night sky. But all he could think of was the brush of her fingertips against his flesh.

"I see. You think you will be my reward for driving the evil spirit from your brother's son." With a trace of anger in his tone, he pushed her hand away. "I want no reward. Especially not this."

By the light of the moon, her face looked stricken. "You do not want me?"

He gave a sound that could have been a laugh had it not been filled with so much pain. Not want her? She was all he thought of. Even in sleep he could not escape the need for this woman. She haunted his dreams. The thought of her was the sweetest torment he'd ever experienced.

But it was her love he wanted, not her gratitude.

Grasping her roughly by the shoulders, he stood and dragged her upward with him. His features were contorted by a savage look that filled her heart with dread.

"I want no martyr in my bed. When you come to me it will be because you love me. Not because you are grateful to me for healing your brother's son." He held her at arm's length and nearly shook her in his rage and frustration. "Now go back to your buffalo robe, Morning Light, and leave me."

"I would be Pale Wolf's woman."

"Pale Wolf." At her whispered words his voice grew ragged. "I'm not some kind of god. I'm a mere man who's being pushed to the limit."

Tears filled her eyes as he released her and turned away. She thought she had understood his needs. She thought they were as great as her own. But once again, she had been wrong about this strange, solitary man. He did not want her. He never had. Her shame and humiliation were overwhelming.

She felt a sob rush to her throat and threaten to choke her. Swallowing, she whispered, "I will go. But know this. You are cruel and heartless. No other brave has touched me as you have, Pale Wolf." She pressed her hands to her breast. "You have stolen pieces of my heart." The sob tore loose, ripping through her and causing her words to be choked and halting. "And without your love I will surely wither and die."

Blinded by tears, she groped her way through the darkness.

Chapter Seventeen

Stung by Dan's cruel rejection, Morning Light turned away and began to make her way through the tall grass. Tears blinded her but she gamely stumbled on.

Suddenly her arm was caught in a trap of steel and she was spun around. Dazed, disoriented, she found herself imprisoned in strong arms and hauled roughly against a wall of chest.

Wild-eyed and terrified she struggled, but she was no match for the hands that pinned her.

She thought, for one breathless moment, that it was a madman who had captured her. Then she found herself looking up into stormy green eyes. Her heart leaped to her throat.

"Did you mean what you just said?"

"That you are cruel and heartless? Yes." She tried to pull away, but he held her firmly.

"No." His eyes narrowed. "What you said after that."

She hung her head. "They were the ravings of a fool. You must forget what I said."

He swore loudly, viciously, then caught her chin and forced her to look at him. "I want to hear you say them again."

"I will not."

The look she gave him was so angry he couldn't help but grin. "Did I really steal pieces of your heart?"

"Yes. You are a thief. I know it is because you have no heart of your own." She turned her head away, refusing to meet his look.

"It is a cold heart, I will admit." He brought his lips to her temple and felt the little tremor that shot through her. Very deliberately he moved his lips across her forehead to her ear as he murmured, "A hard, cold heart that has been waiting a long time for someone to warm and soften it."

Icy, delicious shivers raced along her spine, but still she struggled to resist.

His breath was hot across her cheek as his lips nibbled her earlobe. "Will you really wither and die without my love?"

"You do not speak the Comanche language well enough. I said that I would rather die than give my love to a withered old man like you."

His rumble of laughter touched a chord deep inside her, and she found herself smiling in spite of herself. "Then I must misunderstand my own language as well, Morning Light. Because you spoke the words in very plain English."

"Then that is why I made such a mistake. I should have spoken to you in my own language."

"Do you deny the words you spoke?"

"I deny nothing."

A sudden silence fell between them. A long silence broken only by the sounds of insects and the call of a night bird.

Morning Light became aware of her own shallow breathing. And of the big, callused hands that still held her. Hands that had somehow softened their grasp even while they managed to drag her closer to him, until her body was pressed firmly against his.

She marveled at how easily her softness molded itself to the hard contours of his body. She was so achingly aware of him.

With great tenderness Dan enfolded her in his embrace, holding his passion at bay. He feared that if he gave in to the feelings that surged, he would surely drive her away again. But, sweet heaven, how long could he go on merely holding her? He wanted to crush her to him and savage her mouth with kisses. Instead, he forced himself to stand very still and savor the fact that she was here in his arms.

She closed her eyes and swayed against him, and trembled when he brought his lips to her eyelids. How soft was his kiss. Like the wings of a butterfly, calming all her fears, soothing all her tears. She stood very still, awash in feelings that calmed even while they aroused.

He tasted the salt of her tears and felt her eyelids tremble beneath his lips. Her lashes fluttered, sending ripples of pleasure through him. He held his breath, forcing himself to make no sudden moves. For he feared that the woman in his arms was like a wary doe, ready to take flight at the slightest provocation.

Without realizing it, she brought her arms around his waist and pressed her lips to his throat. That was his undoing. With a sudden intake of breath he dragged his hands through her hair and drew her head back, tilting her face for his exploring lips.

His mouth covered hers in a savage kiss that spoke of hunger. A hunger as deep as her own. In answer, she opened her lips to him, and his tongue invaded the intimate recesses of her mouth. Timidly her own tongue answered.

He took the kiss deeper as his hands moved along her back, dragging her roughly against him until they were so close he could feel the wild thudding of her heartbeat in his own chest.

He drew her head back and kissed the soft column of her neck until he heard her quick intake of breath. She arched herself, giving him free access, and he buried his lips in the sensitive hollow of her throat. As she sighed and moved in his arms he felt the need for her rise and swell until he was half-mad with desire.

With a moan of impatience, he tugged at the laces of her bodice. When they were free, he drew her gown down to her shoulders and burned a trail of kisses across her collarbone.

Her soft doeskin dress barely covered her breasts. For a moment it clung, moving with each measured rise and fall of her breath. He held her a little away, watching as the dress slid lower and whispered to her ankles, where it pooled at her feet.

"Morning Light. You're so beautiful."

She saw the way his gaze moved over her. He made her feel more beautiful than she had ever imagined possible. Desire was clearly visible in his eyes.

She touched a hand to his naked chest and felt his muscles contract at her simple touch. His reaction made her bolder. With a knowing smile she lowered her hands to his waist. But when she encountered the buttons, he had to help her.

"You are beautiful too, Da-Nee."

That was the name she had given him when they were hardly more than children. On her lips it was the sweetest sound.

He gave her a smoldering look. "This is the first time you've spoken my name. I love hearing it on your lips. Say it again."

"Da-Nee." Her lips curved into a radiant smile. "Da-Nee."

The sudden need for her set him on fire.

He caught her by the shoulders and dragged her against him, kissing her until he felt drugged by the taste of her. They dropped to their knees in the grass and he slowly lowered her until she was cradled in his arms.

Her skin was dusky in the moonlight. Her eyes smoldered with fire. A fire that matched his. For both of them, it was a fire that had been dormant for what seemed a lifetime. Fanned by the flames of passion, their desire erupted into an all-consuming blaze.

His hands, his lips, moved over her, avid, seeking, until she moaned and moved in his arms. Her mind no longer seemed to function. Her body had become a mass of nerve endings. She could no longer think, only feel. Steeped in feelings, she lay in his arms, hostage to a desire that she could no longer deny. A strange sense of lethargy stole over her, robbing her of the ability to move.

He burned a trail of fiery kisses from her ear to her throat, then downward to the soft swell of her breast. When his lips closed around one erect nipple, she gasped and arched in his arms. Her body was alive with need. Never had she known such feelings.

Her breathing quickened, as did her heartbeat, until she thought she would explode with desire. With his mouth, his fingertips, he brought her to the first peak.

Dazed, she could only cling to him and whisper his name as wave after wave of feeling washed over her.

When his lips found hers, she had a desperate need to touch him as he was touching her.

With her fingertips, she traced his shaggy eyebrow, the slope of his nose, the outline of his lips. He lightly bit her finger and she drew back with a laugh. Then, emboldened by his teasing, she knelt over him. Her hair swirled around her, adding to his arousal. Tentatively she touched her hand to the mat of hair that covered his chest. When her fingers encountered his nipple, she heard his sudden intake of breath. Alarmed, she paused, but he quickly caught her hand and placed it over his heart.

"Touch me again, Morning Light. I've waited so long for your touch."

Growing more daring, she explored the long, jagged scar that ran from his shoulder to just below his rib cage. But when she started to ask him about it, he pulled her down on top of him and kissed her until she forgot the question.

Inflamed by his kisses, she moved her hand lower and heard him moan with pleasure.

Desire clawed at him. The need for this woman was taking him to the edge of madness.

In one quick movement he rolled her over. His lips covered hers in a savage kiss. While his lips, his hands, continued their torment, he breathed in the wild, sweet fragrance of her that seemed to envelop him. Her taste, her scent, filled him with a need that bordered on pain.

He had wanted to be gentle. She was a woman who deserved tenderness. But needs tormented him, seeking release. When at last they came together, he forgot everything except his need for her.

With a strength that surprised him, she moved with him, taking him higher, then higher still. His lips covered hers and he murmured words of endearment in both English and Comanche, or thought he did.

He plunged his hands into her hair and stared into her eyes. They were wide and expressive, glazed with need, filled with love.

Love. It filled him to overflowing.

He whispered her name as if it were a prayer. And then, together, they soared to the heavens and exploded into a shower of starlight.

They lay together in the grass, still joined. Their faces were slick with sheen. Neither of them was willing to move, for fear of shattering the fragile bond that held them.

Dan pressed his lips to Morning Light's temple, aware of the tremors that still rocked her. But when he tasted the salt of her tears, he lifted his head in alarm.

"I've hurt you. God in heaven, Morning Light. Why didn't you tell me?"

"Shh." She touched a finger to his lips. "You did not hurt me. These are happy tears."

He felt the tension slip away as quickly as it had come. Rolling to his side, he cradled her in his arms and heard her sigh of pleasure.

Through her tears she whispered haltingly, "I had not thought, when I came to you, that I..." She swallowed and tried again. "I only meant to show you my love, to please you...."

He heard the tears in her voice and gathered her close against him. "You did please me." He pressed his lips to her temple. "More than I can ever say. But what is it that troubles you?"

Her eyes filled with tears again, and she couldn't stop them.

"I have never known such feelings. They frighten me. It is always like this?"

With his thumbs he tenderly wiped the tears from her cheeks, then lowered his face until his lips brushed hers. "It is when there is love, Morning Light."

"Do you truly love me, Da-Nee?"

"With all my heart. I never thought it was possible to love someone as much as I love you."

At his words her tears were forgotten. An impish smile curved her lips. "If you love me, why is it your eyes look like this when you are near me?" She made a ferocious face, knitting her brows together into a frown.

"Is that how I look to you?"

She nodded.

Dan burst into gales of laughter. "I look like that so I won't look foolish in front of the others. Would you like it if I let everyone see how I really feel?"

"And how do you really feel?"

He gave a wide, exaggerated grin. With a laugh of delight she kissed the corner of his lips.

The laughter died in his throat when her lips brushed his. It wasn't possible to want her again so soon. But he did. He would never have enough of her.

As if sensing her power over him, Morning Light sat up, her hair swirling forward to tickle his flesh. Her eyes glowed with a woman's knowing look.

"You are frowning again, Da-Nee." Her fingertips lightly brushed his skin and she felt him flinch.

"Witch. You must be touched by the spirits. Do you know what you do to me?"

"Do you wish me to stop?" She brushed her lips lightly across the flat planes of his stomach and felt his muscles contract violently.

He moaned and pulled her down until her face was inches from his. His voice was rough with urgency. "You make me weak, woman. Right now I can't think of anything except you."

Plunging his hands into her hair, he drew her close and covered her lips in a searing kiss. And together they tumbled into a world of unbelievable pleasure. A world where only lovers can go.

In the distance, a single figure stood beneath a rocky outcrop, staring intently at the two figures. One hand closed around the knife at his waist, and he lifted it in an anguished gesture toward the heavens.

The woman should have been his. But she had chosen instead the hated Pale Wolf. She would live to regret her decision. As would her brother, the chief. He would see to it that they all regretted this night. Before he was finished, he would have his vengeance. And they would not soon forget the name of Ishatai, The Coyote.

Chapter Eighteen

In the ghostly light that played over the land just before sunrise, Dan lay in the buffalo robe, staring at the woman in his arms. She lay on her side, curled up against him as comfortably as if she had always slept there. Her hair spilled over his arm, as soft as velvet, perfumed with evergreen.

Sometime during the night, they had awakened in the grass. He'd lifted her easily into his arms and carried her back to his camp, where he deposited her on his buffalo robe. They had laughed softly together, and loved slowly, thoroughly, until they had once more drifted into a contented sleep.

He lay very still, trying to sort through the conflicting emotions that tugged at him. He had always thought that love would be a simple thing. But the feelings he had for Morning Light were far from simple. They were creating new complications in a life that was already complicated.

Always before, he had been alone. He'd known that the decisions he made affected only him. Now this beautiful woman, by her simple act of love, had changed everything. No longer would he be able to think only of himself. Always, she would be first in his thoughts. Her safety. Her comfort.

He had never before felt that he belonged anywhere. Now he knew. He belonged wherever she was. Always he had been alone. Now he felt—whole. Complete. She was the missing piece in his life.

He lay very still, savoring the feeling of peace and contentment that stole over him. This woman had touched a chord deep inside him. Something long buried had begun to grow and flourish once more. He felt as he had many years ago. All those childhood yearnings were blossoming again. He could almost believe that with Morning Light by his side, he could make a difference. His life, his medicine, could count for something.

He watched as her lids flickered, then opened. He saw the momentary confusion in her eyes and felt the first stab of icy fear. What if she regretted their night of love? What if, in the cold light of morning, she turned away from him and returned to her brother's tepee? For a moment his heart stopped beating.

Morning Light studied the man whose arms encircled her. Seeing the little frown between his eyes, she surprised him by leaning up to press her lips to the spot.

"Could it be that my brave warrior is afraid to smile at me?" She touched a finger to the frown, smoothing it away. "Or do you find me so ugly in the light of morning that you cannot bring yourself to look at me with happiness?"

Dan's lips split into a grin. "That's what it was. I was thinking that you'll soon be as plump as Winter Bird."

She attempted to draw away, but he held her fast. Pressing his lips to her temple, he murmured, "And I suppose any day now your teeth will start to fall out like old Running Elk's."

She giggled in spite of herself. "Will you then send me away and find a younger, prettier maiden?"

"If only I could," he said with a sigh. "But you've spoiled me now for any other woman. How could I look at another after seeing your beauty?"

Her laughter faded when she saw the solemn look in his eyes. For long minutes she studied the man who lay beside her. Sitting up, she faced him. Her hair swirled around her shoulders, casting her eyes in shadow.

"I met you once, when you were a young brave. You touched my heart in a way that I have never forgotten. But now," she said softly, "I must know the man you have become."

"What would you like to know?" He placed a hand beneath his head, completely relaxed.

"Were there other women?" she asked timidly.

He swallowed his smile. "Yes."

"Many?"

"As many as there are stars in the sky." He tried to look solemn, but the hint of laughter danced in his eyes.

"I think you—tease. You are not a man to lightly give your heart. But there was a woman. You spoke of her when first you came to us. Her name was Sarah," Morning Light said softly. "And she caused you much pain."

She saw him wince as he caught a strand of her hair and twisted it around his finger. "Sarah Dowd. Her father, Dr. Zachery Dowd, was a teacher who befriended me at medical school. He sensed my loneliness and treated me like a son. And Sarah..." He paused a moment, trying to find the words. "Sarah was lovely. She filled a void in my life." His tone abruptly hardened. "But she could have never survived the rigors of my life here. She tried to persuade me to give up my dream. Before I left for Texas, we severed our relationship."

"Then she did not truly love you, or she would have followed her heart."

Dan watched as the black silken strands sifted through his fingers. He would forever praise heaven for those who could follow their heart. "Her heart lay in Boston. She'll find a man who'll give her the kind of life her father wanted for her."

"She is a fool, this Sarah Dowd. I am sorry for her. And," she added with a smile, "I am grateful."

Morning Light's hand pressed to his heart. Tentatively she touched a fingertip to the raised ridge that ran from his chest to his hip. "Is this a battle scar?"

"You might call it that." He gave a lazy smile at the sensuous touch of her finger. "I encountered an—unfriendly citizen on the Boston docks one night. The butcher who sewed me up must have taken his medical training in a slaughterhouse."

She didn't return his smile. "You spoke of many things when first you came to our camp. You thought you were in that place." She wrinkled her nose. "Boston."

She saw the stillness that came over him. His frown returned. "What things did I tell you?"

"They do not matter." She moved her hands across his stomach and saw the subtle change in him. Though he tried, he could not ignore her touch. Thoroughly enjoying her new sense of power, she moved her hand lower, until he gave a low moan of pleasure.

"Do you know what you're doing to me?"

"It pleases you?"

"It..." he dragged her against him and crushed her mouth with his "...more than pleases me," he muttered thickly. "It drives me mad."

The rest of her questions were forgotten, as were his answers. They came together in a storm of passion.

"Why does the hair grow on your face and chest?" Morning Light looked up from the buffalo robe where she sat braiding her long hair.

Dan stood in front of a cracked mirror, working his straight razor with quick strokes. "Because I'm a man."

"You mean your women do not grow such hair?"

With a grin Dan leaned close and planted a kiss on the tip of her nose. "A few. But they're not a lot of fun to kiss. Their long beards get in the way."

She laughed and tossed her head, sending the braid dancing. "Now I know that you are teasing me." She got to her feet. "It is time I prepared a morning meal for my brother and Runs With The Wind. You will join them?"

He drew her close and gave her a long, possessive kiss. "I know what I'd rather do."

With a laugh she drew away. "That is for tonight. When the shadows cover the land and the others are asleep. For now, you must act as you did before."

"You mean I should frown at you?"

She gave a girlish laugh as she began to walk toward the camp. "Yes. No foolish laughter. Or everyone will know that our hearts have joined."

He watched her walk away as her words echoed in his mind. "Our hearts have joined." He couldn't have found a better way of saying it.

Then he remembered that he had still forgotten to ask her what he'd revealed when he'd been brought unconscious to their camp. Tonight, when they were alone, he would ask.

It was early evening. The day had been full. Dan and Yancy had joined a company of braves who had bagged several more elk. The meat was divided among all the people, who were grateful for the plentiful game. But their concern was growing. The elusive buffalo were still nowhere to be found.

After a fine meal Dan had examined Runs With The Wind, to make certain that the insert was not causing any pain to his foot. When he nodded his approval, the boy surprised him by racing off with the other children, amid shrieks of laughter.

"It is good to hear him laugh," Two Moons said when the boy was gone. "Soon, I think, the spirit will let loose of his tongue and my son will speak."

"Have you not been granted enough?" Morning Light chided. "Your son runs and plays. Soon he will become a fine strong brave like his father. And still you want more?"

The chief gave a wry smile. "I can die a happy man because of the kindness of Pale Wolf. But it is true that there is always something more we desire."

He saw the glances exchanged between his sister and the man who sat beside him. All day they had looked at each other in that same way. And now, as the evening shadows lengthened, they seemed even more aware of each other.

Two Moons watched as his sister made her way to his tepee and prepared his son for bed. Beside him, Dan's eyes were shadowed by the wide brim of his hat. But though his look was veiled, Two Moons knew. His sister had already made her choice. As had Pale Wolf.

Two Moons smiled. He was pleased. The best unions were those between a man and woman who chose each other. Now he would wait. Soon Pale Wolf would come to speak to him. And when he did, he would be bound to the People as surely as if he had been born Comanche. And the next leader of the People would be chosen. Though it was not the custom, these were extraordinary times.

Ishatai knelt on a hill overlooking the camp. His dark thoughts were filled with jealousy and hatred. There had been a time when the chief valued his counsel. Until Pale Wolf had come to them, it was Ishatai who had been welcome in the tepee of the chief. And it had been Ishatai who had been favored with a smile from the chief's sister. Now the council would not hear his words. Even though Two Moons had not yet led them to a buffalo herd, no one was willing to challenge their chief's leadership. What was worse, the woman who should have been Ishatai's had given herself to a man unworthy of her. They were all touched with evil spirits. Even the son of the chief had evil dwelling within him. Yet no one was willing to stand against them. Except him.

Ishatai had a plan. He had seen the signs of the buffalo on his many forays into the surrounding countryside. As yet, he had told no one what he had seen. He was tired of sharing his knowledge with the others, and having them reap the honors. No longer would he call Two Moons his chief. Nor would he reveal to Two Moons the presence of the buffalo herd.

He smiled, thinking about the friends he had made in the camp of the Kiowa Apache. They shared his lust for the blood of the white man. They would be his army. And when he returned with the spoils of victory, the People would revere the name of Ishatai, The Coyote, and scorn the name of Two Moons. And Ishatai would be proclaimed chief by uniting both the Kiowa Apache and the Comanche. And he would claim Morning Light for his woman.

But first he must spirit the woman away from the white dog who had used his powers to win her heart.

With footsteps that rivaled those of a shadow, he made his way unerringly to the stream where Little Bear was watering the horses. For, though she was unaware, she was a very important part of his plan.

When first she spotted the brave, Little Bear's eyes opened wide and she experienced again a feeling of dread. An anger burned in this brave that had him as tightly coiled as a rattler. But when she saw his quick smile, she put aside her feelings.

"What is wrong?" she cried as she scrambled to shore and tethered the horse.

"I had another dream," he said, catching her hand. "Come, where no one will overhear us." He led her up the hill, until they were able to look down upon the camp.

"Tell me of this dream." Little Bear allowed him to lead her to a buffalo robe that he had spread in the grass.

When she was seated, he sat close beside her and handed her a small buffalo horn filled with liquid.

"What is this?"

"Something to warm you."

She drank quickly, emptying the horn. When she shivered in the cool evening air, he drew her close and wrapped his arms around her.

Her voice quivered slightly and she struggled to ignore the pleasure his touch brought. Many of the braves would not look upon her since her return from the white man's camp. But Ishatai treated her with great respect.

"It must have been very important to disturb my work and bring me here."

"I think it is of great importance. In my dream the buffalo returned to the land of our ancestors."

At his words, Little Bear's eyes widened. The buffalo had been in her dream, as well. She would never forget the disturbing feelings that dream had brought.

Seeing her reaction, Ishatai became animated. "A tall warrior in a buffalo robe led us away from the herd and allowed the white hunters to take all they wanted. When the People were finally able to hunt, the herd was dead. And there was great hunger and suffering among the People. Many died. Many more were forced to return to the reservation. The great Comanche nation was no more."

Little Bear's throat was dry. She found she could not swallow the lump that threatened to choke her.

"I have dreamed such a dream," she said softly.

"Then it is as I thought."

She looked up questioningly.

"You and I must save our people from destruction."

"You and I?" She was honored that he would think so highly of her. "How?"

His eyes danced with a strange light. "We will find a way. And when I am ready, you will be my messenger."

A horse whinnied, and he startled her by running down the hill and returning with one of her father's horses. "What have you done, Ishatai?"

"It is said that your horses are the fastest among all our People, is that not so?"

She could not help but smile proudly. "It is so." Her smile faded. "But they belong to my father. They are not for you to ride."

"I will not ride him. He will be yours. And you will measure his strength and speed against my pony."

It was the one challenge he knew she could never resist. Her eyes sparkled. Her smile grew. "You must prepare to lose."

"If you win," he said, helping her onto the horse's back, "I will know that you are a woman worthy to ride beside the next leader of the People."

With a laugh she nudged her horse into a run across the darkening plain, with Ishatai beside her.

He would lead her on a long, tiring ride. She must not suspect what he had in mind. And he would see that they returned when it was too late for her to eat, for he wanted nothing else on her stomach. Then the liquid would have the desired effect.

Chapter Nineteen

Dan lay in his buffalo robe, listening to the slow, steady breathing of the woman in his arms. He had come to a decision. In the morning he would seek Two Moons's permission to take Morning Light as his wife.

He knew he had no right. He had nothing to offer her. Nothing except his undying love. He frowned in the darkness. And a life on the run if his presence should be discovered. She deserved so much better. But she had defied Comanche tradition by coming to him without her brother's permission. No bride-price had been paid. In the eyes of her people, Morning Light was a woman without status. By observing the customs of her people, he would give her the title of respected wife of a medicine man. It was the least he could do to prove his love.

She stirred and moved against him, and he felt desire rising, swift and overpowering. He brushed his lips over hers and felt her immediate response. God in heaven, how he loved her. She had become his whole reason for living.

Thad lay in his bedroll under the stars and smoked one of Lemuel Rollins's cigars. The Indian agent had been making friendly overtures to Thad since he'd agreed to travel with Lieutenant Hall and the soldiers. Though Thad despised Rollins and everything he stood for, he was willing to use the man if it would lead him to Dan. As for the young lieutenant, Thad felt only sympathy for his position. The young officer would never be able to wrest control of his men from the heavy-handed Indian agent. Whatever Rollins was up to, the presence of the soldiers would make it appear legitimate.

What was Rollins up to? The word back at the fort was that they were merely trailing a band of renegade Comanche in order to set an example. There had been rumors of mismanagement of the Indians under Rollins's control. Thad had heard about outbreaks of disease, of a lack of food and medicine. If the rumors were true, the Indians on the reservations would soon revolt and follow the lead of the defiant Comanche, demanding the freedom to roam their ancient hunting grounds.

But there were other whispers and rumors that Thad found even more intriguing. A weathered old horse-soldier, after consuming a bottle of cheap whiskey, had confided that the best scout in their company had helped a thief escape the fort with a store of medicine. Thad blew a stream of smoke into the night air and frowned. Why would a man steal medicine unless he knew what to do with it? Wasn't it natural to assume that the thief could have been Dan?

There was only one reason why Thad was lying in the middle of the Texas plains instead of a comfortable bed back at Jessie's ranch. He was determined to find his brother. He stubbed out his cigar and stretched his saddle-weary muscles. For the first time since he had begun his odyssey, he knew that Dan was somewhere close. He could feel it in his bones.

It was not yet dawn when Dan felt the hand upon his shoulder, shaking him from a sound sleep. Beside him Morning Light stirred and sat up, pushing her hair from her eyes.

"Pale Wolf, you must come."

Dan looked up to meet the worried frown of Crooked Tree.

"My daughter, Little Bear, is burning with fever. Her mother cannot rouse her."

"I'll come at once."

Dan pressed his lips to Morning Light's temple and whispered, "I'll be back soon."

"I will come with you."

"There's no need. Sleep a while longer."

He picked up his black bag and followed Crooked Tree to his tepee. Inside, he was alarmed to find Little Bear lying as still as death in her buffalo robe. Heat poured from her body as he moved aside the covering. When he touched a hand to her distended stomach, her slender body twitched with a spasm of pain.

"What did she eat yesterday?" Dan asked sternly.

Winter Bird shrugged. "Elk meat. A little rabbit. Water from the stream." She seemed perplexed. "But we ate the same, Pale Wolf. And we are not suffering as our daughter suffers."

"Could she have eaten something without your knowledge?"

Winter Bird glanced at her husband, then shrugged again. "You know how it is with children. We are not always with them."

"Little Bear," he said, bending close to her ear. "Can you hear me?"

The girl moaned, and for a moment her eyes opened, but it was obvious she could not see the people who watched her with worried frowns.

"I see death," she whispered through parched lips.

Winter Bird covered her mouth to stifle the sob that tore through her. Catching Dan's arm, she whispered, "You will stay with her?"

He nodded. The fever was severe. The girl was on fire. Already she was delirious.

"I'll stay," he murmured, "for as long as it takes to make her well."

Morning Light rolled to her side and snuggled deeper into the buffalo robe, inhaling the slightly musky male scent of Pale Wolf that still lingered in the folds. The heat from his body lingered as well, warming her body and her heart.

She had never known such peace and contentment. How was it that this man, who was not of her people, could fill her with such love?

Who would have ever dreamed that the man, whose death she had wished for so fervently when first they met, would be the one to win her heart?

She loved him. Loved him with a fierce possessiveness that took her by complete surprise. Though he had made no promises to her, she would be wife to him in every way.

A smile touched her lips as she tossed aside the buffalo robe and added wood to the fire. She would make him a meal worthy of a great warrior. And when he returned, he would be proud to call her his woman.

Slipping the knife from her belt, she began to cut up strips of elk. Her mind worked feverishly. She would dig up the tubers she'd found near the stream. And pick the juniper berries and hackberries growing over the rise. And she would borrow chicory from Sings In The Forest to make coffee. And pemmican. Pale Wolf loved it as much as the children did.

Oh, it would be a grand feast. And when Pale Wolf had eaten his fill, he would take her to his bed again. And she would show him how much she loved him.

She was so absorbed in her plans, she did not see the figure that moved behind her as stealthily as a shadow. When a hand closed over her mouth, the scream that rose to her lips was stifled. Her hand holding the knife was twisted painfully behind her until the blade slipped from nerveless fingers and landed in the sand at her feet. She was lifted in strong arms and quickly bound with strips of rawhide, then tossed over the back of a pony.

The man strode back to the fire and carefully dropped several items, to make it appear they had fallen during the struggle.

As the horse and its riders disappeared over a rise, the pieces of meat that had been so lovingly prepared shriveled and burned until they were bits of ash.

Beside the fire, something glittered brightly in the sand.

Dan remained in the tepee all day, never leaving Little Bear's side. Several times he had to send her grief-stricken parents outside to answer the questions of those who gathered. The chief stood in their midst, listening with the others to the words Crooked Tree and Winter Bird spoke. Before he returned to his camp ne asked that he be told the minute there was any change in the girl's condition.

As the day wore on, the symptoms gradually subsided. Though her fever remained, Little Bear became more lucid, until, by early afternoon, Dan was certain she would recover.

Her parents rejoiced and hurried outside to tell the others. When Little Bear was strong enough to sit up, Two Moons was summoned. The chief entered and knelt beside the girl, who was so weak she could hardly squeeze his hand.

"Once again, Pale Wolf, you have shown us our need for you," Two Moons said solemnly.

"I did very little, except stay with her. I wish I could have done more."

The chief glanced around. "I thought Morning Light was here with you."

Dan seemed surprised by the chief's words. "You mean you haven't seen her all day?"

Two Moons shook his head. "I did not question her absence, because I thought she was here at your side."

Alarmed, Dan stood. "I left her at dawn in my camp. Someone should have seen her by now. Runs With The Wind...?"

The chief shook his head. "The boy has sadly missed her. But, like me, he thought she was with you."

Dan strode from the tepee. As he raced through the Comanche camp and along the shore of the stream, children splashed in the water, and women knelt near the shore, removing their dry clothes from low-hanging branches. Dan searched their faces for the one he sought. But she was not among them.

At Dan's camp, there was no trace of the woman he had left sleeping that morning.

He knelt beside the buffalo robe, lying as he had left it. It should have been rolled up and placed in a cool dry place. The ashes in the fire were cool to the touch. In the sand at his feet, Dan bent and retrieved a knife. He recognized it as the one Morning Light always wore at her waist. She would not have left it there willingly.

He stared around the camp and felt his heart stop. All the signs pointed to the fact that Morning Light had been forcibly taken from this place. But who had taken her? And why?

In the dirt beside the fire he saw something gleaming. Bending, he picked up the coin, then caught sight of the tobacco pouch.

He felt his mouth go dry. These were the unmistakable belongings of white men. He thought of the restless, vicious buffalo hunters. Once again, it seemed, he would have to face his old enemies.

When Two Moons reached Dan's camp, he found him saddling his horse.

"Where is my sister?"

"In the camp of the buffalo hunters." He handed the chief the things he'd found in the sand.

Two Moons examined them carefully, then glanced at Dan, whose eyes smoldered with hatred.

"I should have killed both of them when I had the chance," Dan muttered as he loaded his rifle, then placed it in the boot before carefully checking his pistol. "This time I'll see to it that there's no one left to inflict this kind of pain on helpless women again."

"You are letting anger cloud your mind, my friend," Two Moons said softly. "You are falling into someone's snare."

Dan's temper flared out of control. "Are you saying it wasn't the buffalo hunters who stole Morning Light?"

"I do not know." The chief's eyes narrowed. "But I do know that whoever did this thing had to plan it carefully. The same person who caused Little Bear's sickness, took Morning Light."

"How do you know that?"

The chief saw the blaze of anger in his friend's eyes. "Someone knew he would have to keep you away so that he could put distance between himself and this place before Morning Light was missed. I do not think the buffalo hunters could do such a thing. But someone from among our people could."

Despite his anger, Dan had to admit the chief's words made sense. "Then who...?"

Two Moons met Dan's steady look. "There is another missing from our camp. Ishatai."

For a moment Dan was thunderstruck. Then, pulling himself into the saddle, he muttered, "I won't return until I've found them."

"She is my sister. I know this land better than anyone. I will lead a party of braves to search for her."

"No." Dan's voice was low, angry. "She's my responsibility now."

The chief's gaze met and held Dan's. "So that is the way of it?"

"Yes."

The two men looked up as Yancy came toward them, leading his horse. "Heard what happened," he said, moving a wad of tobacco to the other side of his mouth. "You'll need a scout."

Dan noted the man's bedroll and the extra rifle in the boot of his saddle. "Thanks, Yancy," he said quietly. "I'm grateful for your help."

Two Moons caught the reins of Dan's horse. "Ishatai was one of our fiercest braves. I had once thought he would be the next leader of our People." Fingering the knife at his waist, he suddenly withdrew it and handed it to Dan. "Use this when you spill Ishatai's blood. Tell him that he is no longer a Comanche warrior."

Dan accepted the knife, then clasped the chief's outstretched hand. "I'll bring her back. Or die trying."

He wheeled his mount and urged him into a run. Yancy followed.

Two Moons watched until both horses and riders disappeared over a rise.

"I've found the sign," Yancy said as he pulled himself once more into the saddle.

They had stopped often while Yancy sorted out the various markings in the hard-packed earth.

"Tracks are deeper than normal. One horse carrying two people. He doesn't trust her on her own horse."

"He'd better not turn his back on her," Dan said with a trace of pride. "I saw what she did to those two buffalo hunters. She'll put up a fight if she gets the chance."

Yancy kept his thoughts to himself. But it occurred to him that the Indian knew better than the white men what he was up against. The scout hadn't told Dan that he suspected Morning Light might be drugged with the same poison that had been used on Little Bear. Worse, she could be wounded.

Rage drove Dan as his horse's hooves ate up the miles. A cold black rage that helped to numb the pain. He and Yancy rode in silence until darkness covered the trail. Then they took refuge in a stand of trees.

"No fire," Yancy said as they dismounted. "We don't want to let him know we're behind him."

He took a game bag from behind his saddle and handed Dan some cold meat. "Sings In The Forest packed as much food as I could carry." He grinned and slumped down with his back against a fallen log. "Said she didn't want me to be too skinny when I came back to her."

Dan accepted the meat and ate without tasting it. "What sort of man are we trailing, Yancy? Have you figured him out yet?"

Yancy shrugged. "Hell, Doc. I've seen a lot of men go loco out here. But Ishatai's easy to figure out. He wants to be chief of his own tribe."

"Chief? How can he think about leading when he would turn his back on his people, on all that he hold dear, just for the sake of his own selfish desires? Worse, how can he lead others if he really poisoned a child just to cause a distraction so he could steal a woman?"

Yancy took a long drink from his canteen. "Some men will do anything for power, Doc. Look at Lemuel Rollins. He'd sell his own mother if the price was high enough."

With a hard set to his jaw, Dan went about unsaddling his horse and preparing his bedroll. Drawing the buffalo robe around his shoulders, he thought about rolling a cigarette, then thought better of it and closed his eyes.

His mind filled with thoughts and images of Morning Light. The touch of her, the taste of her, the clean, fresh scent of her lulled him. After the long, hard miles on the trail, sleep came instantly.

Dan and Yancy were awake long before dawn. As soon as there was enough light to distinguish the tracks of Ishatai's mount, they were back on the trail.

As Yancy rode ahead, picking up the faint marks that only he could read, Dan was tormented by fears for Morning Light. He couldn't allow himself to think about what would happen to her at the hands of that madman. Instead he thought about the ways he would seek revenge.

These were strange, new thoughts to a man like Dan Conway. All his life he'd put himself, his needs aside in order to concentrate on his goal. It would have never occurred to him to simply take what he wanted, regardless of the consequences. Others, their needs, their safety, were uppermost in his mind. But now he must try to think like Ishatai.

Where would he take Morning Light? Ishatai had cut himself off from his own people. And his hatred of the white man was evident.

Dan's gaze scanned the distant buttes. Ishatai could hide himself away in one of the many caves that dotted the hillsides, keeping Morning Light his prisoner by sheer force. But Dan wondered if the young brave could hope to live in such isolation for very long. Ishatai needed the adulation of the people. He would soon tire of a life alone.

What then? Dan thought of the attack that had occurred soon after he'd arrived at the camp of the Comanche. Though he remembered little of it, he'd been told that the attackers were from a band of renegade Kiowa Apache. Dan's jaw clenched. That was much more suitable to a brave like Ishatai. The outlaw spirit of the renegades would appeal to Ishatai's fiery nature. The brave's blood was hot for battle. And a warrior like Ishatai would soon be acclaimed leader, a position he clearly coveted.

But where did Morning Light fit into Ishatai's plans? Dan found, when he thought about her, he couldn't think rationally. He knew only that he had to find her. And he would fight anyone who stood in his way.

Chapter Twenty

"You were right, Doc." Yancy's voice was a whisper as the two men knelt on a ridge overlooking a cluster of tepees. "They're Kiowa Apache. Not too many. Looks like most of 'em probably gave up and joined the others on the reservation."

Dan watched the activity below through narrowed eyes. "If the ones that stayed behind are as hotheaded as Ishatai, we may have a war on our hands."

Yancy touched the Spencer eight-shot at his waist. "This old army issue and I have been together for twenty-five years, Doc. We've fought a lot of battles, and haven't lost one yet."

"Stay here," Dan whispered as he began to crawl through the tall grass. "I'm going to try to move in for a closer look."

"The woman cannot be trusted," Ishatai said to the young brave who stood facing him in the tepee. "She must be bound at all times or she will escape."

"I give you my word, the woman will be here when you return."

"When I return," Ishatai said proudly, "there will be food enough to see us through the long, hard winter. I have seen the sign of the buffalo herd. It is big enough to feed all the People, including all the old ones who once walked the earth.'' His eyes glittered. ''And when your people see what Ishatai has given them, they will join my people to fight the white men who swarm like locusts over the land.''

''What about your chief, Two Moons?''

Ishatai gave a short laugh. ''He is an old man who runs from the white soldiers and watches as the buffalo hunters take what is ours. He does not deserve to be leader of the great Comanche nation.''

''I have heard that the People regard him as a great chief.''

Ishatai's frown deepened. ''When Two Moons has joined his ancestors, I will be an even greater leader of the People. Leave me now. I would be alone with the woman.''

The young brave gave a knowing smile as he walked from the tepee. The woman was very beautiful. If she did not belong to Ishatai, he would claim her for his own, for she was a great prize. But, like the others, he feared this Comanche warrior, who seemed possessed of evil. Ishatai had made it plain that he would kill anyone who crossed him. It was the way of the true warrior. He wore the scalps of his enemies with great pride.

Morning Light's wrists bled where the rawhide bound her. Unlike the rope of the white man, these did not unravel, though she continued her frantic efforts to free herself.

Every word spoken by Ishatai had been a knife to her heart. He had located the sacred buffalo but had not shared that secret with her hungry people. And it was he who had enlisted the aid of the Kiowa Apache.

That meant that he was the one who had ordered the attack upon her brother's tepee when Pale Wolf had first been brought to them. This crazed warrior would have permitted the killing of all of them, even the innocent Runs With The Wind. The thought sickened her. What other evil secrets did he harbor in his heart?

She knew, by the cruel smile on his face, that Ishatai would do anything, sacrifice anyone, to assume leadership of the People. Her heart began a painful thudding as he loomed over her.

When the Kiowa brave left them, Ishatai knelt beside her and ran a hand along her arm.

She flinched and tried to pull away. His fingers closed around her arm and drew her toward him, bruising her flesh.

"Now you are my woman," he rasped. "You will remain with the Kiowa until I return. And you will ride proudly at my side when we return victorious to your brother's camp."

"I will never be your woman."

Ishatai's lips drew back in a feral snarl. "You would give yourself to the white dog, who has not even proved himself in battle. And yet you would refuse one of your own?"

"You are no longer one of us. You have betrayed our people," she said with a hate-filled look.

"I would save our people from a leader who no longer leads. The People are hungry. I will feed them." His eyes glittered dangerously. "The sacred buffalo have revealed themselves to me. Does that not prove that I am worthy to be called chief?"

"You are not worthy to catch the droppings from my brother's horse."

At her words Ishatai's hand swung out in a wide arc and connected with her face.

"Now you will know my power," he cried, slipping the knife from his waist.

As he lifted it, she raised her bound hands in front of her to ward off his attack.

"I will make you forget Pale Wolf." He caught her roughly by the front of her dress and ran the blade of his knife through the fabric, slicing it open from neckline to hem. He dug his free hand into the tangles of her hair and dragged her face close to his.

"This is not the way of the Comanche," she spat, struggling with all her might to evade his cruel hands.

"It is my way. My mark upon you will forever remove all trace of Pale Wolf's touch."

"But you will never have what I gave him." Her words came out in a broken sob. "For he has my heart. Always."

He pushed her down roughly and fell on top of her. And as she struggled beneath his weight, Morning Light felt as if her heart would break.

Dan crawled to within a few feet of the camp and pressed himself into the tall grass. On the far side there was great activity as a dozen braves prepared for the hunt.

Hearing the hum of voices nearby, he ducked his head and flattened himself to the ground. As he peered between tufts of grass he saw a brave walk from a tepee and join the others near the string of ponies.

Seeing no one else nearby, Dan began to crawl toward the line of tepees. As he crawled past the first, he heard the sound of a loud slap and the muted sound of a woman's cry. God in heaven. Morning Light.

Blinded by rage he forgot to be cautious and stormed into the tepee.

He paused a moment as his eyes adjusted to the dim interior. Then he rushed forward as Ishatai got to his feet to face him. In the corner, Morning Light lay crumpled like a broken bird. For the space of a heart-beat Dan was distracted by the sight of her. Ishatai seized the moment to spring forward and plunge his knife. At the last second Dan turned, taking the blade in his shoulder instead of his heart.

Pain sliced through Dan, and for a breathless in-stant he dropped to one knee, shaking his head to clear his mind. It took both his hands to remove the knife embedded in his flesh. As it dropped to the dirt at his feet, blood spurted from the wound, spilling down his sleeve.

Ishatai leaped on him, driving him into the dirt, and began pummeling him with his fists.

The thought of this man harming Morning Light filled Dan with a rage unlike any he'd ever known, giving him renewed strength. The two men rolled and tumbled, fists flying.

Realizing he'd met his match, Ishatai suddenly switched tactics. He snatched up the fallen knife and caught Morning Light, dragging her in front of him like a shield.

Reflexively Dan pulled his pistol from the holster.

Holding the razor-sharp blade to Morning Light's throat, Ishatai hissed, "I will kill the woman unless you drop your weapon."

Morning Light wept when she saw the gun slip from Dan's fingers. "Now he will kill us both."

"You are wrong," Ishatai said, pushing her away. With the knife raised threateningly, he shot her a look of triumph as he strode toward the man who stood very still. "I will make you watch me as I kill Pale Wolf and take his scalp. And then you will be forced to live as my woman."

With a victorious smile, he turned toward Dan. He saw the glint of a blade a moment before it was plunged into his chest. His smile dissolved, to be replaced by a look of horror when he realized the wound was mortal.

Dropping to his knees, he stared down at the hilt of the knife, then, recognizing it, lifted a questioning gaze to Dan.

"The knife belongs to Two Moons. He sent a message. You are no longer a Comanche warrior."

Ishatai fell forward into the dirt. His blood mingled with the earth as he gave up his life.

Morning Light flew to Dan's arms and clung desperately to him, absorbing his quiet strength.

"I thought," she whispered between sobs, "you had been lost to me."

He tipped up her chin and pressed a kiss to her trembling lips. "You won't get rid of me so easily."

As they stepped to the entrance of the tepee, they froze. A dozen braves, talking and laughing among themselves, were walking toward them.

"You'll stay here where you're safe." Dan thrust her behind him, prepared to stand alone and do battle.

Just then a voice from the rear of the tepee said, "Better hurry, Doc. I think you've worn out your welcome."

Yancy had split the hide of the tepee from top to bottom. Dan and Morning Light followed Yancy to where their horses were tethered. Pulling himself into the saddle, Dan lifted Morning Light into his arms and they raced away in a cloud of dust.

When the Kiowa discovered Ishatai's body, they poured from the tepee and ran to their horses. But it cost them precious minutes before they were on the trail.

Yancy led the way along a dry creek bed and into high country, where they were soon hidden by thick woods. By evening, they were able to make their way back to the Comanche camp without incident.

"So it was Ishatai who betrayed us to the Kiowa." Two Moons sat across the fire from Dan and Morning Light.

"What is worse, he found a herd of sacred buffalo and did not share the news with the People." Morning Light cradled her young nephew in her lap and watched as his eyes grew heavy.

"He could not keep a thing like that secret for very long. Only today our braves found the herd." Two Moons sighed. "I am glad it was my blade that spilled Ishatai's blood. For to withhold food from hungry people is to condemn them to a cruel death."

Two Moons glanced at Dan, who had been very quiet since his return. "What troubles you, my friend?"

"If there are buffalo," Dan said, "there will be hunters close by. And from what Yancy has told me, the buffalo hunters are protected by the army. If you chase that herd, you might be riding into a trap."

"The sacred buffalo are our lifeblood," Two Moons said solemnly. "Without them, the Comanche cannot survive. Even if we must face the soldiers' guns again, we will follow the herd."

Having heard of the previous army attack upon their camp, and knowing the loved ones they had lost, Dan was aware of the courage it took to make such a statement.

The chief watched as Morning Light rolled his young son into his buffalo robe, then returned to take her place beside Dan. "This is the last night we will spend in this place. In the morning, we will follow the buffalo."

They all looked up at the sounds of happy shouting outside. With the discovery of the buffalo herd, there was rejoicing in the Comanche camp. Adding to the festivities was the return of the chief's sister and the men who had added much to the comfort of the People.

Sings In The Forest stood shyly beside Yancy, never leaving his side. Her great joy was evident by the smile that touched her eyes.

In honor of the spirit that had brought the sacred buffalo to them, the Comanche prepared for the ceremony of the buffalo. In the center of the camp a lodge was constructed that was to be filled with brush cut down by a virtuous woman. This was a great honor, and when the chief bestowed it upon Little Bear, who had recovered fully from the poison, she and her family were filled with pride.

Little Bear could not forget her frightening dream about the buffalo, but for the sake of the others, she pushed it to the back of her mind. There had been enough hardship. For now, she would rejoice and celebrate. She would not dwell on the death and destruction she had seen in her dream.

Little Bear took great pains cutting down the brush and filling the lodge. When it was ready, the young men dressed themselves in buffalo robes and danced around the tepees, circling their way through the entire camp. When they stood in clusters at the edge of the camp, Crooked Tree, an esteemed warrior, pulled himself onto the back of his pony and drove them, like a herd of buffalo, into camp.

Amid shouting and singing, Two Moons held a torch to the newly constructed lodge. With the brush afire, the flames climbed high into the sky. For as long as the fire burned, the ceremony continued long into the night, with the people eating, dancing and singing. And when at last the fire had burned to embers, the braves retired to their lodges to paint their bodies in preparation for the hunt. At dawn the camp would be dismantled and the People would move on together until they reached the herd.

Long before the ceremony ended, Dan and Morning Light slipped away from the others and returned to his camp beside the stream.

"Will you ride with us to the buffalo?" she asked.

He nodded. "I gave my word to Two Moons. Yancy and I have rifles. We ought to be able to provide a little food. It's the least we can do to repay the hospitality shown by your people."

She caught him by the hand. "Come. I will paint your body to ward off evil spirits."

She was surprised when he didn't move. "I have something much better in mind to ward off spirits," he said, dragging her firmly into his arms.

The protest she was about to utter died on her lips as he covered her mouth with his. Heat flared between them.

He lowered her to the buffalo robe, and they quickly lost themselves in each other.

Chapter Twenty-One

Dan stood beside Morning Light and stared at the breathtaking view of hundreds of buffalo grazing on the plains. For as far as he could see, the earth was alive with the great shaggy beasts.

Two Moons sat astride his pony, his eyes alight with pleasure. "Have you hunted buffalo before, Pale Wolf?"

Dan's smile was quick. "The first time, I was fourteen. I used my pa's old Sharps breechloader." His smile grew as the memories swept over him. "It was my first kill and I was allowed to help skin him. We had more meat than we could carry. And the hide was mine to keep. When I went East, I gave it to my little brother. He acted like I'd just given him the moon."

The chief's voice was low. "Then you understand how it is with us? Why we must follow the buffalo?"

Dan nodded. "I understand." His gaze scanned the immense land that stretched out below them. "But there are a lot of places for an army to hide down there. And I still think you're taking a chance."

"The Comanche are buffalo hunters," Two Moons said simply. "Without the sacred buffalo, we cannot survive."

Dan understood survival. Far too often, his own had been in question.

Two Moons solemnly raised his hand and an expectant hush fell over the People as the men mounted their ponies. The women and children found positions where they could observe until the killing was over and it was time to help skin the massive beasts.

As Two Moons lowered his hand, a wild roar went up from the People, and a sea of mounted men spilled over the ridge and converged on the herd.

The air was filled with the sounds of shouts and cries as arrows sang through the air and huge animals began running in crazed circles. The sound of thousands of hooves pounding the ground filled the air and echoed in Dan's chest like thunder, as the animals were driven into a frenzied stampede.

Dan lifted his rifle and waited until he had a buffalo in his sights. With his horse racing across the plains he fired and watched as the animal began to run, stumbled, then suddenly dropped.

A short distance away Yancy took his time, drawing a bead on a great shaggy head before squeezing the trigger. When the buffalo fell, Yancy shouted at Dan and waved his hat.

Dan gave a laugh of pure happiness. He'd learned to love that old scout. Besides, the fever of the hunt was contagious. It had completely taken him over, as it had taken over all of them.

Within minutes he turned his attention to another buffalo and once again brought him down with a single shot. Soon the ground was littered with the bodies of the animals who were lifeblood to the Comanche.

Dan's gaze was drawn to the place where Morning Light and Runs With The Wind were seated, watching the spectacle. It occurred to Dan that they were taking part in something so rare it might soon disappear forever from this land. Coming to a decision, Dan wheeled his mount and rode up beside them.

To the wide-eyed boy, he said, "Come on. I think the son of a great Comanche chief should join the hunt."

He lifted the boy and settled him in the saddle before him. With a flick of the reins, the horse moved out to join the others.

When he had separated another buffalo from the herd, Dan placed the rifle in the boy's hands and showed him how to line up the sight.

Runs With The Wind took his time, waiting until the animal lifted its head to the wind. At a word of encouragement from Dan, the boy pulled the trigger. The report sent him flying backward against Dan's chest.

The buffalo began to run, and a look of disappointment crossed the boy's face. The animal stumbled on a few more steps, then dropped to the ground.

Runs With The Wind lifted the rifle high in the air and gave a shriek of pure joy. Then he half turned and buried his face against Dan's chest, for he knew that a brave Comanche must not cry, even if they are tears of joy.

As the thunderous sounds filled the air, Quent Barker's fury exploded. Standing on a distant ridge, he watched helplessly as the herd he'd been stalking for miles suddenly turned into a black raging cloud moving with the speed of a train out of control.

Turning to Lemuel Rollins, he shouted, "So this is the protection my men and I get from you. While we watch, the Comanche are killing our buffalo."

"I can't help it if they got here first, can I?" Rollins was in no mood to exchange words with Barker. He'd been in the saddle for days, and his muscles, unaccustomed to such a battering, protested every mile. Further, there'd been no sign of the Comanche until today. And now, just when they'd converged on the buffalo hunters' path, the Comanche had appeared out of the blue.

"You promised me the freedom to hunt on Comanche territory. You said all the Indians would be safely back on the reservation."

"And I kept my promise. Until today," Rollins said shortly. "I can't be responsible for every damned renegade in the territory."

"That's my herd," Barker shouted. "My backers have put a lot of money into this hunt, and I've brought my men hundreds of miles. For what?" He leaned close until his face was inches from Lemuel Rollins. "Unless I get those buffalo, my man in Washington will see that you're finished. You won't even be able to get a job shoveling manure. Is that plain enough, Rollins?"

Lemuel Rollins felt the sweat trickle between his shoulder blades and pool at his waist. He saw the others watching him and his face reddened. For a moment he was a boy again, facing the wrath of his father. A white-hot fury bubbled just beneath the surface. He'd vowed that no man would ever again treat him like this. His hand hovered a fraction above the gun at his waist.

"I don't need you to tell me anything. I know how to do my job."

"Then do it." Barker saw the movement and watched the Indian agent's eyes. A man's eyes were always a dead giveaway. If he was going to draw his gun, Barker would know it. He had no fear of this man or any man. To be trail boss of this outfit, he had to be quicker and tougher than anyone else. He was almost hoping Rollins would draw. Then he could give vent to his fury.

For long moments the two men faced each other. Rollins suddenly blinked and turned away.

Disappointment rippled through the group of buffalo hunters who'd been watching. They were bored and restless. A gunfight would have added a little excitement to the day.

Thad watched as the Indian agent stalked down the hill and unleashed his fury on the unsuspecting young lieutenant. Whatever had happened between Rollins and the buffalo hunters camped on the rise above them, it hadn't been good. There was a look of murder in the agent's eyes.

Pretending to be busy cleaning his rifle, Thad ducked his head and listened intently.

"I've found our renegades," Rollins said importantly.

"I'll assemble the men."

"Not yet."

The Indian agent lowered his voice and Thad knocked over a pouch containing bullets. They spilled into the grass, rolling beneath the men's feet, and Thad got to his knees to collect them. As he did he moved closer, until he could hear the words being spoken.

"The Comanche are down on the plain below us, attacking a herd of buffalo."

"Then why don't you want us to attack?"

Rollins shot the young lieutenant a look of disgust and explained, as if to a child, "You ever witness a buffalo hunt, Lieutenant Hall?"

"No, sir."

"Then I suggest you walk to that ridge and see for yourself. The Comanche are loaded with weapons, and their blood is hot for the kill. On top of that, there's hundreds of animals stumbling around, some of them dying, others afraid for their lives. You turn an army loose in that, you'll have more dead by accident than if you lined them up in front of a firing squad."

"Do you intend to just let the Comanche leave with their spoils?"

Lemuel Rollins snarled, "Do I look like some kind of fool? We'll let the Comanche kill the buffalo. And when they're exhausted and sleeping, and their squaws are busy skinning the animals, we'll close in on 'em. Easy as shooting mustangs in a corral, Lieutenant."

As he strolled away, he called, "Have your men set up a tent so I can get out of this sun. And fetch me a bottle of whiskey. It's going to be a long day."

Thad watched as Lieutenant Hall hesitated a moment, deciding whether or not to argue. Then, with a slump of his shoulders, the young officer went off in search of his aide.

Alone, Thad climbed the ridge and was surprised at the number of hunters. He'd heard of the armies of men roaming the plains in search of the last great buffalo herds. But until now, he'd never actually seen them assembled together.

Several of the men sat in the shade of boulders or lay beneath the wagon, their hats over their faces to ward off the sunlight. A group of men were clustered to one side, playing poker. One man stood alone, staring at something below.

Thad joined him and stuck out his hand. "Name's Thad—Matthews," he said, taking his brother-in-law's name.

"Quent Barker." The man couldn't tear his gaze from the fascinating view below.

Thad found himself looking down upon a sight that he'd thought was gone forever from Texas.

For as far as the eye could see, the land was black with buffalo. To one side of the herd, a small band of Indians raced along on their ponies, bringing the great beasts to the ground.

A thrill of anticipation raced along Thad's spine. A part of him yearned to join them. He envied them their freedom. But then Rollins's words came back to him. If the Indian agent had his way, this would be the last freedom the Comanche ever tasted.

"You here to join the Comanche on the hunt?" Thad asked casually.

"Join 'em?" Barker gave a grunt of laughter. "Hell, we're going to help ourselves to their buffalo, just as soon as the army does their job."

Deep in thought, Thad rolled a cigarette and leaned his back against a warm rock as he watched the action far below. Things were clearer now. The government's Indian agent was bought and paid for by the buffalo hunters. He wasn't just searching for a band of renegade Comanches. He was helping the hunters get rid of the competition.

Did anyone in Washington know or care what was being done under the guise of justice?

There seemed to be no way to stop what had already been put into motion. Thad had agreed to ride with the army, but he hadn't agreed to attack helpless women, and maybe even children.

He drew smoke deep into his lungs and exhaled slowly. He didn't like any of this. He despised Rollins, and Barker didn't seem much better.

Maybe he'd pass on this whole thing and head back to Cole and Jessie's.

His eyes narrowed. He couldn't shake the feeling he'd been having ever since he'd set out with the army. Dan was somewhere nearby. The thought taunted him. Hell, he'd come this far. He'd stick around one more day.

In the excitement of the hunt, hours passed like minutes. The sun made its lazy arc across the sky and hovered over the tips of the buttes in the distance.

All around him, Dan noted, the ground was littered with the carcasses of buffalo. Already flies began to gather. The stench of death was everywhere.

The weary men slid from the backs of their ponies and lay motionless in the grass.

Pushed to exhaustion, the horses blew and snorted and slowed their movements, their sides heaving, their tongues lolling. Turned out to graze, they soon converged on a small stream that snaked its way across the land.

When the killing ceased, the women and children stepped from their places of concealment and began to skin the dead buffalo. Soon a great fire blazed, and blackened kettles bubbled with fresh meat. Dozens of buffalo hides were stretched out to dry. On the banks of the little stream the children played games, imitating the great hunters.

Morning Light noticed that Runs With The Wind remained beside the man who had become his hero, lying next to him with his hands beneath his head. Finally, drawn into play with the other children, he fashioned a stick into a rifle and raced along the banks of the stream, shooting imaginary prey.

A shiver passed through her and she felt a portent of doom. The boy was not imitating his father, who had used a bow and arrows, but Pale Wolf, who used the white man's weapon.

The buffalo she was skinning lay forgotten. She suddenly sat back on her heels as the realization dawned. No matter how they tried, they could not stop the inevitable. The ways of their ancestors were already slipping into the past. The way of the white man loomed on the horizon. She feared the choices she might have to make in the future.

She blinked back a tear, then resolutely picked up the knife and continued her work. She would dwell no more on unhappy thoughts. She would think only of her beloved Da-Nee, and the pleasure he would bring her when the work was done. For her, the decision was already made.

Chapter Twenty-Two

"**Y**ou see," Two Moons said as he shared the buffalo heart with his son and Dan. "The spirits are happy. Life is good. The sacred buffalo sustains the People once again."

Dan leaned back against his saddle, replete, content.

"This has become a special time in your life, my son." The chief bestowed his brightest smile upon Runs With The Wind. "The spirit has left your leg. And this day you learned what it is to be a hunter. So, I think, I will hear my name spoken upon your lips."

The boy smiled shyly and wiped his hands on his buckskins. Morning Light had made him a smaller version of the ones she had sewed for his father and Pale Wolf, and Runs With The Wind wore them proudly.

It was a source of pride that he was the son of a great chief, for he loved his father as he loved no other. But he was equally proud of his special relationship with the white medicine man. To Runs With The Wind, Pale Wolf was possessed of great spirits. It was the boy's fondest wish that one day he would be able to heal others like this man did.

Medicine men had always been held in high esteem by his people, and they had been without a healer for a long time. Perhaps he could learn the secrets of healing from Pale Wolf and one day use them to help his people.

"We must rest and gather our strength," Two Moons announced as he rolled himself into his buffalo robe. "The hunt will continue at first light until we have enough food to see us through the winter."

Dan was too comfortable to move. Slumping even lower against his saddle, he covered his face with his hat and promptly fell asleep.

Lying between them, Runs With The Wind curled up and hugged his happiness to his heart. Aside from the day he had learned to walk without the hated limp, this was the best day of his young life.

"Are your men in position, Lieutenant Hall?" Lemuel Rollins squinted into the brilliant blaze of the setting sun.

"Yes, sir."

"The day is spent and their cook fires are beginning to burn low." Rollins checked his rifle. "Comanche don't like to fight at night. Think evil spirits roam the land after dark."

He turned to Thad. "You riding with us?"

Thad glanced at the ridge where the buffalo hunters were mounted and ready. "You've already got three times as many men as the Indians down there. One more won't make any difference."

Rollins shrugged. "Suit yourself. Just thought you'd enjoy killing a few Comanche."

"I'm not here after Indians."

"That's right. You're here looking for a doctor on the run." The Indian agent's smile widened. "Did I forget to tell you? The buffalo hunters reported seeing the doctor in the Comanche camp."

Thad didn't move a muscle, but the tension in him was palpable. "Why didn't you tell me?"

"Must have slipped my mind. Besides, if you think you're collecting the reward, think again. Anyone captured on Indian land is my responsibility. I'm claiming the reward for myself."

Rollins turned to the young officer. "Come on, Lieutenant. Most of the braves will be asleep by now. Even the squaws tending the fires will be dozing. This should be over before it begins."

He pulled himself importantly into the saddle and rode out ahead of the young officer. Over his shoulder he called, "You're going in there a virgin, Lieutenant, but I'll see that you ride out a hero when you rid this great land of wicked heathens."

Thad watched as Lieutenant Hall hurriedly pulled himself into the saddle and urged his horse into a run to catch up with his men.

Shoving his rifle into the boot of his saddle, Thad checked his pistol and mounted. If Dan was down there, he intended, by God, to find him. Then he'd have to figure out how they could slip away during the confusion. The real problem was how to get there without being spotted by the army.

Morning Light stretched out beside the fire. For hours she had carved up buffalo meat until her arms ached from the effort. But though it was tiring work, it was also very satisfying to know that, for another winter, the People would be warm and well fed.

She closed her eyes, thinking about the lodges they would build in the high country. The winter would be a time of solitude and peace. The braves would hunt only occasionally. Like fat, lazy bears the People would hibernate within their lodges, playing with their children, storing their energy for the rigors of spring and summer.

A smile played on her lips. She wanted to give Da-Nee a child. She had seen the love in his eyes for Runs With The Wind. That had only made her love him more.

She heard the rumble beneath her ear and thought of the buffalo. Opening her eyes, she glanced toward the herd that grazed peacefully just a short distance away. Satisfied that they were not stampeding, she closed her eyes again, giving in to the weariness that enveloped her.

She heard the rumble of hoofbeats again, only closer now. For a moment she thought to ignore it. But then she was up, her eyes wide, her heart racing, as the realization dawned.

"Horses," she shouted. "Many horses, bearing down upon us."

All around her the Comanche were roused from sleep as braves reached for their weapons and women and children scrambled for cover. But before they could react, they were overrun by horsemen brandishing rifles.

For Morning Light, it was the replay of a nightmare that had never left her mind. She dragged Runs With The Wind to the ground and covered his tiny body with her own. She watched in horror as the people she loved fell to the ground just a short distance away, their blood spilling into the rich Texas soil.

Dan and Two Moons found themselves pinned down behind Dan's saddle, unable to even use their weapons lest they draw attention to the woman and child lying in the tall grass.

As the shadows lengthened, they saw a second wave of men coming over the rise, brandishing long-range buffalo rifles. The Comanche who took refuge behind the buffalo carcasses had no chance against such power. The bullets passed clean through the dead animals. One time the bullet struck with such force, two braves fell from a single bullet.

Morning Light looked up to see a man crawling through the tall grass directly behind them.

"Pale Wolf," she cried.

Dan whirled and took aim. He had a quick impression of a man with broad shoulders and a muscled arm holding a rifle loosely at his side.

A voice low and deep said, "Dan Conway?"

Dan's eyes narrowed and his fingers tightened on the trigger of his gun. He'd known this day of reckoning would come. He just hadn't expected it during the heat of battle.

"Yes." He lowered his rifle. He would never be able to bring himself to shoot the lawman who'd come to take him back to face justice. Even if it meant facing prison.

"God in heaven," the stranger breathed, "is it really you, Danny?"

Dan peered through the darkness at the tall figure. Moonlight glinted off hair the color of ripe wheat. Recognition jolted through him.

"Thad?" In swift strides he crossed the distance between them.

The others watched in amazement as the two men fell into each other's arms.

A bullet sang overhead and they dropped to the ground. It was several minutes before the men could speak. Then the words tumbled out in a torrent.

"When did you get so tall?"

"Where the hell have you been hiding? I've been to hell and back searching for you."

"How did you find me?"

"What're you doing fighting a Comanche battle?"

There were no answers, only staccato questions.

"How do I get you out of here right under the noses of the army?"

"I can't leave, Thad. This has become my fight as well."

"If you stay here you're as good as dead. My horse is over there in the tall grass. He can carry two."

"I'm not going without them." Dan turned to include Morning Light, Two Moons and his little son, and realized they were watching him with matching expressions of astonishment. He had some quick explaining to do. To all of them

"This is my little brother, Thad," he said, then grinned when he realized his "little" brother was taller than he. "This is Two Moons, Chief of the Comanche, and his son, Runs With The Wind. And this," he said, drawing the trembling woman close, "is Morning Light."

Thad saw the possessive way Dan touched her and suddenly understood.

"Come with me," he said. "All of you."

When they hesitated he waved his rifle. "I know what the army plans. They won't leave until every man, woman and child is dead. Now," he said, pointing toward a darkened outline a short distance away, "trust me."

They crawled out in single file, until they reached an old wooden shack. Overhead, lightning blazed across the sky, and seconds later thunder rumbled. Thad kicked in the door and the others followed him.

In the distance, the sound of gunfire continued, mingled with the fury of the storm.

"This is Adobe Walls," Thad said. "It's the center of operations for the buffalo hunters."

Dan frowned in the dim light. "Then we can't stay here."

"I know. But the army won't expect any Comanche to stay in a white man's building during a massacre. This place sits on the south fork of the Canadian River. We can sneak out the back way at daybreak and swim up the river to safety."

"You will go," Two Moons said to Dan. "And you will take my sister and my son with you."

Dan shook his head. "We'll all go or we'll all stay. But we're not leaving without you."

"No, Pale Wolf. I belong with my people. I cannot leave them. But you must go so that the last of my family can live."

"I will not go without you," Morning Light said, clutching her brother's arm. "You cannot send me away."

"You will go because I command it." Two Moons removed her hand, and held it for several moments, lacing his fingers through hers while he stared into her eyes. "Besides, Pale Wolf and I have talked. A brideprice was settled. And though there was no time for a ceremony, you are now his wife." He saw her eyes fill and touched a hand gently to her cheek. "I can read the love in your eyes. It is what you both want." In a soft voice he said, "You have been a good mother to Runs With The Wind. You will give Pale Wolf many fine sons. And you will tell them about the life that was once led by their people."

He heard the sob in her throat and looked away.

Across the room his son stared at him with unblinking eyes. In swift strides Two Moons strode to him and dropped to his knees. "You understand that, even though I want to remain with you, to see you grow to manhood and become the fine brave I know you will be, I cannot. I am Two Moons, chief of the Comanche. A good chief must put the needs of his people before his own."

The boy swallowed and his eyes brimmed. Ashamed, he turned his head away, but his father cupped his face between his big hands and studied him, memorizing the dark line of his eyebrows, the proud tilt of his chin.

"You will be son to Pale Wolf, but you will never forget your first father. You will grow up in two cultures, that of the People and that of the white man. You will know that there are good and evil in both, but you will honor only the good."

Two Moons's voice never wavered as he stared into the boy's eyes. "When you hear the whisper of the wind, my son, know that it is my spirit traveling always beside you. When you hear the song of a bird, know that it is my voice calling you. And when you feel the heat of a summer day, know that it is my smile of pride and pleasure at the man you have become."

The boy's lips trembled, and the tears he'd been holding back spilled over, coursing down his cheeks.

Lifting him in his arms, Two Moons crossed to Dan and handed the boy to him. "I entrust you with my greatest treasure, my friend. You will see that my son does not forget the ways of his father."

Dan nodded and opened his arms to the weeping boy.

Two Moons picked up his bow and quiver of arrows, and removed a knife he carried at his waist. Straightening his shoulders, he placed his hand on the door.

"Father." The little boy's voice, high and wavering, stopped him.

Runs With The Wind wriggled from Dan's arms and threw himself against his father's form.

The chief leaned down and clasped the boy to his heart, his face twisted with pain. Then he pressed his lips to the boy's head and whispered, "I love you, my son. More than my own life."

Releasing the boy, the chief turned and tore open the door. For a stunning moment he was clearly outlined by a blinding flash of lightning. As thunder echoed and ricocheted across the hills, he strode away without a backward glance.

While Morning Light and Runs With The Wind had finally fallen into an exhausted sleep, Dan and Thad spent the night in quiet conversation. There had been many years to catch up on. Their lives had taken so many strange twists. Yet here they had found each other, less than two days' ride from their sister's ranch.

The storm had blown over. The gunfire had stilled. Dawn light brushed the sky with gold. A slight breeze, blowing off the river, rippled the tall grass.

Four figures made their way from the cabin and picked their way carefully over rocks and ridges until they came to the battlefield.

The army was gone, their orgy of killing ended. The troops had returned to the high ridge to make camp. The herd of buffalo had departed, stampeded by the gunfire, with the buffalo hunters hot on their trail.

Only the dead remained. The bodies of the Comanche, many huddled behind carcasses of dead buffalo, littered the ground. The air was heavy with the stench of death.

In silence the four walked among the bodies, feeling their outrage and revulsion grow. Dan paused beside the body of Yancy, his arm slung protectively over Sings In The Forest, his rifle lying nearby.

Kneeling, Dan touched a hand to the strand of white hair that spilled over the old man's forehead.

"I'm sorry it couldn't be the Rio Grande, old friend," Dan murmured. "I know that's where you said you'd like to be buried. But at least you're with friends who love you."

Little Bear and her mother were still wrapped in each other's arms, crouched behind Crooked Tree, who had died protecting them.

Old Running Elk had fallen on top of his frail, elderly wife in an effort to save her. Her unseeing gaze was still fastened on his beloved face.

On the tallest ridge they found Two Moons, where he had climbed to show his people how to die with pride and dignity. His arm was raised defiantly, his fingers closed around the hilt of his knife.

Dan and Thad moved a few paces away, allowing Morning Light and Runs With The Wind a few minutes to grieve in private. Then, anxious to put this place of death and destruction far behind, Thad motioned for Dan to bring them.

"The sun will be up soon. We have to get across the river before the troops return."

Dan nodded and hurried away. Minutes later they made their way to the banks of the Canadian River and stared in dismay. The swollen waters had risen to a dangerous level. Crossing would be nearly impossible. But staying was out of the question. They were left with no choice.

For long minutes they studied the swirling rapids. It was Thad who finally came to a decision.

"With only one horse we have no choice. I'll just have to take you across one at a time."

"Think your horse is strong enough to fight these rapids?"

Thad ran a hand lovingly over the horse's mane. "I'd trust him with my life. Come on, little buddy," he said, scooping Runs With The Wind into his arms. "You and I are going to take the ride of a lifetime."

Pulling himself into the saddle, Thad snuggled the boy against his chest and eased his mount into the water. At first the horse stumbled, until he found his footing. Then he stepped into the swirling water and with strong, powerful strokes, began to swim the rapids until he reached the far shore.

Precious time was lost because the horse and its burden had been swept far downstream. But eventually Thad deposited the boy on the far banks and returned to claim Morning Light.

For a moment she clung to Dan's hand, unwilling to break contact.

Dan gave her a reassuring smile. "Thad's the best horseman I've ever known. Trust him."

Morning Light turned to Dan's brother, who swept her up into his powerful arms and nudged his horse toward the river. This time the horse was swept even farther downstream, for the rapids were growing more treacherous by the hour. Dan breathed a sigh of relief when he saw the horse clamber up the far banks. As soon as she was safely deposited on dry soil, Morning Light raced to where Runs With The Wind stood, and the two embraced before turning to wave at Dan.

Having safely delivered the two, Thad turned toward the far shore with a hopeful smile. His smile faded at the sight that greeted him.

A line of blue-clad soldiers streamed over the ridge and raced along the shore, their rifles aimed at Dan.

Lemuel Rollins broke stride and pulled ahead, shouting at Lieutenant Hall, "Get that squaw and the kid and take them to the reservation."

Turning to Dan, he shouted, "Doctor Dan Conway, you're under arrest for murder. You'll be held in the fort stockade until the territorial judge arrives to hold trial. And then," he added with a note of triumph, "you'll hang till the buzzards pick your bones clean."

Chapter Twenty-Three

Restlessly Dan paced the eight steps across his cell, then back. Each time he returned to the narrow bunk, he counted off another turn. Nine hundred ninety-nine. He paced again and returned. One thousand. Sinking down on the bunk, he listened while the key was turned in the lock.

As usual, Lemuel Rollins followed the soldier who carried in Dan's meal. It had become a ritual with Rollins. It was not enough that he had finally captured the man who had managed to make him look foolish by stealing medical supplies from under his nose. He wanted more than vengeance. He wanted to strip Dan Conway naked and find his weakness. Then he'd move in for the kill.

"My men haven't found your squaw yet, but they're still searching." Rollins stood back and watched as Dan's eyes narrowed, the only sign that his words had had the desired effect.

The soldier unlocked Dan's door and entered the cell.

The Indian agent's hand went to the gun at his hip and he found himself hoping that the prisoner would make a threatening move. He would have no qualms about shooting the soldier to get to Conway. In fact, it would be better that way. Then he could accuse Conway of being responsible for the soldier's death, as well, assuring the judge's verdict.

Not that Rollins questioned what the outcome of the trial would be. He had already taken for granted that this murdering, thieving doctor would hang.

"Brought your lunch," Rollins said, watching Dan's eyes.

Though he could read the cold fury in them, it was carefully controlled. Not once had he been able to get the prisoner to respond. But he would keep trying until he hit a nerve.

"It's buffalo chips and raw dog meat, just like you ate when you were with the filthy Comanche. Figured you'd feel more at home with Indian slop than white men's food."

Dan saw the soldier glance at him. For a moment he almost thought he saw regret in the young man's eyes. Then the soldier blinked and turned away.

"Last chance to get away, Indian lover," Rollins taunted "Territorial judge just arrived. Your trial is tomorrow."

Dan said nothing as the soldier closed the cell door and turned the key in the lock.

"I ordered my men to start building the gallows," Lemuel Rollins said with a laugh. "Figured we may as well not waste any time. Soon as the judge orders the hanging, we're going to have us a party. All your friends will be here to watch. Quent Barker and his men got back yesterday, after shipping a trainload of buffalo meat east. They said to thank you and the Comanche for doing most of the hard work for them."

He grinned slyly. "I've decided to haul in all the Indians on the reservation to witness what happens to those who think they can defy a legal representative of the United States government." His laughter became a shrill cackle. "I ought to thank you, Dr. High-And-Mighty Conway, for making me famous. Your trial is the talk of the country. By the time you swing, I'll be a real Texas hero for bringing you to justice."

Dan waited until Rollins and the soldier disappeared into the outer office. When he heard the key turning in the lock, he walked to the window and peered outside. On a platform in the center of the parade grounds, workmen could be seen erecting a gallows.

For long minutes he watched. Then he returned to his bunk and picked up the metal plate heaped with steaming food. For the first time since he'd been captured, he gave vent to his rage and frustration. Hurling the plate across the cell, he watched as the food splattered against the bars, staining the floor and walls.

Lying down on the bunk, he pressed an arm across his eyes to blot out the image of a coil of rope hanging from the gallows. An image that was burned into his mind.

"Dr. Conway?"

Dan turned from the window and faced the young lieutenant who was accompanied by several soldiers bearing rifles.

"Come with us, sir. The judge is ready."

A soldier turned the key in the lock and Dan stepped out of his cell. As he did, a soldier bent and began attaching chains to his ankles and wrists.

"I'm not going to attempt an escape, Lieutenant."

"Sorry, sir. Orders from Mr. Rollins."

Slowly, awkwardly, Dan moved along, surrounded by armed soldiers. He was still wearing the bloody buckskins he'd been wearing when he was captured. A thick, dark beard and shaggy hair added to his rough appearance. The judge, newly arrived from the very civilized Saint Louis, would no doubt be offended by the way Dan looked. He was aware that Rollins had planned it that way.

"Where is the trial to be held, Lieutenant?"

"The Indian agent's office, sir. It's the biggest room at the fort. But most of the people will have to stand outside and listen through the open door."

"My trial has drawn a big crowd, I gather?"

The young officer blushed and looked away, unable to meet his steady gaze. "Yes, sir. Mr. Rollins saw to that."

As they made their way from the jail to the Indian agent's office, Dan saw the throngs of Indians, brought from every corner of the reservation, seated in the dust. From atop the walls of the fort, dozens of soldiers walked patrol, their rifles at the ready.

When Dan entered the office, he heard the ripple of excitement that passed through the crowd. As he moved through the crush of people, he caught sight of Quent Barker and Billy, who laughed and pointed.

Lemuel Rollins was seated in the front row, a smug, contented smile curling his lips.

In the second row of chairs sat Jessie and Cole Matthews and their three small children. Dan's heart contracted painfully. He'd been separated from his family for so long now, his own niece and nephews were strangers to him.

His gaze swept the rest of the crowd. There was no trace of Thad or Morning Light or Runs With The Wind.

His gaze returned to Cole and at the questioning look in his brother-in-law's eyes, Cole silently formed the word, "Outside."

Dan glanced at his sister. Her eyes filled and she quickly wiped away the tears and gave him a tremulous smile.

As he sat at a makeshift table, Dan turned his attention to the white-haired man seated at the desk. The man glanced up from the paper he was reading to watch as Dan took his place.

Outside, pushing and shoving their way through the crowd, Morning Light and Runs With The Wind finally edged their way to a window, where they could watch all the proceedings without being seen by those inside. Despite Thad's assurances that they were safe with him, Morning Light was terrified of being caught by Lemuel Rollins. He would surely order them shot, or at the very least, have them sent to the reservation, where they would be separated from Da-Nee forever.

Suddenly all their attention focused on the drama inside the room.

Pounding his fist on the desk, the judge waited for silence, then said in a clear voice, "I am Judge Nathan Carpenter. The accused will stand and listen while my assistant reads the charges."

Hampered by the chains around his ankles, Dan lumbered to his feet and listened intently as the man read.

"It is hereby charged that one Daniel Conway, in a fit of rage, did strike on and about the head one Ethan Sturgis until dead. It is further attested by witnesses that Daniel Conway did then flee Massachusetts to avoid apprehension.''

The judge studied Dan's bowed head. "Do you understand the charges, Dr. Conway?"

Dan looked up. "I do."

"How do you plead?"

For long moments, while the crowd fidgeted, Dan said nothing. Then, in low tones, he began, "It is true that I killed Ethan Sturgis...."

The crowd erupted into a shouting, angry mob.

Outside, Morning Light brought a hand to her mouth to keep from crying out. It was the cruelest torture she had ever endured, to be this close to the man she loved and be unable to stand beside him and give him comfort.

Judge Carpenter pounded his fist on the desk and glared at the crowd until they fell silent.

"How do you plead, Dr. Conway?"

As Dan opened his mouth, a voice from the rear of the room said with authority, "He pleads not guilty."

The crowd surged to its feet to see the speaker. Angry voices were raised in protest.

Again the judge pounded on the desk and ordered his assistant to clear a path for the speaker.

"Step forward," the judge called, "and explain yourself."

Dan stared in disbelief at the sight of the tall, dark-haired man wearing a plain black suit, shiny at the knees, and carrying a wide-brimmed black hat. The man was bearded, with dark, solemn eyes punctuated by bushy dark brows.

"Who's the preacher?" Billy asked Quent Barker.

"Damned if I know. Maybe he's come to say a few words over the prisoner before he swings."

Both men snickered.

Hearing them through the open window, Morning Light felt her heart grow heavy.

"My name," the man began quietly, "is Jacob Miller. I attended school in the East with Dan Conway."

"What do you know about the murder?"

"I was with Dan the night it happened," Jacob Miller said in a loud, clear voice.

The crowd erupted into shouts and jeers. Angrily the judge brought his fist down on the desk and demanded silence.

"Did you see Dr. Conway kill Ethan Sturgis?"

Jacob Miller nodded. "But you must hear the entire story, if you are to judge the guilt or innocence of this man."

For a moment the judge seemed taken aback by Jacob Miller's statement. Then he leaned forward. "All right, Mr. Miller. Tell the whole story. But tell it quickly."

"Dan Conway became my friend in Boston," Jacob Miller said, meeting the judge's stern gaze. "My only friend. You see, I am a Quaker, and there are those who take offense at anyone who worships in a different way. Dan Conway, however, has a very special gift. He is able to accept people as they are. He offers his friendship freely to anyone." His voice lowered. "Ethan Sturgis, on the other hand, was a dockworker who enjoyed causing trouble for many people. He once singled me out for a violent beating because he knew that I, as a Quaker, would not defend myself."

Again the crowd erupted, as heads craned to see this strange creature who would not fight even to save his own life.

"And that is why Dr. Conway killed Ethan Sturgis?" the judge asked.

"No, sir."

The judge waited patiently. "Go on, Mr. Miller."

"On our last night together, before we were to leave for our various homes, we celebrated with dinner at a friend's. Dan Conway and I left together around midnight."

Jacob Miller's voice carried throughout the room. The crowd had gone strangely silent. Outside, the sound of hammers stopped as the workmen completed the gallows.

"A mist was rolling in as we made our way along the docks. We didn't see anyone until Ethan Sturgis lunged at us. He seemed..." Jacob Miller fumbled for the right word "...perhaps drunk, or deranged. He hurled insults at Dan and the doctor for whom Dan worked as an apprentice. In a rage, he accused Dan of luring the sick and infirmed from the docks to a clinic, where unnecessary surgeries were performed upon them. He also accused Dan of stealing bodies from the paupers' cemetery."

"For what purpose, Mr. Miller?" the judge interrupted.

"To study. Many medical students did such things."

"To your knowledge, did Dan Conway ever do such things?"

"No, sir. Dan Conway would have never stooped to such practices."

"You are certain, Mr. Miller?"

The man seemed to stand taller. In a voice that rang with authority he said, "Dan Conway is the most honorable man I have ever met."

"What happened after Ethan Sturgis made such accusations?" the judge asked quietly.

"When Dan denied any knowledge of such things, Sturgis drew a knife and attacked Dan. The battle was vicious, and during the course of it, Sturgis used his knife to lay Dan open."

Again the crowd reacted, and the judge was forced to pound his fist on the desk until the crowd fell silent.

"Go on, Mr. Miller."

Jacob Miller glanced at Dan, who stared straight ahead.

"Dan and Sturgis wrestled for the knife. When at last it was over, both men lay bloody and battered. I summoned help and had them taken to a home nearby, where a rough dockworker often cared for the sick. He called himself a doctor, though his methods were quite primitive. At any rate, under his care both men managed to survive."

"Are you saying that Ethan Sturgis did not die, Mr. Miller?"

"Not right away. In fact, for a little while, he seemed to be improving, though his wounds were critical."

"What happened then, Mr. Miller?"

"While he was recovering, Dan Conway became obsessed with the things Ethan Sturgis had said. During his years in Boston, he had been befriended by a very wealthy, successful doctor, to whom he eventually became an apprentice. Dan confided in me that he'd had questions of his own about the doctor's secrecy. But until Sturgis gave voice to them, Dan had put such questions from his mind. Now, he was determined to learn if the accusations were true.''

"Who was this doctor, Mr. Miller?"

"His name was Dr. Zachery Dowd."

Excitement rippled through the crowd. The doctor's fame had spread even to Texas.

Jessie and Cole exchanged worried looks when they saw the way Dan stiffened.

"What was the relationship between Dan Conway and Dr. Zachery Dowd?"

"Besides being apprentice to Dr. Dowd, Dan considered him a friend and teacher. Dan mixed all his drugs, compounded his salves and accompanied the doctor on his rounds. In exchange, Dan earned enough, along with two or three other jobs, to finance his schooling."

"Two or three other jobs?" The judge glanced at Dan before returning his attention to the witness. "How could the man find time to eat or sleep, let alone attend medical classes?"

Jacob Miller shrugged. "Life was difficult for all the students, sir. But life was especially hard for Dan Conway, because of his background. He had not had the advantage of an Eastern education, and so he had to work harder than most to complete his assignments."

"Was he a good student, Mr. Miller?"

"He was one of the finest in our class, sir."

"Can you tell me anything more about this, Mr. Miller? What did you learn about Dr. Dowd's practices that had been called into question?"

"While Ethan Sturgis was recovering from his wounds, Dan confided in me that he had been asking questions, and learned that much of what Sturgis had said was true. Dr. Dowd had a group of young students who actually recruited the sick from the docks and brought them to Dr. Dowd's clinic, where surgeries were performed on them. And though he could never prove it, Dan also suspected that Dr. Dowd gave permission to his students to dig up bodies from the graves in a paupers' cemetery, for there was never a shortage of cadavers in Dr. Dowd's classroom. But when Dan went to the docks to ask Ethan Sturgis to testify in court about what he knew, he learned that Sturgis had died."

There was no sound in the room. Jacob Miller's humble attitude and soft words had a calming effect on the unruly mob.

"What did Dan Conway do about his suspicions?"

"He reported them to Dr. Dowd and the staff at the medical school."

"What happened then, Mr. Miller?"

"Dr. Dowd flew into a rage. He vowed to ruin Dan Conway unless he recanted his suspicions. Further, he forbade his daughter, Sarah, to ever see Dan again."

"What was the relationship between Dan Conway and Sarah Dowd?" the judge asked.

"There had been talk of marriage. But, of course, that had been when Sarah had assumed that Dan would accept her father's offer to become his partner in Boston. When she and her father learned that Dan intended to return to Texas, the marriage plans were abruptly ended."

"How did Dr. Dowd intend to ruin Dan Conway?"

Jacob Miller shrugged. "I do not know, sir. I left for my home in Ohio to pursue my own career. That was the last time I saw Dan Conway until today. If I had known that Dan would be accused of murder, I would have come forward at once.''

''Mr. Miller, did you know that the one who accused Dan Conway of murdering Ethan Sturgis was Dr. Zachery Dowd?''

A stunned silence fell over the crowd in the makeshift courtroom.

Jacob Miller shook his head. ''No, sir, I did not.''

The judge turned to Dan. ''Would you be so good as to tell me the rest of the story, Dr. Conway?''

Dan nodded. Somewhere inside, his heart was beating and his blood was pulsing. But he felt only a strange numbness.

''When I learned that Sturgis had died, and that the doctor who worked on the docks had to explain his death to the authorities, I thought it would be a simple matter to clear up. After all, I had only fought the man in self-defense. By the time the authorities had completed their work, I was made to look like a cold-blooded murderer.''

Jacob Miller interjected, ''There were those in Boston who would probably believe the worst about Dan Conway, because he angered many good people by going out among the rugged dockworkers and bringing medicine to them. That made him a misfit in the eyes of many.''

The judge watched Dan carefully. ''Are you saying that an important man like Dr. Zachery Dowd, known far beyond Boston, insinuated himself into this case for revenge?''

Dan's eyes were bleak. ''Who's to say how love can so quickly turn to hate? Or how trusted friends become enemies? I only know that Dr. Dowd swore that he'd see that I never practiced medicine again.''

"If he knew the charges against you to be false, why did he not simply permit you to return to Texas, where he would never have to see you again?"

Dan clamped his mouth shut on the words that sprang to mind. Instead he said nothing. But a little muscle worked at the corner of his jaw.

In the silence that followed, a soft woman's voice said, "My father feared that if he allowed Dan Conway to return to Texas, he would lose his only daughter. And that would have been worse than death to Zachery Dowd.''

The crowd was electrified as a beautiful young woman stood and pushed her way through the crowd until she was standing before the judge.

She wore a blue organdy gown that accentuated her tiny waist and rounded hips and fell in soft folds to the tips of dainty leather boots. Soft blond hair fell in perfect ringlets down her back. A pretty white bonnet with matching blue ribbons was nestled in her hair.

Watching through the window, Morning Light felt her heart plummet.

The crowd strained to hear every word this beautiful creature spoke.

"I am Sarah Dowd," she said in a nervous, breathy voice. "When I heard of the trial, I came from Boston to testify on behalf of Dan Conway. For, you see, Your Honor, my father is no longer alive to speak the truth."

"What is the truth, Miss Dowd?"

She glanced at Dan, then forced herself to look away. "Everything Dan Conway has told you is the truth." A tear trickled from the corner of her eye and rolled down her cheek. "My father believed that he had lost everything of value, his practice, his reputation, and his daughter. But he had not lost me. Seeing how he was suffering, I knew I could never leave him.

"Later, when my father realized what he had done, and the price he had forced me to pay, he could not bear the guilt and humiliation. He killed himself with a lethal injection of poison. And I was so distraught at his death, I could not think about anything or anyone else. I allowed myself to become buried in grief. It is only now, when I realized that another innocent life would be lost, that I was able to face up to what had been done to this good man."

The judge studied the bearded man in chains and dirty buckskins and wondered why he found himself believing all this. There was a quiet strength and dignity about the prisoner that demanded respect.

"Would Dr. Dowd have lost his only daughter, Dr. Conway?"

Dan shook his head. "Sarah and I had already agreed that she would remain with her father. Her love for him was far greater than her—feelings for me. Whatever had been between us was destroyed when I voiced my suspicions about his medical ethics."

"Is Mr. Miller's story true? Did you kill Ethan Sturgis in defense of a life?"

Dan nodded. "I did."

"Do you think Dr. Zachery Dowd intended to see you hang for a crime that was really self-defense?"

Dan shook his head. "No. I believe the doctor was desperate to spare his reputation, not only for his own sake but for the sake of his daughter, who was the dearest thing in his life. I would like to believe that Dr. Dowd, had he lived, would not have allowed this thing to go this far. I think, in his youth, he was a man of high moral principle, who, somewhere along the way, went astray. He was once my friend. I would like to remember the good things about him.''

In a quiet voice the judge said, "You are a most forgiving man, Dr. Conway." He turned to Jacob Miller. "Why did you not come forward before this?"

"I regret that I knew nothing of it. I thought the matter had been settled after I left Boston."

"Then how did you happen to be here, Mr. Miller, if you did not know about your friend's trouble?"

Jacob Miller smiled. "Dr. Conway's family is most persistent. His brother, Thad, found me on a train headed here and forced the conductor to stop the train so that I could ride ahead with him."

Dan glanced up, a gleam of hope in his eyes. If Thad had found Jacob Miller, he had surely escaped the soldiers that had been hunting him.

"Why were you on a train headed here, Mr. Miller?" the judge asked.

"I am in receipt of this order from the president of the United States," he said, offering a document to the judge. "Commanding me to report to this fort and take charge of the badly mismanaged Indian affairs. It seems that President Grant was unaware of the shoddy treatment of the Indians here at the reservation until it was brought to his attention in a letter from someone who had firsthand knowledge. That same person recommended me for the job because he thought I, as one who had often been mistreated because of my beliefs, would see that humane treatment was offered to all of God's children."

The judge read the document, then glanced around the room until his gaze settled on Lemuel Rollins, seated importantly in the first row.

"Lieutenant Hall," the judge said, "you will take Mr. Rollins into custody until a trial can be convened. Mr. Rollins, the government is charging you with withholding food and medicine from the very people you were ordered to help. Further, you are charged with taking money from the buffalo hunters in exchange for allowing them to violate treaties between the United States government and the Indian nations."

The crowd became deathly quiet as Lemuel Rollins was escorted from the room by armed soldiers.

Quent Barker began to shuffle out of the room and signaled for his men to follow. But before they could leave, a contingent of soldiers surrounded them. They, too, were led away to the stockade.

The judge peered over the rim of the document and fixed Dan with a steady look. "President Grant praises you, Dr. Conway, for risking your life to uncover the evidence documented in this letter. Further, he requests that you offer your valuable assistance as a doctor to Mr. Miller in his new post as chief of Indian affairs."

"I'd be honored to help Jacob Miller."

Judge Carpenter gazed out at the sea of faces and said, "I have often wondered if I would recognize a true hero if I met him. This day I have met him. Dr. Conway, I salute you."

It took a full minute before the impact of his words registered.

"You mean I'm a free man?"

"You are indeed, Dr. Conway. This trial is adjourned."

For long minutes Dan stared at the young woman who had cleared his name.

Touching a hand to her shoulder, he said gruffly, "My heartfelt thanks, Sarah. I know the pain and anxiety this journey must have cost you. And please accept my condolences on the death of your father."

"Thank you." She blinked back the tears that threatened. "Now that I've seen this place you spoke of so lovingly, I can understand your eagerness to return to it." She touched a hand to his cheek in an achingly sweet gesture.

From her place by the window, Morning Light struggled to swallow the lump in her throat that threatened to choke her. Catching the little boy's hand, she led him quickly away.

Sarah Dowd trailed a finger through the dark beard that covered Dan's cheeks. "I would have never fit into this world, Dan, any more than you would have fit into mine."

"I know, Sarah." He bent and brushed a kiss across her cheek, and watched as she turned away and placed her hand on the arm of a fashionably dressed man.

Accepting Jacob Miller's handshake, Dan found himself surrounded by soldiers who clapped him on the back and offered their handshakes.

The next familiar face Dan spotted was Cole Matthews. Dan's brother-in-law stood head and shoulders above the crowd. On Cole's shoulders was a dark-haired little girl whose hands were wound around his neck.

Beside Cole stood a slight young woman with wheat-colored hair and eyes as blue as a Texas sky. In her arms was a chubby infant. A boy of about six, with pale hair, stood between his parents.

At the sight of his sister, Dan's stern gaze melted and he crossed the distance between them to take her into his arms.

For long minutes she hugged him to her, fighting the desire to weep. When the tears started, she buried her face against his chest.

"At last you're free to come home and be with your family. That's why you never returned to us, isn't it, Dan? You knew the authorities would find you at our ranch."

"Yes. Tears, Jessie?" He grinned, tugging on a lock of her hair. "I thought you were too tough for that."

"I used to be," she said with a shaky laugh, wiping the tears with the back of her hand. "Since I've had babies, I seem to cry at the darnedest things." Sniffing, Jessie shoved her eldest forward. "Dan, meet your nephew, Jack," she said. "We named him for Pa."

Dan accepted the boy's hand, then drew him close and hugged him.

"The girl is Lisbeth," she said, "and the baby is Frank."

Dan saw his sister's smile in the curve of tiny lips, and Cole's dark stare in the eyes of the little girl on his shoulders.

Cole stuck out his hand and Dan grasped it. "Those were mighty fine words the judge said in here. We're proud of you, Dan."

"Thanks, Cole."

Turning away, Dan pushed his way through the crowd until his brother, Thad, grabbed him in a fierce hug.

"I knew you'd win, Danny. When we were kids you always won."

The two brothers embraced again.

"Morning Light?" Dan said as soon as he could catch a breath. "Are she and the boy all right?"

"I figured you'd be worried about them," Thad whispered. "They're fine. But they wouldn't come inside. They insisted on staying out there, where Rollins wouldn't see them. They figured they could mingle with the other Indians and not be noticed."

Seeing the fevered look in Dan's eyes as he struggled to push through the crowd, Thad moved ahead, clearing a path, with the rest of his family struggling to keep up.

When they reached the front porch, Dan turned impatiently to his brother. "I thought you said Morning Light was here."

"I left her and the boy right over there by that window."

Dan turned to stare at the sea of faces. The Indians brought in from the reservation numbered in the hundreds. Already some of them were drifting through the gates of the fort on their return trek.

"I'm not leaving here until I find them."

"Maybe they don't want to be found," Cole said gently. "They've been through a lot. They're frightened, and exhausted, and for the past ten days they've been trying to adjust to a strange new way of life at the ranch."

"I have to find them."

"We'll help," Jessie said quickly.

Dan turned to his sister and placed a hand on her shoulder. "Go home, Jessie."

"What about you?"

He smiled gently. "I've been taking care of myself for a lot of years now. I'll manage just fine. And when I find them, we'll join you."

"You're taking a lot for granted." She touched a hand to his shaggy beard and studied his eyes, so grave, so weary. "Cole could be right. She may not want to be found."

"You don't understand, Jess. If I came back without her, I wouldn't be home."

Jessie felt the tears start again and turned away.

"I'll stay with you," Thad said.

"No, Thad. You've done enough. More than enough. What you did for me went way beyond duty or even love, and I'm grateful. But I have to do this one," Dan said, turning away, "alone."

Chapter Twenty-Four

A dust-covered horse and rider topped a ridge and paused. Sliding from the saddle, Dan stared down at the darkened outlines of the tepees below. An occasional fire still blazed, although most had burned down to glowing ashes.

For four days he had ridden the land of the reservation, searching for the woman and child who'd managed to elude him. Many of the Indians he encountered along the way had urged him to give up the search. It was, they said, like sifting through the sands of the desert for a single gold nugget.

Morning Light and the boy were more precious to him than gold. They had become his reason for living. All his hopes, all his dreams, were hollow and empty without Morning Light and Runs With The Wind to share them.

He would strip apart every camp, every tepee, if he had to. He would never stop searching for them.

Many Indians had seen a lone woman and child, and Dan had followed every lead. But none had proved to be Morning Light and Runs With The Wind.

This was his strongest lead yet. Dan had been told by several Kiowa Apache, remnants of a once-large tribe, that a woman and child had followed a ragged band of Comanche from the fort. Though these Comanche were not meat eaters, their customs would be similar. He was convinced that Morning Light would try to stay with her own people.

Dan studied the barren land below. Jacob Miller's new job would be the most challenging of his life. These proud, rugged people, who had roamed the plains for hundreds of years, would not survive another generation without thoughtful planning and vigorous work.

Jacob was up to the task, Dan thought. Of all the men he'd met, Jacob Miller was the most conscientious and the most diligent. He would help these people or die trying.

As for Dan, he had already vowed that he would do all in his power to bring his own brand of healing to the People. It was not just proper medicine they needed, to heal their bodies, but a healing of the spirit, as well. Somehow all people must learn to live in harmony. That would be his true goal. That would be his gift of healing.

In every Indian camp he had seen the signs of sickness and neglect. But despite such signs, he felt, for the first time, stirrings of hope for the Indian nations. There was a warehouse filled with clothing and medicine. With Rollins gone, these things would go to the people intended. Though it would never make up for the land taken from them and the way of life being denied them, he vowed that their lot would be improved.

He knew now why he'd returned to Texas. His medical practice would be open to everyone. And he would carry his knowledge to the most remote regions to see that no one was denied his skills.

His frown deepened. None of it would mean anything unless he could share it with Morning Light. Where was she? Why had she fled his family?

She had cared enough about him to wait until the judge rendered a verdict. That proved that he still meant something to her. But the fact that she had deliberately disappeared had to mean that she didn't want to be found.

His hands balled into fists at his side. Two weeks. They had been apart for two long weeks, during which he'd endured imprisonment and trial. But none of it had been as difficult as these past four days. A sense of urgency drove him.

While he had thought of nothing but her, she would have had plenty of time to think about what she wanted, and to compare his way of life with the one she had always known.

He thought about Sarah. She had been convinced that she loved him. But she had been unable to leave the comfort of her father's home for a life in the Texas wilderness. His feelings for Sarah had never been as strong as the love he felt for Morning Light. But what of her feelings for him? Was it the same for Morning Light? Had she decided that she could not share his life?

In agitation he pulled himself into the saddle. He couldn't wait around any longer, tormenting himself with these doubts. He had to find her. And regardless of her decision, he had to know.

His body protested the movement. He'd been riding for four days now without rest. But even when he'd tried to force himself to sleep, it wouldn't come. His mind refused to let go, even for a few hours.

With this camp so close, he couldn't risk even a few hours. He had to know if the ones he loved were nearby.

He urged his horse into a trot.

Morning Light lay in the tepee beside the sleeping boy. As his chest rose and fell in a slow, steady rhythm, she fought down the tears that threatened to spill from her eyes.

Would the nighttime always be like this? Would the demons always come to haunt her? Would the image of Dan's beloved face always appear in her mind's eye to bring the pain around her heart?

During the day, it was possible to stay so busy that there was no time to think. She worked until she was too exhausted to do any more. Then she would fall upon her buffalo robe and be asleep instantly. But within an hour or two she was awake again, with thoughts and images swirling through her mind to torment her.

Always the thoughts were about Da-Nee. The pride she had felt when he had faced the angry crowd in the fort. And the love she felt whenever she thought about the special times they had shared. And then would come the shaft of pain when she realized that it was the beautiful white woman who had saved him from the gallows.

Morning Light had seen the look on the woman's face when she had touched a hand to his handsome face. The love Sarah Dowd felt was there in her eyes.

Morning Light had not seen Da-Nee's face. By the time she had turned to him, her eyes had been too filled with tears. But she knew. A woman always knew these things. How could he not love the woman who had come by iron horse from a thousand miles away to save him? Sarah Dowd had given proof of her love for him. An honorable man like Da-Nee would not soon forget such a thing.

Morning Light hated the tears that filled her eyes. They were a sign of weakness. She wiped furiously at the tears with the back of her hand, but she couldn't stop them. They fell faster, streaming down her cheeks, spilling onto the buffalo robe.

At the muted sound of a horse approaching, she sat up. Her hand went to the knife at her waist. Moving to the flap of her tepee, she peered into the darkness. At first she saw only the darkened outline of the other tepees nearby. Then a horse and rider came into view.

Her heart stopped. For a moment she thought the man looked like Da-Nee. But that was impossible. He was many days' ride from this place.

Stepping from her tepee, she remained in the shadows and watched as the horse and rider drew nearer. She clutched her knife firmly in her hand.

Dan had expected a sentry or two to challenge his arrival. Then he realized that many of the Indians no longer needed to guard their camps. For the first time, they knew a measure of peace and safety. The wars between the various Indian tribes had ended. And with Rollins gone and Lieutenant Hall in charge, the Indians knew that they were safe from cruel attacks by the army.

As he urged his mount toward the center of the camp, his gaze was drawn to a flicker of movement beside a tepee. His eyes narrowed. This tepee was isolated from the others by several hundred yards.

As he watched, he saw a slender figure suddenly pull back, blending into the darkness. He felt a thrill of recognition and brought his horse around.

For a moment he could see nothing but inky blackness. Then gradually, as he strained through the darkness, he could make out the shape of a woman as she shrank back against the hide. As he watched he felt the first real thread of fear begin to curl along his spine.

He hadn't really thought this through. He had merely blundered forward, determined to find her. He had never accepted the thought that she might not want to be found.

What if Morning Light had already decided she couldn't live with him? What if her first taste of life with his people had destroyed their fragile bond?

He knew only one thing. If Morning Light rejected him, all his victories were hollow.

Despite the outcome, he had to know.

He swallowed. His voice was gruff. "Morning Light."

For a moment the shadow shrank back farther. Then, slowly, hesitantly, she stepped forward, clinging to the knife.

"Why have you been hiding from me?"

"I do not hide." The words nearly stuck in her throat. But now that she had spoken, she felt her fears subside. She was sister to the great chief, Two Moons, and *pia* to Runs With The Wind. She would not shame them by showing any fear.

He swore savagely. Now that he'd finally found her, his wild rush of relief had given way to anger. An anger that caught him by complete surprise.

"You ran away." He knew his tone was accusing, but he couldn't seem to control himself.

She drew herself up to her full height. "You do not own me. I am free to go where I choose." She swept a hand to indicate the camp. "These are my people. They have given me a home with them."

"You wish to join your people, to live among them always?"

"Yes."

He felt his heart contract and pushed aside the pain. He had known that he was risking much by allowing himself to love her. He'd gambled and lost before. But this time, the pain was worse than anything he'd ever known.

With difficulty he lowered his voice. "If that's what you really want, I won't interfere."

To Morning Light he looked so fierce, seated on his horse, glowering at her with that frown that had become so dear to her. It was the image she would always carry in her heart.

"I never wanted to force you to live among my people," he said. "I just hoped that once you got to know Jessie and Cole and their family, that you and Runs With The Wind would be able to accept them and love them the way I do."

"I do love them," Morning Light said quickly. "Your sister, Jessie, was so kind to us. And so patient. A life such as she leads would be..." Morning light struggled to put into words what she was feeling "... beyond anything I have ever dreamed."

"You didn't hate the ranch?"

"Hate it?" Morning Light gave a short laugh. "It was so beautiful. And the children are so sweet. Your brother, Thad, gave Runs With The Wind a pony of his own, and he and your sister's children rode and played for hours. I have never seen him so happy."

While she spoke, he slid from the saddle and took several steps toward her, studying the light that came into her eyes as she described her love of the ranch.

"If you were happy, why did you leave?"

Her smile faded. "I did it for you, Da-Nee. You need no reminders of your life with the Comanche now that you have returned to your people."

"I want you and Runs With The Wind to be with me." He clenched his hand at his side and watched as she began to shake her head.

"It cannot be. Even if this is your custom, my heart could not bear it."

"I don't understand you, Morning Light." His tone was low and angry again.

He wanted to force her to get on his horse and ride with him. He wanted to shake her. He wanted to crush her in his arms and make her love him. He wanted to take her here, now, and prove how much he loved her.

Instead he forced himself to say patiently, "Our customs are no different from yours. I want you to live as my wife. I want you and the boy with me always."

"I cannot share you with Sarah Dowd," she said fiercely, feeling a terrible shame wash over her at the vehemence of her words.

"Share me . . . ?"

"Sarah Dowd is a fine woman. It took much love for her to come so far to clear your name. You will find much happiness with her. And now that your high chief, who sat in judgment of you, said that you were a great hero, you will be highly regarded among your people. There will be celebrations to honor you, and you will be given your choice of fine maidens to please you."

Dan went very still. "So that's what this is all about." For long minutes he studied Morning Light, seeing for the first time the trace of tears on her lashes. His voice was no longer edged with anger. "You think that the judge's words have somehow changed me."

"You are . . ."

"The same man who was brought unconscious to your tepee and nursed back to health. The same man who rode beside your brother, and lay with you when the shadows covered the land."

At his last words he saw the color that flooded her cheeks and felt the heat begin to return to his heart. He hadn't lost her. Yet.

"I'm the same man who paid a bride-price for you, and promised to take care of you and Runs With The Wind for the rest of your lives."

"You will not be bound by such a promise," she said softly.

"I want to be bound by it." His tone was gentle, teasing. "Do you wish to be free of me?"

"Never." Her eyes flashed, her nostrils flared. "I do not lightly give my heart, Da-Nee. But I will not be a burden to you."

"Burden?" He caught her by the arm and dragged her close. "You are the sweetest—burden I've ever been given. I want you with me always. You and Runs With The Wind. We are a family now."

At the intensity of his words, her voice caught in her throat. "You are not merely fulfilling a promise to my brother?"

"I love you, Morning Light. More than anything. More than my own life."

"And Sarah Dowd?"

"You should not have run away so quickly. You would have met Sarah's husband. And you would have known that I love only one woman. I love you."

"Oh, Da-Nee." She threw her arms around his neck and hugged him fiercely. "You have stolen all of my heart. And I cannot imagine life without you. But I was willing to try, rather than bring shame to you."

"You'll always be my source of greatest pride," he murmured against her lips.

He kissed her, long and deep, and felt the familiar rush of heat.

"We will wake Runs With The Wind," she said against his lips. "He will be so happy. Though he has tried to hide his sorrow, I know that he has been grieving for you."

"Not just yet," he said, touching a finger to her lips to still her words. "The morning is soon enough to give him the news."

"But we are wasting precious time..."

"It won't be wasted," he whispered against her cheek.

"But..."

"God in heaven, have mercy." He chuckled, running kisses across her cheek to her ear. "It's been so long since we've been together, and I've been storing up a whole lot of love."

"Oh, Da-Nee." She settled herself against his chest and felt the strength of his arms around her.

This was a man she had vowed to hate. But the heart could not be denied. She would share his love, his culture, as he would share hers.

As he lowered her to the cool grass and covered her lips with his, Dan felt the familiar rush of heat. This was his destiny. This woman, this land, this strange mix of people and cultures.

He'd meant only to return to his home and use his knowledge to help the people. He'd never dreamed he'd come this far. He'd found a love greater than anything he ever could have imagined. And in her arms he found the greatest challenge, and the richest reward, of all.

Epilogue

The ranch was typical of those springing up around Texas. It consisted of two low buildings, with a covered breezeway between. A corral of mustangs stood close by. Cattle were lowing in a green field beyond.

As the two horsemen approached, a big shaggy dog sprang up from his shady spot and raced toward them, tail beating the air.

"Hello, old boy. Where's your mistress?"

Dan slid from the saddle and untied his black bag.

Runs With The Wind led both horses toward the stalls and saw to their food and water, while Dan strode toward the house. Finding it empty, he hurried out back, where he knew he would find his wife.

Morning Light had one of the mustangs on a lead rope. Murmuring softly in Comanche and English, she inched her way closer until he stopped fighting her and allowed her to run her hand along his velvet muzzle.

Dan watched, fascinated, as she gently coaxed the horse to allow her to drop a saddle over his back.

"You're not going to ride him, are you?"

She looked up, then shot him a smile of pure pleasure and dropped the rope.

Crossing to him, she touched a hand to her swollen stomach. "Not until after the child is born. Thad said he and Cole will buy all the ponies I can provide."

Dan wrapped his arms around her and drew her close for a long, satisfying kiss. "I never realized I was going to marry a woman who could earn more money than a doctor."

"That is because your brother and Cole pay in cash, while most of your patients pay in chickens and eggs and skinned rabbits."

"Every little bit helps."

"Yes. I have cooked two of those rabbits for your dinner."

"Then, come on, woman, and feed your hungry man."

"In a moment. First I must remove the saddle and lead rope from my horse."

"Leave it for the hired hands."

"I am not accustomed to having others do my work."

"That's why I pay them."

"Yes. With chickens and eggs and skinned rabbits."

Runs With The Wind stood in the doorway and watched as they approached, arm in arm. Soon their family would welcome a baby. The thought made him smile.

He thought often of his father, and at times, when he felt the sun warm upon his face, and the whisper of the wind by his side, he would talk to Two Moons and tell him of his happiness. Dan and Morning Light did all they could to keep the memory of Two Moons alive, and for that, the boy was grateful. Runs With

The Wind considered Dan and Morning Light his family now.

Dan was teaching him about herbs and medicines, and the art of healing. And Morning Light was sharing her skill with horses, which had always been a source of great pride to the People.

"Come on, son," Dan said, dropping an arm over his shoulders. "We're going to serve up the supper tonight while this plump hen catches her breath."

"I am not plump."

"You are." He lifted her into his arms and deposited her in a cushioned rocker by the fire. Kneeling, he placed his hands over the soft mound of her stomach and kissed her with a kind of reverence. "And to me, you are the most beautiful creature on earth."

Morning Light sat back and watched as Dan and Runs With The Wind carried the food to the table and prepared her plate. The baby within her moved, and she felt a rush of such emotion, tears filled her eyes. She had never dreamed she could know such happiness.

She wanted to give Da Nee many fine, healthy babies. But for now, this man, this boy, and this baby within her, were her whole life. And together, just maybe, they could begin to heal the wounds that scarred this beautiful land.

* * * * *

Harlequin® Historical

IF YOU THOUGHT ROMANCE NOVELS WERE ALL THE SAME... LOOK AGAIN!

Four exciting Historical romances every month

Each month, authors like Ruth Langan, DeLoras Scott and Dallas Schulze whisk you away to another time and place....

And don't miss our annual Historical Christmas Story collection, which will be sure to have you stringing up the mistletoe—this year featuring Bronwyn Williams, Maura Seger and Erin Yorke.

But there's more! In July 1993, we're celebrating the Fifth Anniversary of our launch with a Western Historical Story collection, three of the most exciting, rough-and-tumble love stories ever set in the Wild West. Be sure to join in the fun!

HARLEQUIN HISTORICALS—
A touch of magic!

HHT